This book is a work of fiction. Names, characters, places and incidents are either the product of the author's imagination or are used strictly as a fictional device. Any resemblance to actual persons, living or dead, or to actual events or locales is entirely coincidental.

A proportion of all royalties from sales will be donated to the British Red Cross to assist with their work in various war-torn parts of the world.

Copyright © 2017 Anthony Talmage. All rights reserved.

ACKNOWLEDGMENTS

To my Labradors Purdy and Sunny, who take me for a long walk every to help me devise my plots and create my characters

Preface

According to Transparency International, an organisation dedicated to fighting corruption in governments around the world, billions of pounds of corrupt funds pour into the UK and US every year. TI's statistics reveal that 20 of the 22 bodies in the UK charged with supervising the movement of money fail to meet official standards of transparency. Forty-two per cent of the most serious type of reports of suspicious activity in legal services were assessed to be poor quality or incomplete, raising concerns about 'gaming' of the reporting system. Just £1134 is the average fine issued by Her Majesty's Revenue and Customs to firms breaking money-laundering rules. Zero sector supervisors in the UK were considered by TI to provide a 'proportionate and credible deterrent' to those who engage in complicit or willful money laundering. In short, however comprehensive seem the authorities' anti-laundering measures, they are trumped by the launderers' ingenuity.

One

The scar on my left cheek itched. It always itched when I got excited. I double-checked the numbers for the umpteenth time. According to Venture there was only one winning ticket for this week's 'rollover' prize. And I was holding it.

I slid the scrap of paper back across the coffee table. 'Congratulations Mrs Pearson, what does it feel like to be worth £17 million..?'

Annie Pearson shook her head uncertainly. 'According to your paper, Emma, it's going to bring me nothing but trouble.'

She waved a liver-spotted hand at my double-page spread in last Thursday's Daily Globe, which lay on the sitting room carpet between us. Like the rest of the series, it featured a National Lottery winner whose overnight fortune had brought in its train disillusionment and despair.

The Gorgon had reckoned the way to push up circulation and make her mark with The Chief was to pander to the baser traits of human nature.

So each week a parade of squabbling families, disintegrating friendships, and the winners' increasing wretchedness gave gratification to all 3,261,533 readers of Hugo Pentecost's flagship tabloid.

And now had come a new twist. Annie Pearson pointed at

the headline. This week's screamed: 'LOTTO LEN UNDER GUN GUARD AFTER KIDNAP BID'. Underneath ran the tag...'Underworld Targets Jackpot Winners...'

Annie said, 'That's one of the reasons I asked you to come and see me. I'm over 80, my dear, and far too old for that kind of unpleasantness...'

'Mrs Pearson...'

'...Annie, please...'

I picked up The Globe and said kindly, 'Annie...I'll tell you a trade secret: these people wanted the publicity. They volunteered themselves. And they have a particular appeal to my editor because their wins have, if you like, backfired on them. But you'll never be in that category. All you need do is tick the box for no publicity, keep quiet and no-one will ever know.'

Annie said anxiously, 'I don't want anyone, anyone at all, to find out about it.' As an afterthought she added, 'To think I only bought the blessed ticket on impulse because I had a pound change left over. I suppose I wanted to see what all the fuss was about...'

I smiled reassuringly, 'As far as I'm concerned, Annie, your secret's safe with me. But a piece of advice: When you make your claim emphasise to Venture that you insist on remaining anonymous. They won't like it but they'll have to respect your wishes and keep your identity secret.

'So,' I said surreptitiously switching off the recorder on my smartphone, 'claim the money, go on a cruise, and then live the rest of your life in luxury.' I wagged a finger at her and prodded it at Lotto Len's picture. 'And don't give a thought to these lurid stories because they belong to a different world.'

She held my eyes in a steady gaze. For an octogenarian she was still a smart woman. Her white hair was neatly brushed and her clothes were tailored to fit a once attractive and still elegant figure. At length she spoke, 'Keeping my name out of your paper was one reason I rang this morning. The other was to ask for your help.'

I glanced at the clock on Annie's mantelpiece. It was 11.30am. Theo would be wondering where I'd got to. When JJ had transferred Annie's call to my desk this morning I'd said nothing to Theo Burgess, my news editor.

He'd have told me not to waste my time. An old biddy claiming to be the winner of this week's lottery? A trillion-to-one chance. More likely another lost soul wanting some company. And for some people talking even to a journalist was better than nothing.

If the caller had lived outside London, in the sticks somewhere, I would have politely fobbed her off. But, at that time of day, it was only a 40-minute drive through the morning traffic from Shoe Lane to Chiswick. So I'd decided to check it out.

But, by now, Theo would be getting nervous. In case The Gorgon went on one of her newsroom rampages. Theo claimed that my being around seemed to have a soothing effect on Magenta Bennett, scourge of the hacks under her control.

And I knew why. She'd been full of meaningful looks and friendly touches recently. Which meant I would soon be obliged to tell her my sexual orientation was strictly hetero. Not that, I thought wryly, I'd had much opportunity to prove it lately.

The Gorgon's notorious temper tantrums were usually linked with obsessions faithfully reflecting The Chief's latest whim.

Flavour of the month at the moment was 'rightsizing the core workforce.' So Magenta, universally referred to by disgruntled journos as 'Gorgon' Bennett, now had the Sword of Damocles to add to her instruments of terror.

I looked back at Annie. She was still gazing at me steadily. She said, 'You know, you do remind me of my daughter. You've got the same green eyes and kind face she had. I noticed the resemblance the first time I saw your picture in the paper...'

A shadow crossed her features. 'Her name was Caroline. She was killed in a riding accident when she was just 18...' Abruptly she was back 40 years, re-living the pain. '...It was a filthy day but she insisted on taking her pony out for a hack. It slipped and rolled on top of her...'

She shuddered as she saw the scene in her mind, probably for the thousandth time. Then she blinked it away. 'It's hard to believe she would have been nearly sixty if she'd lived. I could have been be a great-grandmother by now. Things could have been so different...'

She expelled her breath in a long sigh. 'But the point is my husband's dead and I have no family, not even any nephews and nieces...And the friends I had are all gone. I keep myself to myself and I'm content in my little flat here and with my husband's company pension, I've enough to live on...'

'Mrs Pearson – Annie - I don't want to be rude, but I have to get back to the office.' She seemed not to hear me. She said, 'Do you know what the most difficult thing is for someone of my age?' I replied firmly, 'No, Annie, I don't.'

'Well, I'll tell you. It's the loneliness. If you've got no family and no friends, you become as good as a prisoner in solitary confinement. And then you lose your nerve to go out into the world. But, after a while you persuade yourself that it's not so bad after all.

'You tell yourself that there are definite consolations to

being on your own. You can be totally selfish without feeling guilty...'

I shuffled and pointedly looked at my watch. I should ring Theo and tell him where I was. Annie talked on, oblivious '... Then, your solitary routine becomes your most precious possession. Without realising it, you cling to it blindly. And anything that threatens it makes you panic.'

I got to my feet, intending to divert Annie from her introspection. But it seemed to bring about a sudden, inner resolve. She looked up at me. 'And that's how I felt when I realised I'd won the wretched lottery. I was afraid.' Her eyes darted again to my last story. 'I couldn't cope with my life in turmoil...the upheaval.'

'Annie, you said something about needing my help...'

'...I'm going to get begging letters, people are going to be banging on my door at all hours, I won't be able to go to the corner shop without being pestered.'

'But I told you, Annie, you can keep your win a secret. I won't tell anyone. You can put all your money in a building society and live off the interest. You can carry on as if nothing's happened.'

She snorted, 'I'm not a fool, Emma. You of all people should know these things always get out.' She sat back and looked at me, as if weighing something in her mind. 'I wouldn't be at all worried if my daughter were still alive. She would have handled everything for me.'

I reached out and touched her hand gently. 'But Caroline's not alive. So you'll just have to trust yourself in this. It won't be as bad as you think. All you've got to do is telephone Venture and they'll look after everything.'

She shook her head. 'Strangers...I don't want to rely on strangers.' She was watching me thoughtfully. 'Caroline may not be here any more. But you are, Emma...Why can't you act on my behalf with the lottery people?' I went to say something and she stopped me. 'I've been thinking a great deal about this. You're the perfect person. On the one hand, you're someone who knows all about newspapers so you'd be able to keep my name out of them. And, on the other, you're someone I feel I can trust. I've read your column since it started and you come across as a nice person. And, now I've met you, I'm sure I'd feel very secure knowing you were looking after things for me.'

With both hands she steered the ticket back to my side of the table. I looked at it and then up into her faded blue eyes, which were staring levelly into mine. I said soothingly, 'That's really very kind of you, but you don't need me. One phone call and you'll get all the help you could possibly want from experts…'

'…Very well.' Annie pushed herself slowly to her feet and leaned across to retrieve the ticket. She began to walk purposefully out of the room. I said, 'Annie, what are you going to do?'

She said wearily, 'I'm going to flush the damned thing down the lavatory.'

I leapt up. 'You can't do that, it would be…criminal…'

She looked round. 'Can't you understand, my dear? I'm alone and frightened and I couldn't cope with the responsibility. If you can't help me I'd rather keep things as they were. If I destroy this ticket, I can pretend none of this ever happened.'

I sank back into my chair. Perhaps, I thought, if the old lady had time to sleep on things she'd change her mind. In the meantime, I'd play along. 'If that's what you really want, Annie, of course I'll help you...'

Immediately, she dropped her show of vulnerability and her

voice took on a business-like tone. She began firing questions at me.

'Are you married? How old are you? Where are your parents?'

I said cautiously, 'No, I'm not married. I'm 28, my parents are divorced. My mother lives in Bristol and my father married again and is in Kent with my step-mother. I have an older sister and two nieces in Hornsey Rise.'

I continued in a rush, 'I love my job as a reporter, although my mother doesn't think it's the sort of career suitable for a lady. And I have a flat in St John's Wood where I contentedly co-habit with my two blue Burmese cats, Oscar and Kate.'

Abruptly, Annie changed tack. 'Forgive me if I'm getting too personal, but I'm curious. How did you get that scar on your face?'

Involuntarily, I fingered it as I switched my mind back 16 years. I said, 'Like your Caroline, I was mad on horses. When I was 12, I had a bay pony called Flea. One day I was bending down to pick up his tack and something startled him. He kicked out and hit me in the face.

'I knew at the time he didn't mean it, but it still hurt. I had a hoofprint on my cheek for days and the scar's what's left.'

I don't know why, but suddenly I wanted to confide in this old lady. 'To be honest, Annie, I've got a bit of a complex about it. Just after it happened my mum tried to play it down. She said it wasn't a scar, just a mark. And then we began calling it Mark as a joke. I know it's not really a disfigurement as such. But I can't help feeling it puts people off me…'

…'You mean men..?' She hesitated for a moment, looking awkward. These days, of course, it doesn't follow it would be a man, but you know what I mean.' I nodded. 'As it happens, I was thinking of men.'

She said baldly, 'Is that why you haven't married?'

I realised I'd only talked about myself like this with one other person - JJ. It was probably because Annie was a stranger and I'd bottled things up - especially after Nick.

I smiled ruefully. 'I'm not sure. A scar on a woman's face does tend to undermine the self-confidence. Funnily enough, after I got engaged I never gave it a thought.

'Then, about six months ago, we split up and all the old hang-ups came back. I've tried to rationalise why the relationship went wrong and I'm sure it was nothing to do with a one-and-a-half-inch line, which I cover up most of the time with make-up.'

'So, what do you think the real reason was?'

I eyed her for several seconds before answering. 'He was a policeman in Special Branch. He put his job first and me second. But he expected my priorities to be the other way round.

'I tried, but after a while the unfairness of it got to me, so I broke off the engagement and we went our separate ways. I haven't seen him since.'

Talking about it scratched at the old wounds again and I was appalled at myself. I could feel the pinpricks of tears beginning behind my eyes. I blinked them back fiercely.

Annie reached out and squeezed my arm. 'Forgive me if I've been presumptuous. But thank you for being so open with me. And allow an old woman the privilege of offering you some personal advice: life's too short to worry about trifles - and that tiny blemish is a trifle, believe me. You're a lovely young woman. In any case, any man worth his salt will love you for what you are inside as well as out.'

I felt myself blushing and wondered what this respectable old dear might think if she could see me indulging my animal passions. Although I hadn't done that for a few weeks now. My last liaison's name was Gerry, a crime reporter on the Mail.

It had been a case of two adults, mutually attracted, fulfilling each other's physical needs. But, as usual for me, it had been a joyless union and neither of us had wanted to repeat the experience.

Annie broke into my thoughts. 'I'm very sure now that you're the one to help me. You will won't you, Emma?'

'Alright, Annie.' I smiled at her. 'Now, please, get on that phone and stake your claim.'

'Before I do that I want to settle the matter of your fee.'

I laughed. 'My fee? But, all I'm going to do is keep your name out of the papers. And, metaphorically hold your hand until you feel reassured enough to…'

'…Emma, my dear. I obviously haven't made myself clear. I want your advice and help and friendship for as long as it takes for my life to get back on an even keel again. That might take months. I…I…want to be able to feel I can rely on you as I might my own daughter.'

Her voice became determined again. 'Now, I know this will take up a great amount of your time so I'm happy to pay you a proper fee for your services-…

'…I don't want a fee, Annie.'

She held up her hand. 'I would feel happier that way. Now, let me see…For all the extra work you might be put to in protecting my privacy, plus helping me sort out everything… would, say, half a million pounds be fair?'

I stared at her incredulously. 'Did you say half a million? That's five hundred thousand pounds?' She nodded eagerly.

'Mrs Pearson, are you sure you know what you're saying? Half a million pounds is an awful lot of money to pay for some temporary help which you can get free of charge, from experts, just by picking up the phone.' I added, 'Once Venture know you're holding the winning ticket you'll have advisers lining up from here to Kew Gardens. And they'll stay with you until you're happy the money's been invested exactly in accordance with your wishes...'

She said vehemently, 'That's precisely my point. For every adviser there's an adviser's wife and family who'll get told about this old widow who's just come into a fortune she doesn't want and doesn't need. They'll all go out and tell their friends and their friends will discuss it down the hairdressers and in the pub and, before you know it, I'll be in all the papers. And that's just what I want to avoid.'

She looked at me artlessly, 'But, if you took the ticket and claimed the money on my behalf - just as Caroline would - and word did get out, it would be you dealing with all the publicity and I'd be safe here with my privacy intact.' She waved her hand dismissively. 'And in any case a mere half a million is small change compared with the rest of the money.'

'Annie, you're not behaving rationally. You can't hand over something that's worth £17 million to a complete stranger...'

'You're not a stranger. And, on the contrary, I believe I'm being extremely rational. This time last week I was content and comfortably off in my ordered little world. Now, I'm faced with chaos. But, in you I think I've found someone I can trust to protect me from all that...' She chuckled. 'You'll be, what do they call it these days? My minder.'

I persisted, 'But, how do you know you can trust me? What's to stop me from taking this ticket now and pretending I'd bought it? It would be your word against mine.' She surveyed me gravely. 'If you betray my trust there's nothing I can do about it. But what will I have lost? I'll still have my cosy routine intact and the threat of overnight notoriety will be gone. I shall be very sorry for you, of course...'

'...Sorry for me, why?'

'Because you will have to live with your conscience for the rest of your life. And, believe me, it would destroy you in the end.' Abruptly her expression changed and she smiled brightly. 'But, if you don't betray my trust, as I know you won't, I'll get the best of all worlds: I'll have the money, which I shall enjoy discreetly donating to worthy causes; I shall have a new friend and companionship in you, who reminds me so much of the daughter I lost, and I'll have my anonymity.'

'Annie, I can't take your lottery ticket. It would be too much responsibility. Supposing it was stolen, or I lost it?'

'Don't you want to earn half a million pounds?'

'Of course I do. But that's the point. I wouldn't be earning it.' I added brutally, 'I'd be taking advantage of an elderly woman who appears perfectly sane, I admit, but for all I know could be mentally unbalanced.'

Annie said with mock severity, 'I'm not ga-ga yet.' Then she asked, Do you believe in fate?'

'I'm not sure, why?'

'I told you a little white lie earlier. I've already rung the lottery office to stake my claim. But, when they asked for my name and address I froze and just put the phone down. And as I did, I saw your photograph in the paper and it was as if Caroline was looking at me. Telling me it would be alright. Telling me to trust her. So, I decided I had to speak to you. Now I know I did the right thing.'

The ticking of the clock over the fireplace seemed unnaturally loud. I thought for a moment and then made up my mind. 'I'll tell you what I'll do, Annie. I'll take the ticket, lodge it with my bank for safe keeping and then come back in a couple of days to discuss it again when you've had more time to get used to the idea.' Her face creased in a delighted smile as I put the precious slip of paper into my purse. For good measure, she said, 'I'm not going to change my mind you know.'

I sighed and asked her if she had anything I could write on. After a brief forage in a bureau drawer she handed me a sheet, blank except for her name and address printed in the top, right-hand corner.

I wrote in capitals: RECEIVED - ONE LOTTERY TICKET DATED JUNE 11, 2018, CONTAINING THE WINNING NUMBERS OF 12, 14, 37, 41, 43, 46 WHICH THE OWNER, MRS ANNIE PEARSON, HAS ENTRUSTED TO MY CARE. Underneath I added, 'Signed Emma Holgate, reporter for The Daily Globe.'

I scrawled my signature and handed it to Annie. I said with mock stern-ness, 'Here's a receipt. You must keep it safe because, if I should get run over by a bus, that's your only proof the ticket belongs to you.' Annie continued to beam at me. She folded the paper and tucked it into the letter rack lodged among the ornaments on top of her writing desk.

Two

On the way back to The Globe's Shoe Lane headquarters, I stopped at Barclays and handed in an envelope, with its £17 million contents, for safe keeping. The clerk made me sign across the seal before sticking a clear tape over my name. That done, he went off to lodge it in the bank's safe.

I needed time to think. I parked off the Bayswater Road and walked for 20 minutes in Kensington Gardens. The early summer air was filled with the scent of roses and the sun glittered brightly off the surface of The Long Water. And by The Serpentine mums and toddlers fed the ducks, oblivious to my churning thoughts.

I arrived at my desk at 1.15pm and was greeted by a fretful Theo, his bald head wrinkled with worry.

'Christ, Emms. Where've you been? No, don't bother to tell me...' He shot a glance over his shoulder. 'She who must be obeyed has been chewing the carpet over you. She reckons she's onto the scoop of the century and says she wants to see you instanta.'

I looked at Theo, puzzled. Ever since The Gorgon had arrived as The Chief's new broom nine months before, she'd confined me to the feature pages. At first, I had protested saying it was a waste of my experience as an investigative reporter. Her response was to lecture me on obeying orders. And I'd been stuck with personality pieces and the lottery series ever since. That's why I was surprised if The Gorgon had decided to take me out of mothballs.

Theo shrugged, 'Don't ask me what she's talking about. You know what she's like. She won't tell me anything if she thinks she can take the credit for it with Pentecost.

'Anyway, she's been doing the okey-cokey in and out of her office door looking for you for the past hour so you'd better get in there smartish. Oh, and by the way, I said you were working on a backgrounder for next Thursday's column but I don't think she believed me.'

He frowned at me. 'But, if she should ask, don't make me look a complete prat. And since she obviously fancies you it might help me stay out of the shit if you put on your most winning smile...' So, I thought, Maggie's gropings had been noticed.

I knocked on The Gorgon's door and went in. The top of her desk was hidden under pages of rival papers which she'd been looking through. Her computer was like a drowning swimmer's head just visible among hostile waves. We called her The Gorgon because she was a monster. It was alleged she'd used her pneumatic and brassy charms to sleep her way to the editor's chair.

What she lacked in journalistic skills, she made up for in decibel levels, bawling out any minion whose efforts might have prompted an unflattering communique from the proprietor. Magenta, or Maggie, as she hated being called to her face, had her sights set on higher things than the editorship of Sir Hugo Pentecost's scurrilous tabloid.

She saw herself running a major slice of The Chief's multi media enterprise which included print, on-line, satellite TV and Radio and cable. He was now also dipping a corporate toe into apps for smartphones, tablets and phablets. And, as a belt and braces, was also tweaking android systems to keep his Organisation ahead of the pack. Every time The Globe published a sensational exclusive, The Gorgon was convinced she was one step nearer her goal of taking over the satellite empire.

Her greeting was characteristically pithy. 'Where the fucking hell have you been? Theo gave me some crap about a backgrounder. What planet's he on? Wherever you were you should have left a note on the computer log..?'

'Sorry, Maggie, I had to check out a call I had first thing from someone who said she was this week's rollover jackpot winner. Theo wasn't around so I left a message with Fiona but she must have got it garbled.' I added brightly, 'Anyway, I couldn't let the call go in case it turned out to be genuine. You know how hard it is to screw any info out of Venture when they're being coy.'

Her interest perked up. 'And was it genuine?'

My loyalty to Annie won over Maggie's vaunted ambition. 'Fraid not. Just a lonely old dear wanting some company.' Surprisingly, Maggie didn't seem annoyed. 'Just as well because I wouldn't want you distracted from this one.' She gestured for me to sit in one of the easy chairs she keeps for VIP visitors and she lowered herself into the other one opposite.

She leaned forward, 'I've had a tipoff which could give us the scoop of the fucking decade. Before I tell you what it is I want to make it absolutely clear that you report directly to me on this one. If dog-breath asks you, say I promised my sources that only one of my journalists would be given the information. That should salve his wounded pride. And then you keep me in touch with everything you find out. If I'm not here ring me on my mobile.'

I agreed. 'So what's the story?' She was still leaning forward. But she lowered her voice as if it might penetrate the double-glazing, allowing someone amid the dry staccato of newsroom keyboards to pick up her words and sell them on to the Mirror. 'This serial murderer who's got us all sweating our tits off...' The Gorgon was talking about The Big One. The story that every national, provincial evening, weekly, on-line outfit, tv and radio station in the country were vying with each other to get a different angle on.

So far, all we'd been able to do is run the police Press conferences, interview the families and print the usual 'PHANTOM STRIKES AGAIN' headlines with nothing new underneath, except the victim's name. The rest of the facts had become terrifyingly predictable. So far six people, with no apparent connection, had been ritually slain by a madman with a 9mm handgun.

Ordinarily, such a weapon would kill cleanly at close range. But our murderer used his to carry out a deadly ritual. He filed crosses into the tops of low-velocity bullets. And then, confronting his quarry, he would place the barrel against their abdomen and pull the trigger. The victim would die instantly, effectively disembowelled by the spread of the soft lead. The eviscerated organs acted as a natural silencer so no-one in the vicinity heard a thing.

Those on the receiving end of this treatment were dead before they hit the floor. Curiously, if the act was carried out skilfully, they showed hardly any external sign of injury. It was only at the post mortem that the police were informed they had a macabre homicide on their hands. Six similar murders in total so far and detectives were still no nearer catching the perpetrator.

The media had gone into a frenzy over it, dubbing the killer The Phantom because, despite their efforts and those of police forces across the country, no witnesses had so far been found. The case was becoming the biggest cause celebre since Jack the Ripper.

'...We reckon there's method in The Phantom's madness.' The Gorgon was smirking triumphantly. I said, 'Don't tell me we've got a different angle on the story at last?' ' Better than that, Emma my love, I think this ritual nonsense is just a blind. I think our killer's a cool professional carrying out the bidding of organised crime.'

'Hang on a minute...How do a string of random murders suddenly turn into contract killings?'

'Ah, that's just where everyone's gone wrong. They've assumed there's no connection between the victims. But there is...' The Gorgon was obviously enjoying playing Holmes, so I obligingly slipped into the role of Watson.

'Sorry, Maggie, I can't see it. They've all come from different parts of the country, they're unrelated and unknown to each other. The police and every crime reporter in the land have tried to find a link.'

The Gorgon's smirk widened into a grin. 'What's your column been majoring on over the last couple of months?'

'Lottery winners...You know that.'

'Yeah, and your fodder's been the venal, the grasping and the egocentric who've been too stupid to opt for no publicity. They wanted all their mates to know how lucky they'd been. But, after the novelty wore off they blew it. But what they didn't realise was that, by going public instead of keeping their big mouths shut, they probably saved their own lives...'

My scar began to itch again. 'Now you really have lost me. What's The Phantom got to do with lottery winners?' Maggie leaned back and closed her eyes, savouring the knowledge she was about to impart. 'Those punters who are slow off the mark in claiming their jackpots are being tracked down by a crime syndicate and murdered for their winning tickets...'

Three

The Gorgon was leaning forward again. This time she was touching my knee. By the look on her face she was already inwardly savouring The Chief's congratulations for another explosive scoop. I shifted and she withdrew her hand.

'Let me get this straight,' I said, 'Your tipster claims some Mr Big is behind the serial killings. But they're not random because each victim is a jackpot winner whose ticket is subsequently stolen by the hired killer?'

'Exactly.' I shook my head. 'Sorry to be a party pooper, but it just doesn't add up. For a start how does Mr Big track down the winners and get to them before the official Venture people? Secondly, if some gang were killing off the winners, who's been claiming the money? The same person - the killer - can't pretend to be lucky every week, someone might get suspicious...'

The Gorgon didn't appear to notice my sarcasm. And she wasn't deflated by my logic either. Instead, she sat there with a big grin on her face. 'How they do it is ele-fucking-mentary, my dear Watson. Mr Big has bribed someone on the inside at Venture to pass on the names.'

She clasped her hands together in excitement. 'It's so simple...Look, suppose you were a winner, what's the first thing you do..? You ring up Venture and stake your claim. Some nice helpline wallah checks the numbers with you over the phone. If they match the winning line they ask for the security code on the ticket. If that checks out they take your name and address and says someone from Venture will call on you the next day - to verify that your ticket's genuine, has the right date on it, and is indeed the winner...etc. And all this is automatically recorded on the Venture computer.'

I risked interrupting her in full flow. 'Suppose I don't bother to check my numbers the same night. Say I'm out somewhere and don't remember until Monday?'

'No problem. There's someone manning the phones the whole time. And winners have 180 days to make their claim. Within that timeframe it doesn't matter when you contact them. The crucial thing is that, as soon as you phone in, Mr Big gets your name and address passed to him straight away.'

She went on, 'The lottery line staff get lots of false alarms with people thinking they've won - but the stupid buggers have actually got their numbers muddled. So all the insider has to do when she thinks she's spoken to the genuine winner is pass on the details and erase the recording from the computer log. Later, after the murder, the substituted claimant - Mr Big's rep - registers his ticket and this time normal procedures apply and no-one's any the wiser.'

I said doubtfully, 'But if there are rostas of different lottery line answerers, and only one insider, how do the criminals ensure their woman - or man - is the contact for the jackpot winner every time?'

'They don't. But even if their strike rate's one in 10, they're still being phenomenally successful.'

'So, what happens after the mole passes on the winner's details?'

'Mr Big dispatches The Phantom, who arrives on the scene claiming to be from Venture. Probably flashes an ID with Venture's logo on it. That way, the killer's welcomed into his victim's home with joyful smiles. The Phantom asks to see the ticket and when he's got it, he administers the coup de gras, and disappears.'

I shook my head, 'But how does The Phantom manage to get his victims on their own? They're obviously not all single people living alone.'

'The Phantom selects his victims very carefully to give himself the best chance of getting away cleanly. Probably the lottery insider wheedles out of the claimants their marital status and family details. And then she spins some yarn about confidentiality and not telling anyone, even your nearest and dearest, until it's been confirmed.

'Added to that the mole probably arranges a precise time for the supposed lottery rep. to call, making sure there'll be no-one else around. If there is, The Phantom gives them the chop, too. I mean, what's a couple of deaths compared with £10 million or so?'

'But,' I argued, 'Even if I, as a winner, was able to keep calm enough to follow instructions and stay shtum I'd still probably tell those closest to me. And surely they'd be a mite suspicious if their beloved was about to be a multi-millionaire one minute and dead the next...And then no-one can find the winning ticket...'

The Gorgon leapt out of her chair, leaned over and pinched my cheeks affectionately. 'Got it in one, honey. Despite the insider's persuasiveness, some punters did blab about their wins and when different grieving relatives told the same story to Venture's security people, the NCA were called in.'

I decided to feign ignorance. 'NCA? What's that?'

Maggie sighed impatiently. 'The National Crime Agency. They were set up to help co-ordinate major investigations into organised crime across the country. A sort of British FBI if you like.'

'Why the NCA and not, say, the Met?'

'Secrecy. The Government wanted a lid kept on this. Imagine what it would do to lottery takings if punters got wind of what's going on. The NCA have the clout, and the network, to handle this discreetly. Or they think they have...' She gave me a broad wink. ' But they've reckoned without The Globe...'

I said, 'So the NCA have confirmed there's definitely a connection between the serial murders and the lottery?'

'At first Venture wanted to pooh pooh it. But a certain conscientious detective wasn't having any. He's come up with some pretty convincing evidence. I'm not saying any more but I've been given access to that info. That's why I know this story's kosher.'

I said, 'But what about the point that The Phantom can't claim the winnings every week, so who does?'

The Gorgon waived her hand airily, 'Who cares? Mr Big could whistle up an army of nobodies for a cut of the prize, no questions asked. He probably gets them to lie low while all the fuss over the murder dies down. Then they emerge from the woodwork weeks, or even months, later and claim the prize.'

She completed her logic, 'And, should anyone check back on dates and locations, and match them up with the killings, the claimant would still turn out to be someone as innocuous as a commercial traveller saying he bought the ticket on impulse when passing through the town. Who could prove otherwise?'

I thought for a moment. 'So what your informant's saying is: a Mr Big is milking the lottery by bribing someone on the inside and hiring an assassin on the outside?'

The Gorgon said triumphantly, 'Yes, but that's not the end of the story. This scam's just the tip of a very murky iceberg. It's all about money-laundering. To be more precise: drugs money-laundering. Our Mr Big's using the clean lottery cash to wash funds for drug syndicates.'

'So who is Mr Big. Has your tipster told you that?'

'Look, blossom, if I had all the answers why would I bother telling you all this? That's one of the things I want you to find out. With all the contacts you've got with the lottery people, plus your background knowledge, you'll be able to get under the skin of this one quicker than anybody else.'

She said with determination, 'So, I want you to drop everything and concentrate on this exclusively. If you need help use JJ. But I want to splash this in a week.

'You've got to firm up the link between the jackpot winners and the serial killings. And get at least enough to print a speculative piece on the money-laundering and drugs links...' She put her hand back on my knee and slid it just under the edge of my skirt and squeezed. 'I know you all think I'm a hell-cat sometimes but I can be very appreciative to those who please me.' I suppressed a shudder and stood up.

Affecting not to notice she said, 'One more thing, darling, if you use JJ don't give him the complete picture. And I'll tell dog-breath I've asked you to follow up something on The Phantom killings. And all this is strictly on a "need to know" basis. The fewer who know about it, the less likely it'll be that some bastard out there'll flog it to the Sun or Mirror.' She eyed a spot on the wall above my head. 'But, I think I'll give The Chief a flavour of what's brewing; he likes to be forewarned when a blockbuster's in the wind.'

She said briskly, 'We'll go with a..."Are-you-buying-a-ticket for-your-own-execution..?" front pager next Monday. And then watch those wankers in E1 and SE1 scorching their arses trying to catch up. And while they're still shitting themselves we'll run the money-laundering angle the next day.'

I left her gleefully anticipating a sackful of brownie points from Sir Hugo Pentecost - known in media circles and the financial pages as The Chief - and threaded my way back to my desk. JJ, whose computer terminal sits opposite mine, craned round his screen with a quizzical expression.

JJ, or Jeremy Bartholomew Jerome as he was christened, is the best mate a girl could have. Some people think he's a loner just because he doesn't show any interest in socialising down at the Cheshire Cheese. But he and I get along fine. It was his wise words and brotherly hugs that helped me through my Nick Marlowe trauma. And, over the last few years, he's matched me bottle for bottle through long nights of unscrewing other screwed-up affairs.

He has a scruffy flat in Notting Hill Gate and lives on his own, but he's never asked more from me than friendship. He once told me he'd been planning to marry someone but it hadn't worked out. Perhaps we're both a couple of oddballs. Anyway, his last long-term relationship was 15 years ago. Now, he seems content to alternate his time between his work and his hobby. He's a film buff. And he's always quoting bits of old movies and can tell you who was in the credits from Top Billing to Best Boy.

Before perks like foreign trips were given the chop by The Chief's gurus from the Harvard Business School, one of JJ's thrills was to be sent to cover the annual Oscars ceremony in Beverly Hills. Because of his love for the industry he made a lot of friends in it, including some big names. At the end of last year, even The Gorgon was mightily impressed when Ridley Scott rang up and invited JJ to the set of a film Ridley was shooting in Brighton.

Yes, JJ's my best friend. I love him. Platonically.

He said, 'What did the Editor-from-Hell want? It can't be blood-sucking time, it's not dark yet.'

'Now don't be acerbic, JJ. Under those Vampire wings beats the heart of a simple maiden who, like the rest of us, just wants to be loved.' He said coldly, 'I can't stand what she's doing to Theo. She treats him like shit and the way she calls him "dog-breath" behind his back... She's deliberately trying to undermine his authority. And it's not as if she's any good as a journalist.'

JJ was off. This was one of his favourite themes. He rumbled on, 'At least Theo's done the rounds as a hack. But she's never even worked on a weekly. Straight from a post-grad journo course into The Chief's fast-track training scheme. And from there to Night Editor, where she funked it in her office while others covered her back.

'And now, at the ripe old age of 30, she's lording it over the newsroom like Citizen Kane. And she seems to delight in humiliating the very man who could make or break her reputation...' He growled, 'If I was Theo, I'd put a contract out on her.'

Which reminded me. I told JJ The Gorgon wanted me to follow up a confidential tip she'd had and he was to be my leg-man. JJ said he had a dental appointment but would only be out of the office two hours at the most and would work late if necessary. He raised his eyebrows when I told him the first thing I wanted him to do was to ring round his contacts and try to match up the retailers of winning lottery tickets with the locations of The Phantom murders.

Four

Later that afternoon a disbelieving bellow from the other side of the office brought the newsroom to a standstill. Theo was leaning on his knuckles staring down intently at his computer screen. Then he looked up. 'Christ! Everyone check Incoming stuff from the agencies. Now!'

Eyes swivelled back to their monitors. Theo said excitedly, 'If it's accurate we've got our front-page lead for the morning. And I want to get the full SP into the first edition...'

He bawled across to me, 'Emms, as Maggie's asked you to work on a serial killings angle you might as well pick this one up and run with it...' He addressed the rest of the reporters, now galvanised out of their post-lunch torpor '...and anyone not committed can work on background stuff for the inside pages.'

He looked back at his computer screen, 'According to our stringer in West London The Phantom's struck again. The flash is still coming up...' Theo read aloud what the agency reporter was filing from miles away via his laptop and dongle. '...Police won't confirm or deny the elderly woman had been shot with a 9mm handgun.

'However a spokesman said the killing had all the hallmarks of a series of other murders which have occurred in various parts of the country over the past year and a half. The spokesman refused to disclose the dead woman's name but neighbours say she's a kindly woman who keeps herself to herself called Annie Pearson...'

I accessed the copy on my terminal and stared, stupefied, at the next slug of the story. The body had been discovered by a neighbour who lived in the block of flats I'd been sitting in that morning. He was quoted as saying he'd heard a muffled bang and thought something on next door's cooker had exploded. He went to check and found a woman on the floor. He'd phoned for an ambulance and the paramedics had called the police when they discovered their patient had been shot through the abdomen.

Theo yelled, 'Emms, quick as you can, firm up "The Phantom Strikes Again" line and I'll get everyone else who's spare to work on backgrounders. You just concentrate on who the old girl was, how she's been killed and, more importantly, why? I mean what's this dum-dum maniac want with a harmless old geriatric?'

The blood had drained from my face and Theo's voice was oscillating in my head. '...And try to stack up a definite connection between her murder and the others. I know we've tried already on that one but there has to be something they've all got in common.'

Dumbly, I acknowledged his order and walked as inconspicuously as I could to the toilets which were off the landing. I got there just in time before the contents of my stomach heaved into the lavatory pan. I stayed on my knees with my head cradled on my arms until I'd got myself more or less under control. Annie Pearson, the vulnerable old lady who'd decided to put her trust in me. The sweet old widow still mourning her dead daughter from all those years ago now, suddenly, dead herself. Ritually slaughtered like some animal.

And, if Maggie's tip-off was accurate, Annie had probably been murdered because of the ticket I had walked off with. But, how did The Phantom track her down? Annie had told me this morning that when she called Venture she'd confirmed she had the winning numbers but had hung up as soon as they'd asked her name. So, if she hadn't said who she was, and where she was calling from, the only explanation had to be that Mr Big's insider had noted Annie's number and from that had obtained the subscriber's name and address.

I tried to reconstruct in my head what might have happened. The Phantom had gone to Annie's flat pretending to be from Venture. But Annie would have been surprised that they knew who she was. Perhaps she thought I had told them. Not realising she was entertaining a murderer on her doorstep she might have invited her visitor in and told him I was handling all lottery enquiries on her behalf. Or, if she hadn't said anything about me, there was still my receipt which Annie had tucked so chirpily into her letter rack.

Either way, when he'd found out what he wanted, The Phantom had then killed Annie as cold-bloodedly as his other victims. But why? It didn't make sense. Why kill Annie for nothing? But, whatever his reasons were, I had to assume The Phantom now knew I had the ticket. And, what's more, he knew where to find me.

'Are you OK, Emms? Your face is as white as one of the Addams Family.'

I gazed vaguely across my desk. 'Yes...yes...I'm fine, JJ. I get nauseous sometimes when my blood sugar drops too low.' I prattled on trying to cover my shock. Instinctively, I took refuge in rehearsing familiar grumbles. 'It's these 14-hour shifts. My friends think I've got it made when I tell them I have four days off a week. They don't think about the other side of the coin. Let them try working three days with only a break for sleep - if they're lucky.'

He said, 'You know what they say...If you can't take a joke don't work in Fleet Street...' I said, 'Or shouldn't that be Wapping? Or the Isle of Dogs? It doesn't seem to have the same ring though as the Street of Shame does it?' I changed the subject, 'How was the dentist?'

'Oh, fine. Just a filling. While I was waiting I used my mobile to phone round a few contacts.'

He glanced at some notes he'd written on his pad. 'I got lucky with a couple of calls and, so far, it does seem as if two of The Phantom's victims lived in the same towns in which the winning lottery tickets were sold...' He looked at me steadily. 'Have we got some kind of connection, here?'

'Look, JJ, Maggie's paranoid about this. She's convinced she's onto the exclusive of the decade and she's so scared about it leaking out that she's keeping everyone on a "need to know" footing. But, I can't work with you like that so I'm going to tell you what she told me. But, if she happens to mention it, you know nothing. OK?'

JJ agreed and I relayed what The Gorgon had said. As I talked he looked shocked and then brightened. He whistled softly. 'Hey, if we can prove some connection between this latest murder and the location of this week's lottery outlet we'll know for sure we're onto something.'

'Right, concentrate on that,' I said. I surveyed the swarm of activity round us. 'But, tell no-one what you're doing and why. If you come up with something let me know straight away. If I'm at home, call me there. What we don't want to do is even hint to anyone else that there's a link between The Phantom and the lottery...Because if we do, that's Maggie's exclusive gone and she'll be looking for human sacrifices - you and me.'

JJ grinned. I said, 'So, you chase the top secret stuff and I'll flounder about with the rest of Fleet Street trying to dress this latest killing up with something new... ' For the remainder of the afternoon and evening I tried not to think of that scrap of paper worth £17 million sitting in my bank's safe. Or the ruthless assassin who had me in his sights. My only comfort was that it was unlikely he'd want to kill me before he got his hands on Annie's winning ticket.

And he wouldn't know I was aware of a connection between the murders and the lottery. So, he'd assume I was a sitting target. That gave me a small advantage. I pushed all this to the back of my mind while I became the questing reporter. I spoke on the phone to the police, our stringers, Annie's neighbours, the district hospital and even the local sub-postmaster where Annie used to draw her pension.

I pieced more fragments together as each edition came and went until we had everything we were going to get. As I worked, fear lurked like a panther in the back of my mind, waiting to spring at me as soon as I had nothing else to think about. I assumed that as the police hadn't been in touch, they had not found my receipt. Which meant Annie's killer had taken it with him.

The final edition to hit the streets had the front page

screamer...'PHANTOM STALKS CAPITAL.' Underneath, it read...'Serial Killer's OAP Victim.' Theo congratulated all of us on what we'd achieved, before telling us to go home. But I wanted to stay and so did JJ. He sat opposite me industriously typing into his computer's personal notes file, which was protected by a code word known only to its user. Not for the first time I looked at his spare frame and genial features and thought what a waste it was that he didn't have a partner to share his life with.

I said, 'So, what have we got so far?'

He said five out of the seven serial killings he'd managed to check were in the same locations in which the winning tickets had been sold. But, he hadn't so far been able to establish a connection between Annie Pearson and a local outlet. And, no-one had actually linked the victims to the lottery. Also, the eventual claimants had wanted no publicity and had all dropped out of sight. Surprise, surprise.

According to a friendly contact in Venture's PR department, this was puzzling. Because, she'd told JJ, the Press always managed to track down the jackpot winners. But these few had become invisible, taking their fortunes with them.

'You've done a great job, JJ. Now, let's go home and start again in the morning.'

'Got time for a quick one, before the pubs close?'

I gave him a weary smile. 'Tomorrow, maybe. Tonight, I'm bushed. I just want to get some sleep.'

As we were leaving, The Gorgon emerged from her office and wanted a full briefing on what we had so far. I told JJ to call it a day and for the next hour I went over everything with Maggie. As I left she was still in her office waiting, no doubt, for the phone to ring and the purring congratulations of The Chief on a front page that would sell an extra 200,000 the next day.

At that time of night it would take me only 15 minutes to drive back to the flat in St John's Wood. A jumble of emotions churned inside me as I tacked through the streets of the West End. I drove past Broadcasting House, around Regent's Park and to the apartment in Eamont Street where Nick and I had planned to set up house together.

It was a warm evening for late May and, as usual, I had left the windows in the first-floor apartment open to let the air help clear away the claustrophobia of the office which I always brought home with me. The thought that kept re-surfacing was how vulnerable I was. I lived on my own and there was a homicidal maniac on the loose who saw me as his next target. But, I thought, there was a blockbuster of a story somewhere in all this. If I kept my nerve I could do even better than Maggie's putative scoop of the decade.

I also now held a winning lottery ticket worth £17 million. And only I, and The Phantom, knew about it. A surge of excitement bubbled up through the fear. As long as that ticket stayed safely in the bank, it was my invisible shield.

I knew there was something wrong as soon as I saw Oscar and Kate sitting on the step. They were growling and grumbling, their tails twitching. Normally, they would have used the cat flaps to let themselves in. And by this time they'd have been fed by my neighbour, Mrs Ormrod, and be stretched out languidly on the settee awaiting my arrival home. Instead, they stalked around my legs as I opened the door to the shared passage. Mrs Ormrod's flat was on the left and mine was opposite. Her door was shut but mine was open. And the lights were on inside. Maybe she'd forgotten to feed Oscar and Kate and had let herself in with the spare key and was in there now opening tins to give them a late-night snack.

I pushed the door wider and stepped inside. Mrs Ormrod was lying face-up on the kitchen floor. If it wasn't for her eyes, wide open and staring sightlessly at the ceiling, she could have been asleep. I knelt down beside her and the stench of a blocked lavatory wafted up my nostrils. A red stain had spread across the linoleum from under Mrs Ormrod's back. I felt my insides heaving and I leapt for the sink. For the second time that day I vomited until there was nothing left in my stomach.

Five

Within an hour the flat was swarming with police. They admitted we were looking at The Phantom's eighth victim. In charge was Inspector Tom Marsden, assisted by Sergeant Karen Pickford, the same two who were running the investigation into Annie's murder.

They made a contrasting pair. Marsden was about 40, tall, slim with a sallow complexion and hollow eyes. Karen was about 26, slightly built with an elfin face topped by short, curly, blonde hair. They both looked weary, resigned to a long night on top of an already long day.

We sat in my front room, amid a shambles of overturned bookcases and emptied drawers. Pictures were smashed and askew, books had been ripped apart and pages littered the floor. Even my pot plants had been emptied out and their leaves plucked off leaving the stems looking naked and vulnerable.

The cushion fillings had been scooped from their covers and scattered everywhere. The Phantom had left no carpet unturned, I realised, in his search for Annie's lottery ticket. I repeated again exactly what I'd found when I'd walked through my front door. All the while Marsden was trying to make sense of his day. Eventually, he said, 'It's remarkable, Ms Holgate, even for London, to have two murders within a few hours of each other and with the same MO.

'But it's even odder that the second one goes on to involve a reporter who's spent the last six hours ferreting for information on the first. Could there be a connection, I wonder?'

I looked at him tired-eyed. 'What are you getting at?'

He jerked his shoulders. 'Well, for instance, had you ever met Annie Pearson?' I hesitated and then shook my head and tried to deflect his line of questioning. I was never any good at lying and I was sure that someone with Marsden's experience would be able to tell I was hiding something.

Switching into my questing journalist persona I said, 'Have you found a motive for the old lady's murder?'

Marsden looked at me sternly, 'Let me remind you, Ms Holgate, that you're not a reporter now but a key witness in a murder enquiry. It's not for you to ask questions.' I shrugged and said I was only trying to help.

Karen broke her silence. 'We're not certain about the motive but he was obviously searching for something because Mrs Pearson's flat had been ransacked just like this. From what I can see, your neighbour must have disturbed her assailant as he was turning your place over. The police surgeon says she must have been killed shortly before you arrived home.' She added musingly, 'So, The Phantom coolly murders one old lady. And, a few hours later on the same day, pops across London for a repeat performance.

'And, whatever he was looking for must have been important enough for him to carry on his search, even after killing Mrs Ormrod and risking being caught in the act by you. And, if that had happened, we might now be looking at three homicides.' She asked suspiciously, 'What could you have here that he didn't find at Mrs Pearson's?'

My head was starting to thump and Mark the scar was itching infuriatingly. 'I wish I knew,' I lied. 'But why should it be me with the connection? Why not Mrs Ormrod? Maybe she just happened to be in my flat feeding the cats when the killer called. She would have heard him knocking at her door and might have opened mine to ask what he wanted.

'The Phantom could have assumed he'd got the address mixed up, walked into my flat thinking it was Mrs Ormrod's, killed her and then started looking for whatever he'd come for...' I improvised.

Karen looked up at Marsden, who grunted unconvinced. He suggested I find somewhere else to sleep, as his team would be in residence for at least the next 8 hours going over every inch of the place. But, wherever I went, I was to 'hold myself available' for further questioning. I rang Theo at home and told him what had happened. He was deeply shocked but enough of a journalist to make me go over every detail in case they could be used in The Globe's next edition. He told me to charge a hotel room to the paper, but I said it probably wouldn't be necessary. Then I dialled the only person I knew I could lean on.

An appalled JJ drove across from Notting Hill, swept me up in a comforting hug, and took me back to his flat. He made up his spare room and it was 2 o'clock before I finally collapsed into bed. Tired as I was, the events of the day boiled around in my head. I had to get them in some order before the morning. The Phantom was obviously desperate to get his hands on the winning lottery ticket. Maybe whoever he was working for was getting impatient.

And, besides possessing their passport to £17 million, they now knew I knew what they were up to...

Six

It seemed I'd been asleep for only a few minutes when the chirruping of an insistent early bird penetrated my coma. But it wasn't a lark. It was my mobile phone, which I'd forgotten to switch off. I groaned and looked at my watch. It was 7 o'clock. I put the phone to my ear. A familiar voice said, 'Hello, Emma. It's Magenta.' She sounded odd. Subdued. Perhaps she couldn't sleep and had been hitting her jellies again. Office gossip said she always kept a bottle of Temazepam handy to bring her down from her other narcotic indulgences.

And she never called me Emma, always Sweetie or Darling. Or her most patronising sobriquet, Blossom. Her voice sounded flat. 'Theo (not dog-breath?) called me about your situation. Said you should take a few days off. Get away somewhere...'

I said, 'Thanks, Maggie. But I'd rather work. I'd feel safer at the office and I want to get on with your story...' Brief silence. 'No, Emma. I'm dropping it...'

'...Dropping it?' Instantly, I was fully awake. 'But, it could be the scoop of the decade...You said as much yourself...'

'...I was hasty. And I've found out my informant misled me. I didn't think it through properly. Let wishful thinking get the better of me. Now, I realise I was being...er...fanciful. Sorry.'

She sounded desperate, as though she wanted me to be convinced. 'So drop it and take a week off, you must have had a terrible shock. There are more important things than work you know...' Now I knew there was something amiss. The Gorgon sounded like Mary Poppins. Had someone got to her? Had she been warned off? What was going on?

'OK, Maggie. But I don't want a holiday. I'd rather come in.'

She sighed heavily, 'Alright, if you insist. I think I might be able to find you something to keep you occupied. In fact I left Theo a note about a project I'd like you to work on. I'm at home at the moment but I should be in by nine. If you get to the office before me, Theo'll brief you. See you later.' She broke the connection. For a while I lay there puzzled. I decided I wasn't going to get back to sleep so I got dressed. JJ treated me gently, fussing round me and insisting I ate a leisurely but hearty breakfast. Later, after the worst of the rush-hour traffic, we drove together to The Globe. I left my car in my resident's allocated space.

On the way JJ brought up the ransacking of my flat. He said, 'What was he looking for? I mean, he did the same thing at Mrs Pearson's. What was he searching for that he thought the old lady and you had?' I looked at him and shook my head.

JJ ploughed on, 'If there is a connection between lottery wins and the murders, had she just won the jackpot?' He laughed. 'Don't tell me. You and she are part of a syndicate and The Phantom's stalking you all, one by one...' He saw my wintry smile and apologised, 'Sorry, Emms. My gallows humour sometimes runs away with me. It's not funny, what you're going through.'

We arrived in Shoe Lane at half past nine. We took the lift from the underground car park to the editorial floor. When we stepped out onto the landing we were pounced on. A group of early arrivals, who were round the coffee machine, surged towards us. Geoff Travis, The Globe's City Editor, spoke first. 'What a terrible experience for you. If there's anything any of us can do to help, just ask.' He must have seen my lip tremble because he pushed on hastily, 'Have you heard about The Gor--er--Magenta?'

JJ and I looked at each other and shook our heads. Geoff said excitedly, 'Dead. Killed in a hit and run. Apparently, she was just getting into the office limo outside her house when a scruffy vehicle mounted the pavement and hit her. Police say it was probably some joyrider on drugs. They'll probably never catch who did it. More than likely he's already torched the car and he's back home with a dozen alibis.' My mouth had dropped open and my mind was trying to compute this latest shock when Theo spotted us through the double doors and motioned the two of us to follow him. The rest went back to their desks, shaking their heads and whispering. We trailed past empty desks and into Theo's office where he closed the door. He stretched out a hand and put it on my shoulder. 'You alright, Emma?' I shrugged.

Then, with sincerity in his voice he said, 'I know Maggie was a cow but she didn't deserve this. What a waste. Some kid looking for kicks just wipes another human being off the face of the earth.' He smiled crookedly. 'The Chief's asked me to take over the helm temporarily.'

I asked, 'Did he say anything about a major exclusive Maggie had under wraps?' Theo looked puzzled. 'Not a thing. He just said for me to keep him in touch if the police come up with anything. Why, what was she working on?'

'I don't know,' I lied. She just seemed pleased with herself about something and made it clear she expected to be awarded more Brownie points when she told Sir Hugo.' JJ opened his mouth to say something so I shot him a warning glance and he closed it again. Theo picked a piece of paper up from his desk and said, 'I found this note from Maggie this morning. She must have written it last night before going home.

'It says she wanted you to do a profile on The Chief...' He wrinkled his brow, 'I suppose it comes at a propitious moment; I mean it'll take you away from the coal face. And it'll stop any conflict of interest between you as a reporter and you as a witness in a murder investigation.' Theo shook his head in wonderment. 'She might almost have known...'

'Known what?' I asked.

'Well, it's just that there you were last night working full bore on The Phantom killings. But, before anyone could know that by this morning you'd be actually involved in one of them, she writes me a note instructing me to take you out of the front line and ease you into a quiet backwater? Very prescient.'

JJ said, 'I don't think it's got anything to do with second sight. You know what The Chief's like. Loves to appear in his own columns. To be photographed in the Royal Enclosure at Ascot, at the Lord Mayor's banquet...hob-nobbing with the rich and powerful...All that sort of crap...I expect that when Maggie, still full of herself last night, rang The Chief he probably brushed her blockbuster aside, seeing the requirements of his own ego as of far more pressing importance.'

Theo said, 'Mmmm, maybe. Anyway, mine's not to reason why... Emms, if you feel up to it arrange an appointment to see the old coot.' Theo looked at the note again. 'Says nothing here about you, JJ, so you can get back to the grindstone and carry on where you and Emma left off last night.'

As we made to leave, Theo exclaimed, 'Jesus, I almost forgot. There are a couple of spooks waiting upstairs for you,

Emms. They say it's got to do with a police matter. They arrived about half an hour ago.' There was a strange expression on Theo's face as he spoke. It was a mixture of concern and a smirk. 'One of them says he knows you...'

I told JJ we'd compare notes later and left him to join the growing groups talking in hushed whispers about The Gorgon's rude departure from this life. My mind was still trying to cope with the deaths, in quick succession, of three people I knew. Instinctively, I switched into my journalist's detached mode.

I walked up one floor to the carpeted area we keep for the benefit of VIPs. As I pushed open the interview room door my heart jumped and started pounding wildly. The two men were sitting in easy chairs talking in undertones. When I walked in they both stood up. One of them, a tall, slim, dark-haired figure came forward and put his hands on my shoulders. We looked at each other silently. Then he said, 'Hello, Emms.'

Seven

It was a shock seeing Nick again, after all these months. He looked well. A little tired, perhaps. But he had the same glimmer of humour in his eyes and the way his lips quirked at the corners still made me go weak inside.

Now I knew why Theo's expression had been so odd. He'd known Nick and I when we'd been together and he'd watched my struggle to get life back on an even keel when we'd split up. I'd imagined a thousand times how I would handle meeting Nick again if we happened to bump into each other somewhere.

I'd be cool. Controlled. Together. He'd be flustered, tongue-tied and awkward. My exit would be with a nonchalant quip leaving him impressed and cursing his stupidity for letting such a prize out of his life. Instead, I gaped and I could feel a flush spreading from my neck to my face. My scar reddened deeply and itched infuriatingly. Speechlessly I allowed Nick, who seemed in perfect command of his emotions, to lead me to his companion. He said, 'Emma...I'd like you to meet a colleague of mine, in fact he's my boss, Jim Allardyce...'

Allardyce was about 50, as tall as Nick, but thicker set. A square face was topped by a shock of wiry, greying hair. His eyes were a penetrating blue but with laughter lines at the edges. The creases on his face betrayed his years of association with human weakness. He was the sort of person one could trust on sight. 'How do you do, Miss Holgate. I'm a fan of your column, and particularly your recent series on lottery winners. Most instructive. Almost makes me glad I've never had the lucky numbers.' I smiled weakly.

We all sat down, facing each other round a low, glass-topped coffee table. Nick kept his expression neutral, so I couldn't tell what effect meeting me again after all these months was having on him. A vague feeling of disappointment swirled through me. The least he could do. I thought, was to look as though he was finding it difficult - encountering again the woman he once planned to make his partner for life.

He leaned forward, his clasped hands resting on his knees. 'Emms, we heard about the terrible thing that happened to you last night. Are you OK?'

I was about sarcastically to say I was just fine, totally under control. After all it would be a pretty poor journalist who'd let the butchery of her next door neighbour, followed by the violent death of her editor, knock her off balance. Not to mention Annie. But, before I could speak Allardyce shot a reproving glance in Nick's direction and said kindly, 'Forgive Nick's rather gauche question, Miss Holgate...'

Perhaps, I hoped, Nick wasn't as self-controlled as he made out. And his brain had lost its co-ordination with his mouth. Allardyce was still speaking '...Of course you're not alright. Who would be after finding a mutilated body in their kitchen? However, Nick tells me you're a resilient person and, frankly in the circumstances, we had to see you rather quickly...'

I spoke for the first time and was surprised that the words came out without a tremor. 'I'm sorry. What do you mean, in the circumstances..?'

Nick blurted out, 'We think you might be next on The Phantom's list of victims.'

I blinked. For a moment I'd forgotten all that. The shock of seeing Nick here, in the familiar surroundings of my own territory, had driven recent events out of my mind. But he was now telling me what I'd already worked out for myself. What I hoped he and Allardyce didn't know was that I had a lottery ticket worth £17 million burning a hole in the safe at my bank.

And logic dictated The Phantom wouldn't kill me before he got his hands on it. And somewhere in all this mess was the key to Maggie's mega-exclusive, which I wanted to myself. I wasn't going to be a meek lamb to The Phantom's slaughter. I was going to track him down...and whoever he was working for. But first I needed more information. I said, 'Why on earth should The Phantom be interested in me?'

Nick deferred to his boss who started speaking. 'I'd better explain that we're not from a conventional police force. I'm a Commander in the National Crime Agency...Do you know of it?'

I nodded and he seemed pleased. He explained, 'The NCA was set up to bust organised crime and I pick my team very carefully. I asked Special Branch to release Nick to head up my section dealing with money-laundering...You may not realise it but this is a burgeoning industry in Europe mainly because international crime bosses regard us as a soft touch - whereas the US, having had something of head start, has cracked down hard and is making it extremely difficult for syndicates to operate.'

'But I thought the European banks were showing a united front on terrorist funds and dirty money?' I said.

The corner of Allardyce's eyes creased in a smile. 'That's what we're all supposed to think. But, in reality, it's a real hit or

Ticket to a Killing

miss affair. Our law's based on suspicion. Every employee in the finance industry is required to report any transaction they think is dubious. They have compliance officers whose entire job it is to check for suspicious movements of cash.'

His expression turned serious. 'But, either our systems, or individuals in them, are sloppy. Boxes are ticked without lateral thinking. This means that many suspicious transactions get through. Whereas in the US they've got special Investigation units, with sophisticated computer networks that track any unusual movements back to their sources...'

Nick chipped in, 'So the syndicates run to the UK where we're so incompetent it's laughable. It's said the biggest laundering operation is the City of London itself. But, even so, the big boys realise once we get our act together they'll be squeezed out again...Unless they come up with a foolproof way of exchanging their dirty money with no risk.'

I said, 'And you're about to tell me they've cracked the problem.'

Allardyce nodded, 'They've discovered a whiter than white source of cash that gives them the provenance they're looking for. It's called The National Lottery.'

Nick said, 'It's so simple but 100 per cent effective. They win the lottery. When they get their cheque for, say, ten million pounds they split the money into tranches of one million each and then add to it nine million of drugs money.

'They then split the 100 million and pay it into 10 different bank accounts. If any questions are asked as to where the ten million came from they produce the lottery as their alibi. Neat, Eh?'

Allardyce continued, 'But the fact that they don't actually win the lottery is a minor detail. Their agents "acquire" the ticket and thus, to all intents and purposes, become the owners. Who can prove that the ticket isn't legitimately theirs?'

I said, 'And they acquire the winning tickets by tracking down and murdering the real owners?' Allardyce looked startled and then recovered. 'Precisely. And, once the money's legitimised as it were, as an extra safeguard they then electronically squirt the one hundred million to other bank accounts all round the world where it becomes impossible to track back.'

Nick intervened. 'So you see, getting hold of lottery tickets is worth up to ten times the face value of the win. And from an international crime syndicate's point of view well worth the risk of killing a few innocent people. And there we have the link between these serial killings and the lottery.'

Allardyce said sombrely, 'If this isn't all bad enough, we've got wind that there's something else, even more sinister, being cooked up. But that's all we know at present. We're pulling out all the stops to crack this wide open now to see if we can get to the bottom of what it is.' He said almost as an afterthought. 'Although this has nothing directly to do with the Tory government, none of this would have happened under Labour. Because they have a declared policy to limit lottery winnings to a million.'

I looked at him, puzzled. He said, 'Well, a million's not enough to make it worthwhile for organised crime, so they'd have taken their business elsewhere. But while these massive "rollover" prizes are being paid out, the money-launderers are making hay while it lasts. At present they seem content to target the UK but we believe they might have Europe in their sights.'

Nick cleared his throat and said, 'Emms, getting back to why we think you're in danger. First, I have a confession to make. I gather Magenta must have told you about a tip-off concerning a connection between the lottery and The Phantom murders? Well that tip-off came from me. You see we hoped that if a paper with The Globe's clout started digging around, it would panic the syndicates into making a fatal mistake. But, we miscalculated...' He looked at me sorrowfully '...Somehow they found out what Magenta knew, saw it as a threat, and killed her.'

'Killed her? But it was a joy-riding kid who lost control...' Nick shook his head. 'It was no accident. They had to do something quickly before she passed her knowledge on. A hit and run is crude - but it's effective.'

But, I thought, she had passed it on. To me. And then she'd intended telling The Chief. But had she? No-one knows whether she actually managed to contact him. Yet, somewhere between briefing me yesterday afternoon and ringing me at seven this morning, she'd been got at. Either she'd been threatened or otherwise persuaded to drop the story. Was JJ's theory right? That Maggie's scoop of the decade had fallen victim to the proprietor's ego? Nothing more sinister than that?

Or, incredibly, was Sir Hugo Pentecost somehow involved? Too far fetched, even for a tabloid newspaper. But if he wasn't, who else had twisted her arm? And whoever her persuaders were, had she told them that she'd already passed the information on? I said, 'But why bother to silence her when they know the NCA is onto them?'

Allardyce said, 'Ah, but that's the point. They probably don't know it was us who was Magenta's contact. Being a journalist she probably didn't reveal her sources - especially when we got her to swear not to. No, It's more likely they think one of her staff's done some intelligent digging and put two and two together. Once they've got rid of her all they need to do is find the journalist hot on the scent.'

Nick continued, 'We have a theory they might think that journalist is you. Your by-line's been on your lottery series for weeks now and they know your reputation for investigative journalism. They probably drew an educated conclusion and that's why they sent their hired killer to your flat yesterday. It was nothing to do with the earlier murder. They probably trashed the place to throw us off the scent.

'Although they couldn't get to you last night, they knew where your editor would be this morning and decided to silence her first. Now, you're the only danger left to them and that's why we're here now.'

I said thoughtfully, 'I can follow your logic except for one thing: How did they find out Maggie knew what she did? If it was that secret she'd hardly have blabbed it about.' Allardyce said, 'Just what we'd like to know. Solve that one and we're a lot closer to finding the boss. Find him and we've got The Phantom...'

He regarded me seriously '...And that's why we need your help...'

Eight

We talked for another half an hour. I could hear the murmur of voices outside the door as The Globe went about its daily business. But in our small corner we were in a world of our own. A world of murder, international drug trafficking, money-laundering and crime barons growing fat on the back of human misery.

Allardyce paced the room, his hands thrust deep in his pockets as he painted a picture of what law enforcement agencies in 50 different countries were up against. 'We're like a few Canutes trying to hold back waves of filth. And the corruption's getting everywhere - the police, politics, legitimate business, industry, even the Church...

'We make arrests, of course, but every time we cut one head off, two more grow in its place. It may sound pompous, Miss Holgate, but it's a real threat to democracy. Governments seem powerless and are reacting by sticking their heads in the sand...' He nodded towards Nick...'We see what's happening and it's a nightmare. What we need is to inflict a decisive blow against the overlords. Then we'd be some way towards putting their syndicates out of business. But, we have to have a starting point. And that's where you, Miss Holgate, come in.' I told him to stop calling me Miss Holgate. Emma would be fine.

Nick said, 'Whether we like it or not, you've become a target of The Phantom. This means that if we keep close to you we'll be close to him. Because, somewhere out there, he's waiting his moment...' A frisson of fear ran down my spine. 'You're saying you want me to play the sacrificial goat?'

Allardyce said stiffly, 'Don't think we like the idea. But, you're the only real lead we've got. It also seems to me that you stand a better chance than those other poor devils…'

'…Why, because I'm forewarned?'

'No, because you're fore-armed. I'm asking Nick to stay close to you, as your protector as it were, until all this is over.'

'You mean he's going to be my bodyguard?'

'Precisely so. Since you need protection anyway we thought you, and we, could work together. I've called off Marsden and Pickford. If they need anything further from you they'll direct their questions through us. They didn't like it but I pulled rank and they had no choice.' He continued brusquely, 'This is how it would work: You continue normally at The Globe and we monitor your every move. If The Phantom should try anything, we'll have him. And that could lead to his boss. And that, in turn, might result in us closing down the drugs network and the money-laundering syndicate.'

Allardyce peered at me expectantly, 'Well, Miss Hol…Er…Emma?'

I looked out of the window and down at the street below. The black London taxis looked like toys, manoeuvering their way around two lorries delivering the next batch of newsprint for The Globe's ever-hungry machines.

Mentally I ran through my situation. I possessed a lottery ticket worth £17 million, which no-one knew I had. Except whoever had killed Annie and taken my receipt: The Phantom? He and his boss were probably becoming more than a little impatient

Ticket to a Killing

to get their hands on it. But, while they didn't know where it was, I was safe.

Meanwhile, Nick and Commander Allardyce had an alternative theory which also made me a target: That I had information dangerous to The Phantom and Co. All of which put the criminals in a dilemma. But they couldn't have me murdered until they had the ticket. On the other hand, as long as I was on the loose, I might write a story for The Globe linking the National Lottery with the serial killings. Which would blow their scam wide open. So, I pondered, what would I do in their place? A bribe? Intimidation? Kidnap? I turned round. My two companions were waiting silently for my answer. 'How, exactly, is Nick going to follow my every move?'

Allardyce cleared his throat awkwardly, 'I won't beat about the bush, Emma. I understand you and Nick were...er...engaged at one time. It seems apposite for the purposes of our exercise, as it were, if you and he should...um...effect a reconciliation.' Nick was looking embarrassed. He said placatingly, 'All we'd need to do is go through the motions. Just until this Phantom business is licked. You have to admit, it does have the virtue of simplicity. You and I appear to be trying again so no-one thinks twice about us being seen around together.' He reasoned, 'No-one, except Theo, knows I'm in the police because if you remember you used to insist that we kept it quiet. You didn't want to upset your friends, you said. So, we become a couple again and I can keep a really close eye on you...'

Allardyce interjected, 'But we'd like your association with the NCA to be a bit more than just a passive involvement. We think it would be an excellent idea if you actually work for us - temporarily of course - which would make it easier for Nick. He could share confidential information with you and you could be given access to our computer system.' He added with a grin, 'You'll have to sign the Official Secrets Act, of course.'

I wasn't as hard-boiled as I was making out so the prospect of Nick keeping watch over me was a comforting one. But, I didn't want those old wounds, which were only just beginning to heal, opening up again. On the other hand, I told myself, what choice did I have?

'OK, I'll go along with it. But I want you both, but particularly Nick, to understand that our apparent reconciliation is for show only and strictly business.' They both nodded. Then I said, 'But there is something that puzzles me. Why don't you just let me run a story on all this? It'll be like putting a bomb under the syndicates and they'd have to call The Phantom off.'

Allardyce shook his head regretfully, 'Would that we could. Your editor said the same thing. But, as we told her, if we did that they'd all go to ground and then pop up somewhere else when the heat's off. We only gave her the info on the strict understanding that she made lots of commotion but didn't use the story until we said it was OK. After all, she'd still have an exclusive when it was all over.'

So, I thought, The Gorgon had been duplicitous to the end. She'd intended to splash the story and had given me a week to get it together. I said, 'So, nothing of this must get out until your say-so?'

'Right. What we need is to get to their top man and destroy their chain of command. Then it'll take them years to recover, by which time our anti-laundering computer systems will be in place.' He added warningly, 'And, while I think of it, you must keep our arrangement strictly between us, OK?'

I agreed. 'So where do we go from here..?'

Nine

Theo looked at me expectantly as I stopped at his desk. 'Anything we can use in today's Phantom follow-up?'

'Sorry, Theo. Just routine questions. What's JJ working on?'

'He's trying to stitch something together we can bang an exclusive tag on.' His face took on a pleading look, 'Give him something the others haven't got for Christ's sake. If I'm to stand any chance of getting this chair permanently The Chief'll want to see some flair. You know how he loves flair. You can see The Sun and The Star's headlines now, can't you..? "...GLOBE HACK IN PHANTOM DRAMA..." "...PHANTOM STRIKES IN GLOBE GIRL'S FLAT..." Marsden seemed unusually forthcoming at this morning's media conference so everyone's got the same stuff...'

I said, 'But they haven't got "...PHANTOM MISSED ME BY MINUTES - Emma Holgate's Own Story..." have they?' His face brightened. 'Hey, you're a genius. Go to it. Tell JJ everything. Don't leave a thing out.'

I said resignedly, 'And I suppose after that you want me to get on with the Pentecost profile?' Theo nodded. 'Make him feel good, Emms. I've told him you're a hot-shot journalist and the best feature-writer we've got. So, turn on the feminine charm. I need all the gold stars I can get.'

'Anything new on Maggie's hit and run?' I asked.

'Not a thing. What could there be, anyway? A hit and run's a hit and run's a hit and run. I'll put the story on the front page with a black border round it. Good job she's not here or she'd be running it as the lead.' He sighed philosophically, 'As the poet said "...All paths of glory lead but to the grave..."'

As I walked through the newsroom, curious eyes followed me. They were wondering how I could turn up for work after what had happened last night. Geoff Travis waved from his desk under the window. Well done, Emma, work'll be good therapy. No point in brooding at home.' As though he realised he'd got his sympathies in the wrong order he added, 'Still knocked for six over Maggie...'

Home. That reminded me. Oscar and Kate. I rang my number and a ponderous voice answered. He said he was Pc Carter and who was I? I said I was ringing to check up on my cats. 'No need to worry, Ms Holgate. They've been fed and there's enough Kittykat in their bowls for another week I should think. Oh, and we've tidied the place up for you. You won't be able to tell anyone's been here - and that includes your...er... unwelcome visitor.' I thanked him and turned back to JJ.

I gave him a censored version of my conversation with Nick and Allardyce, majoring on my churned emotions when I'd unexpectedly encountered the man I had loved. After JJ sympathised, I explained that we couldn't use the story about The Phantom's link with the lottery and money-laundering. But that we'd have it exclusively when the NCA had cracked the case.

I remembered my promise to Allardyce and decided I shouldn't say anything, even to JJ, about working under cover for the law. Then we got down to concocting 'my personal story' of how I found Beryl Ormrod's body. I left no detail out so that by the time we'd finished it read like a thriller. Theo should be satisfied.

At the insistence of the police I had to give my own Press conference later in the day. It was a novel experience being on the receiving end of an inquisition. I held a lot back and eventually my fellow journalists trooped out grumbling. They knew The Gobe's story would be better than anything they'd be printing.

Ten

You could almost smell the money. Hand knotted Persian carpets on the floor; a Gauguin portrait and a Pissaro townscape of Dieppe on the walls. Underneath them, in little alcoves, a bank of computers showing Stock Market prices in London, Tokyo and New York. There were also television screens for video-conferencing or watching the CNN news. When the technology wasn't needed it could be swivelled back to be hidden behind carved, wooden panels.

It was late afternoon and I was in Sir Hugo Pentecost's penthouse suite in Docklands. Under a brilliantly-lit tropical fish-tank was a leather chesterfield settee and matching chairs. A restful spot to wait for inspiration, I mused. Or to cook up your next multi-million takeover. A picture window looked out onto a panorama of London split by the snaking blue highway of the Thames. In front of it was a magnificent, antique desk and, behind it, my boss - The Chief.

I'd seen plenty of pictures of him, and we'd once passed each other at a charity ball. But, as he stood up and leaned forward to shake my hand, I realised how accurate JJ's description of him was. He was in his fifties, 6ft tall and pear-shaped, with a smiling, jowly face and sparse hair. He must have weighed at least 18 stone.

According to JJ, Sir Hugo Pentecost, self-made millionaire, media grandee and kingmaker, was a dead ringer for Kasper Gutman, played by Sydney Greenstreet, in the 1940s black and white film The Maltese Falcon. And he sounded like him too. But, the clipped sentences and old world charm belied the ruthless rod with which he ruled his global empire. The affable charm concealed a massive ego and ferocious determination.

'Miss Holgate. A pleasure, indeed.' He waved me to the chesterfield and sat opposite. His chair sighed softly as his corpulent figure subsided into the leather. He ordered tea which appeared on a silver tray with matching teapot. His major domo poured the brew into fine porcelain cups and withdrew silently.

Sir Hugo said soberly, 'First, allow me to express my sympathies for your...ah...ordeal last night. And then for poor Miss Magenta to be struck down like that...' He shook his head disbelievingly '...To think that two such terrible events should happen to members of my own staff. Foolish, I know, but I can't help feeling somewhat responsible.'

I thanked him for his concern and reassured him that the two incidents' connection with The Globe was purely co-incidental. He seemed satisfied with that and, apart from making a flattering comment about my resilience, turned back to the matter in hand. 'I understand you wish to write a profile on me?' He saw the look on my face. 'Forgive me, dear lady, you regard this assignment more as a three-line whip of course. I'm sure I would in your place. However, I feel I must explain that the request came from your editor, not the other way round.'

I realised I'd forgotten to activate the recorder on my phone. It was still in my bag and I didn't want to have to take it out now and admit to my boss I often used it as a substitute for laborious note-taking. So, under the guise of reaching for a pen, I rummaged and tapped the record function. It might not pick up the entire conversation from that distance but it would have to do. Then I sat with my pen poised. 'Sir Hugo, perhaps we might begin with a bit of background. There's plenty in the cuttings, I know, but you can't always believe what you read in the newspapers.'

'A sense of humour, yes I like that. And not one to be intimidated by the presence of one of the world's most influential mortals. I do so tire of sycophants. I can see you and I are going to get along famously. Yes, famously.'

For the next hour he told me of his humble beginnings as the only son of Polish parents who had fled their homeland and settled in Swindon, in Wiltshire, after the war. Hugo had gone to a grammar school, which was followed by an apprenticeship at the Wiltshire Gazette where his father worked as head printer. I said, 'So, in a way you followed in your father's footsteps when you made the media your career.' His genial expression slipped for a split second and his face became a mask of bitterness. Then it was gone and he was smiling again.

'Alas, dear lady, my father and his adoptive country fell out rather badly. He never got over it and died a premature death. I never talk about this particular episode in my life and I expect you to make no reference to it in your article...' If that's what he wanted...it was his newspaper. But, it was strange I'd seen nothing about, what was obviously a noteworthy episode, in the files. I steered him onto safer territory. He told me that, after learning the business from the bottom up, the young Hugo managed to persuade a bank to lend him five thousand pounds to take over a run-down family newspaper.

It prospered and by the time Hugo was thirty, he owned a

string of publications throughout the south of England. Along the way he had changed his name by deed poll from Jazinski to Pentecost which, he thought, had a ring of dynamism and renewal about it. Later, he took an interest in commercial television, buying into a regional station in Southampton. Such was his flair with new technology that he always managed to stay one step ahead of the competition. Twelve years after that he had his own satellite television station in the US. From then until now his domain had grown exponentially until he owned newspapers, tv and radio stations, on-line operations and social media sites across the globe.

Meanwhile, he was diversifying into other industries, gobbling up companies in the US, Australia, Canada and South America. Officially, he was knighted in 2014 for his services to the media. But cynics claimed he had purchased his honour by throwing his newspapers and broadcasting operations behind the Conservative Party. Next step, so they said, was the House of Lords.

I shook my head in genuine admiration, 'With so many enterprises around the world, how do you keep track of everything that's going on?'

'A perspicacious question if I may say so. I confess a few years ago I would have been floundering. I'd never be able to attend all the meetings I'd need to direct operations. But, and I say this in all modesty, I could double my workload and still cope. You see I have two invaluable servants and through them I keep in touch with everything.'

'Two servants..?'

'Indeed yes. One is my technology. I have the very latest that science can offer. All my enterprises are linked to me either here or at my financial headquarters by a network of computers and personal devices.

'Forgive the arcana, but the technophiles call it groupware. So, I'm like the spider sitting at the centre of the web. At the touch of a button, or at a keystroke as the jargon would have it, I can control my entire empire...' He heaved himself out of his chair and walked to a console on his desk. 'I can videoconference with any of my managers without leaving this building. And I can call up on my terminal here any of the accounts of any of my world-wide holdings.

'I can even follow transactions as they're happening thousands of miles away. All I need to do is shuttle occasionally between here and my finance hub in the Channel Islands and I know, day by day, hour by hour and minute by minute what's going on.'

I said, 'That's very impressive. But, isn't it dangerous to rely on computers to control everything? I mean our system at The Globe's always crashing and when that happens people who've never known any other technology start seriously panicking.'

'How right you are again, dear lady. But, I have anticipated such an eventuality so everything is supported by a second network: belt and braces as you might say. And, in the unlikely event of both systems imploding, everything is backed up in my own server farm. So we never lose anything.'

'You said just now you have two servants. If technology is one, what's the other?'

'Not a What, my dear Miss Holgate, but rather a Who? I'm referring to George - my secret weapon.'

'Like George the automatic pilot?'

'You are a caution, Miss Holgate, and that's a fact. He very well could be described as a kind of pilot could George Bixby. Though I say it myself, George is one of my greatest finds. He is a veritable genius. What Dr Stephen Hawking is to theoretical physics, George Bixby is to cyberspace. He writes my software, re-designs my hardware and runs my digital world as God runs the universe. He may be small in stature but he's a giant among men...'

I was puzzled. I'd looked through the files on Sir Hugo before coming to the interview but I'd never come across anyone called Bixby. 'Is he new on the staff?' I asked. The Chief's jowls wobbled with mirth as he shook his head. 'No, no, no, Miss Holgate. He's just a shy, retiring type. Never happier than when he's grappling with the mysteries of deep data mining or augmented reality, or streaming game technology. Like a troglodyte in his cave, he's content to be in the dark so long as there's a screen glowing in front of him.'

'So where is this George, I'd like to meet him.'

'Alas, Miss Holgate, the bird has flown - literally. Only today he has gone to Guernsey on one of his regular trips. As I mentioned earlier I have offices there, and my server farm, and George visits whenever it takes his fancy and performs what you might call a financial and technological health-check to make sure everything is in order.'

'So, he's privy to all your most confidential dealings?'

'Just so, dear lady, just so. He is, as I've said, the God of my cyber universe from whom no secrets are hid.'

'This must make him a very powerful person.'

Sir Hugo waved his hand deprecatingly, 'That kind of power is for ordinary mortals. George needs no such thrill. He's at his happiest when he's pushing out the frontiers of digital technology. I leave him a free hand and supply him with, at times, quite considerable resources to develop his pet ideas. And he's perfectly happy with that. You'll see what I mean when you eventually make his acquaintance...'

'You said he's small in stature. Is that significant?'

'Once again, like an arrow, you unerringly pierce to the heart of the matter. Like his fellow genius, Stephen Hawking, George is, what one might call in these politically-correct times, physically challenged. To put not too fine a point on it George is a midget. A dwarf...'

Sir Hugo explained, 'He was born of normal parents but the poor fellow was afflicted with glandular problems and stopped growing at 3ft 6in. It gave him a rather...er...jaundiced view of life I'm afraid...But sometimes nature can temper her wild excesses with compensatory gifts. George's compensation is his intellect. And he has a special bent in the realm of digital technology. He plays the computer keyboard with dazzling virtuosity.'

He gazed at the ceiling as he reminisced. 'I first found George when I took over a small commercial TV station. They had him poked away in a basement mending computer consoles. They had no idea they were harbouring the veriest simulacrum of an Einstein in their midst. I released him from his cage and, like a wild bird, his creative spirit soared.

'He created computer software and hardware that enabled me to strip out echelons of overmanning and run my companies at immense profit. Yes, Miss Holgate, George and I were made for each other.'

'So you stay one jump ahead of the opposition by staying one jump ahead in the technology?'

'Just so. And I will always be the leader because no-one can match George's genius. If he left me and set up his own IT company he could make millions for himself. But, he likes what he's doing and has no desire for change. For which small mercy I am truly grateful.'

'So what's your tame Einstein working on at the moment that's going to revolutionise the world?'

Sir Hugo's expression turned serious. He strode to the

window and looked out at the ranks of office buildings jostling for space across the river. He hummed to himself and bounced on the balls of his feet. Then he turned round again and fixed me with a messianic stare.

'I like you, Miss Holgate, I really do. And therefore I'm going to trust you. But what I'm about to impart is strictly not for publication. Is that understood?' I agreed. He went on, 'Let me ask you first what you know about computer viruses.'

'Isn't it a special code that's put into a computer file that corrupts the data?'

'An admirably pithy summary. Yes, and it can spread from one computer to another wrecking months or years of work. You perspicaciously suggested earlier that I was courting danger by relying so heavily on technology. Of course you were right.

'Thousands of companies the world over are being attacked every day by viruses and millions, even billions, of dollars are being lost.'

When he saw my face he decided I needed my skimpy knowledge of the subject fleshed out. He said helpfully, 'The viruses are either what are known as "polymorphic" - that is they keep changing shape to avoid detection - or "stealth", which hide and pounce unexpectedly. Then there are the sub-categories...resident viruses, direct action, overwrite, boot, macro directory file infectors. I swear the next global war will be a battle of the viruses. Whoever wins will rule the world.

'Of course there's anti-virus software that tests for all the known variants. But as fast as this arrives on the market, some hooligan hacker's invented a new form of sabotage...'

I said, 'But George has come up with something to stop them?'

'Better than that, dear lady. George Bixby's found a

foolproof way of neutralising any form of virus, in existence now and yet to be invented. He calls his brainchild "Rainbow."'

He looked at me balefully. 'Just in case you don't appreciate the significance of his discovery, Miss Holgate, I should explain that whoever installs his system would be guaranteed virus-safe for ever. I looked suitably impressed. 'That's quite an invention. So Pentecost Industries are all set to make billions selling this round the world?'

He waved his hand dismissively. 'I'm in no hurry. First things first. I shall market test it in my own companies. Thereafter, we shall see.'

I said casually, 'It's a good job George is an honest sort. I mean if he wasn't, then presumably he could create a virus that could do the opposite - foil all attempts to detect it and ruin the data. Just think of the havoc he could cause to your rivals...'

'For a moment Sir Hugo looked startled. Then he said silkily, "I suppose the same could be said if the Police Commissioner should turn to crime, or the doctor should decide to poison his patients. Tut! tut! You journalists do have such a cynical view of humanity. I suppose it's an occupational hazard.'

I said levelly, 'I'm sorry. I was being mischievous. You've been very helpful this afternoon and I appreciate your confidence. I think I've got enough to write my profile.'

'Oh but you've only got half the story, dear lady. You must come to Guernsey and see what we get up to there. It's the heart of our financial operation...' He leaned forward to peer at a calendar on his desk. 'As a matter of fact I'm going there tomorrow. Perhaps you'd care to join me and I'll show you how I actually exercise that control I was talking about.' He added persuasively, 'Also, you'll be able to meet George Bixby. He'll still be there squirting millions around the globe from his "mission control."'

Sir Hugo was the boss. And I wasn't going to argue. But how could I explain my bodyguard? I said thoughtfully, 'I should be delighted, Sir Hugo. But, as I'm due a few days off, I wonder if you would allow me to combine business with pleasure? You see...' I hesitated '...I hope you won't mind if I mention a personal matter. You see...my fiance and I split up about six months ago. But we've decided to try again. In fact it was only today we made the decision.'

I explained, 'They say it's an ill wind. But when Nick heard about the murder in my flat he came across to see if I was alright and, I suppose emotions were running high, before we knew it we were apologising to each other for past mistakes and...well...we agreed to have another go...'

Sir Hugo beamed, 'My dear lady. How fortuitous. Of course you must ask your young man to join us.' He stared at me as if he'd just made up his mind about something. 'In fact, you will both be my guests. And as I own the Breton Hotel - one of the island's finest, though I say it myself - I can guarantee you'll lack for nothing while you're there...'

I went to object and say we'd make our own arrangements but he held up a hand. 'I absolutely insist. Let's say I wish you to acquire, first hand, a feel for the culture of a Pentecost enterprise. Yes, yes, it will all fit in beautifully: You can complete your research and I can feel some small satisfaction in smoothing the path of true love.'

Sir Hugo said he would inform the hotel and a car would pick us both up tomorrow and take us to City Airport, where his private jet would fly us to The Channel Islands.

Eleven

Before I left Docklands, I rang Theo to tell him of The Chief's royal command and asked him to tell JJ what was going on. Then I drove back to the flat to feed Oscar and Kate. When I pushed open the door, I was amazed. The police team had done a good job at repairing the damage. There was no sign of last night's chaos.

I looked through the inner door to the living room. Everything was just as it was two days ago, except it was a lot tidier. The books were back on the shelves, the carpets had been vacuumed and the ripped cushions had been re-stuffed and sewn up with a neat hand.

My sister, Wendy, lived with her accountant husband, Harry, and my two nieces, Nicola and Vicky, in a three-storey, Victorian house in Hornsey Rise. I rang her there and spent the next 15 minutes calming her down. After hearing about the murder, she'd been trying to reach me all day but no-one had seemed to know where I was.

I told her I was fine; The Phantom had been after Mrs Ormrod and had cornered my neighbour in the wrong flat. I don't know if Wendy believed me but it might stop her worrying. She agreed to collect Oscar and Kate the next day and look after them until I got back from Guernsey. My cats always went to Hornsey when I was away on assignment, so the routine was a familiar one to them.

Next, I rang Nick who was just as frantic as Wendy. He'd gone back to The Globe after lunch to start his protection duties and found me gone. By the time he'd got to Sir Hugo's place, I'd left there. He was about to dial my flat for the fourth time when I'd rung him.

After the explanations, I told him of Sir Hugo's offer to both of us and Nick seemed excited. I reminded him of our agreement and he said it was nothing to do with our relationship and he'd explain later. He said that, since we were going to be thrown together over the next few days, it might be an idea if I stayed the night at his flat. I was too weary and scared to protest. But I made the point: I wanted a separate room.

I had a few days leave owing to me at work so I decided to pack enough for up to a week in warmer climes. I was in the middle of deciding what sweaters to take for the cool evenings, when the phone rang and I spent the next 10 minutes in earnest conversation. Then it rang yet again, just as I had heaved my case through the front door and was turning the key in the lock. I fought my way back in and picked up the receiver before the answerphone had a chance to click in.

From the atmospherics on the line the call could have been coming from twenty fathoms down, off the coast of Albania. A distorted voice said, 'They seek him here, they seek him there, they seek The Phantom everywhere...' There was so much mush the voice was barely recognisable as male. And it had a weird Donald Duck quality about it.

I was so flustered I said the first thing that came into my head. 'How did you get this number?' I asked. 'Not only have I got your number but I know all about you, even to the dress you're wearing today. Polka-dot would be a fair description, wouldn't you say?'

He must have been following me. If he really was The Phantom, I'd been within a few yards of Public Enemy Number One and hadn't known it. I tried to think back over the day, to recollect any sinister face. A blank. 'Who are you, really?' Static and phasing again. Donald Duck said, 'We were ships that passed in the night. I was so sorry to have missed you yesterday. I'd been looking forward to a cosy chat about a matter of mutual interest...'

As calmly as I could I said, 'You're not The Phantom. Someone as clever as him wouldn't risk staying on this line while the police traced the call...' A derisive laugh through the echo and the static. 'The technology has yet to be invented that could trace a digital, pay-as-you-go mobile phone which I shall throw away after our chat. I could be calling you from the other side of the moon.'

He added sinisterly, 'But in fact, I'm very, very close. I know your every move.'

'If you know my every move,' I challenged, 'where was I going just before you rang this number.' The caller's reply drained the blood from my face. 'To make arrangements for your romantic break in the Channel Islands with your ex-lover...'

Fear coursed through me. Only Sir Hugo, my sister, the office and now Nick, knew that. Of those four only Sir Hugo could have passed the information on to The Phantom. I dismissed the thought as soon as it surfaced. Why would he? Nothing was making any sense.

Maybe if I kept this caller on the line he'd trip himself up. 'How do I know you really are The Phantom? Prove it...' The hoarse and desperate voice that came out of my mouth seemed

Ticket to a Killing

to belong to someone else.

'Why are you being so tedious, Emma? But, if you insist...Do you recognise these words: "Received - one lottery ticket dated June 11, 2018, containing the winning numbers of 12, 14, 37, 41, 43, 46, which the owner, Mrs Annie Pearson, has entrusted to my care..."'

The caller continued, 'Happily for me, dear partner in crime, this document contains your very legible signature.'

I asked evenly, 'What exactly is it you want?'

A satisfied sigh. 'That's better. Partners should co-operate, don't you agree?'

Fear was being replaced by anger. I said, 'What's all this about partners?'

The Phantom answered, 'Were you thinking that now she's dead, your need is greater than hers?'

Before I could respond he went on, 'What were you planning? To wait until all the fuss had died down and then cash in the ticket and keep all £17 million for yourself? Tut tut. Not on, I'm afraid. My principals wouldn't allow it. They want to retrieve their investment...'

'...If that ticket's not mine,' I said defiantly, 'it certainly doesn't belong to you, or your principals - whoever they are.' Then as if having an afterthought, I said, 'But, perhaps if I could meet them personally, we could come to an arrangement...'

Silence.

I careered on, 'Alright then, all I have to do is go to the police and hand the ticket over and explain...'

'...Explain? Explain what? That you somehow seem to have acquired a lottery ticket worth millions belonging to a woman now murdered. Don't you think they'd be a mite suspicious? Especially if some public-spirited citizen sent them your receipt.' The voice continued with remorseless logic, 'If that happened, they'd conclude you went to see Mrs Pearson in your capacity as a journalist. And, when you saw this geriatric with a piece of paper worth £17 million, you suddenly realised this was your once-in-a-lifetime opportunity. You took advantage of a poor, confused, frail old lady.

'You conned her into parting with the ticket, in exchange for a worthless piece of paper. Later, you returned to her flat, murdered her, retrieved the evidence and used your own newspaper to compound the assumption that poor Mrs Pearson was yet another victim of that psychopath, The Phantom.'

·I said fiercely, 'They'd never believe such a wild story. And you know it wasn't like that.' The voice through the ether took on a soothing tone. 'There's no need for us to fight, Emma. We should be working together for our mutual benefit. My associates are pragmatic people. They realise you've tucked away the ticket somewhere safe - a bank, perhaps?

'So, they need your co-operation to retrieve their investment and I've been authorised to offer you a deal...'

Twelve

When I arrived at Nick's cottage in Highgate I was suddenly nervous about being alone with him. I didn't know how I was going to react. I'd kept my feelings battened down ever since I'd seen him with Allardyce in the interview room this morning.

The house was one of those modernised, Edwardian terraces with exterior character intact, while the insides had been ripped out to accommodate essentials for life in the 2020s - dishwasher, automatic washing machine, microwave oven, satellite TV, around-the-house sound system and a smart metering system for saving energy.

He greeted me with a neutral kiss on the cheek and showed me to the spare room. By the time I'd unpacked and had a shower Nick had pulled the curtains to shut out the fading light and the table in the lounge-diner was laid. Red candles in filigree holders were flickering romantically.

The smell of lamb casserole seeped out of the kitchen. It was always a joke between us when we were living together that Nick was a better cook than me. He poured us both a drink and we sat down in armchairs opposite each other. He said awkwardly, 'Emms, this is a strange situation. I promise I won't get heavy about us but I do want to say that I was really pleased to see you again this morning, despite the circumstances.'

I hesitated before answering. 'Nick I meant what I said about keeping things on a business footing...' He held up his hands in a gesture of surrender. 'OK, I'll leave it there.' He consulted his watch. 'We've got half an hour before the meal's ready so let's talk shop. In fact, I've another confession to make.'

I looked at him wondering what he was going to say. Was my phone bugged? Did Nick know about the call from The Phantom and the £17 million lottery ticket sitting in my bank?

Nick didn't seem to notice the flash of alarm that must have crossed my face. Not to mention Mark burning redly. Nick said. 'We leaked the link between the lottery winners and The Phantom to Magenta for a specific reason - it wasn't just to put pressure on some crime baron: it was to gauge the effect it had on one specific person.'

Nick leaned forward, put his drink on the table and took a deep breath. 'Brace yourself for this...For some time now we've suspected your boss Pentecost's up to his neck in one of the biggest criminal empires the UK has ever known. And before you say that's impossible, remember Maxwell.

'That's why I couldn't believe our luck when you told me on the phone earlier that we've been invited to be his guests in the Channel Islands. It's just the chance we've been waiting for to get a look behind the scenes. As you can imagine, we're having to tread very, very carefully on this. Sir Hugo's a respected member of the Establishment, with a lot of powerful friends who'd only be too delighted to rubbish the NCA and all it stands for.'

'Pentecost? A crime baron? You're right I do think it's impossible, despite Maxwell. And why would the

Establishment want to rubbish the NCA?' I said.

'There are plenty of politicians who hate the idea of a British FBI and we've had to fight for funds every step of the way. Some would rather let Pentecost get away with murder than see us succeed. So, you see, if we're to prove our case every piece of evidence has got to be copper-bottomed'

A piece of the jigsaw dropped into place. It could have been how The Phantom knew about my planned Guernsey trip. If Sir Hugo was involved he could have briefed his hired killer. But, despite the Maxwell precedent, I still couldn't see The Chief mixed up with drug traffickers and international crime syndicates. It wasn't his style.

I asked Nick, 'What could possibly be in it for Sir Hugo, who's already a billionair, to risk everything for just more money - money he could never spend in his lifetime anyway?' Nick rubbed his jaw reflectively, 'I'm not sure. But I suppose it could be to do with power. When people like Pentecost get a taste for it, it becomes just like a drug. The more they have, the more they need. And also the thrill. To be a scion of respectability while at the same time being involved in the UK's most notorious murder sensation since the Yorkshire Ripper, probably beats even cocaine.'

I shook my head. I still wasn't convinced but Nick pressed on. 'While he gets away with it, he lives life on the edge. Every moment is sweet, every success becomes a triumph. Maxwell must have felt something of the sort as he cooked his books and robbed thousands of pensioners. But this makes Maxwell seem like the vicar who ran away with the offertory.'

Nick looked at the clock and smiled apologetically. 'That's enough shop for now. Dinner should be ready. And I've got a chilled bottle of Sancerre. You can bring me up to date on what you've been doing for the last six months...'

For the next two hours we talked and talked. It was as though we'd never parted. My heart still leapt every time Nick smiled that crooked smile of his and he still gave himself away by unconsciously blinking rapidly to cover his emotions. By the time we'd finished a second bottle of white wine all the old emotions were tumbling around inside me. Why had we split up? Why had we tortured ourselves when it was obvious we both needed each other so much?

Nick pinched out the candles and came round to my side of the table. He leaned down and kissed my neck. A delicious shiver ran through my body. 'I still love you, Emms,' he breathed into the softness of my skin. I raised my face and our lips met in a long, sensuous kiss. It had been so long...A heady desire cascaded through me like a swollen river. As Nick drew me to my feet, and we clung to each other, I began trembling uncontrollably.

A small voice in my head reminded me insistently of my earlier resolutions. But it was drowned out by six months of repressed need intensified, perhaps, by the events of the past two days...'Oh, Nick. I've missed you so.'

'And, I've missed you, darling...' Our lips met again and the tips of our tongues touched, lazily at first and then with more urgency. We broke away and hand in hand stumbled into the bedroom. Nick began undoing the buttons on the front of my dress. His right hand scooped my left breast and massaged it gently.

I could feel my nipples harden, making rivet-like dents in my bra. Nick eased my dress off my shoulders and it slipped to the floor. I stood before him as I'd done so often when we were together, in just my underwear. Which he would love to remove, slowly and sensually.

But, suddenly, the dam of passion in us both gave way and

Ticket to a Killing

we were lost in a frenzy of undressing. Then, naked, Nick slipped to his knees and buried his face in the tangle between my thighs. Then he began burrowing deeper.

An aching need surged through my loins. I wanted him badly. I pulled him to his feet and began kissing his neck and chest, working my way down to his flat, muscular stomach. My tongue flicked and all the while Nick's head was raised heavenwards. His eyes were closed and he began groaning softly.

With each movement Nick's groans got louder. Abruptly, he gripped my head between both hands and eased me away. 'Not yet,' my love,' he said, gasping. 'I want to give you pleasure.' He motioned me to lie on my back. As I did so, he pushed my legs apart and slipped inside me. A spasm of ecstasy stabbed through me and I threw my arms round his buttocks and pulled him even deeper into me.

The more Nick probed, the more exquisite became the shattering paroxysms. Together we undulated, moaning and keening as the tides of bliss surged through us like electricity. Our rhythm harmonised as I ground my pelvis into his. He wetly kissed and licked my lips and ears as he thrust with his hips. Together, bucking and humping, like a crazy see-saw, our tempo quickened. Finally, he cried, 'Yes, Oh yes. Now. Now,' and he became racked with shudders. My pelvis arched and I surrendered to the waves of pure pleasure that flooded through me.

For a moment we stayed there, our bodies throbbing and our lungs gasping. Then Nick spoke. 'That was wonderful darling.   Welcome   home...'

Thirteen

Later, as we drank our coffees and recovered our decorum, we talked again about Nick's suspicions of Sir Hugo and how the NCA had tried, and failed, to get any real evidence against him. Nick said gloomily, 'Allardyce's hope that catching The Phantom will lead to Pentecost seems a longshot to me. But, it could work the other way round.'

'How?' I asked.

'Well, if only we could know when one of Pentecost's minions was going to pay in the lottery cash, we'd have a starting point. Because, if we did know, and Pentecost is using the money to launder drugs funds through his own secret subsidiaries, we could track the payment's movements through the banking system. Then we'd have some solid evidence.'

My body was still glowing from our love-making and I was finding it hard to concentrate. 'How would we have solid evidence?' I asked. Nick said, 'Ironically, it would be provided through Pentecost's own computer system. You see his love for all things digital and hi-tech could trip him up in the end. Because all his transactions are recorded on his back-up system,' I nodded and told Nick some of what I'd learned at Canary Wharf.

Nick went on, 'Once the cash has been paid in and then

squirted to accounts round the world, it'll all be recorded. If we could somehow get hold of that particular Pentecost computer file our boffins could unscramble the information and we'd have a complete picture of Pentecost's network. Nick was warming to his theme and he started pacing up and down as he talked. 'Our theory is that this network - like a spider's web - mirrors the drug syndicates' own organisation. So, once we know the accounts which the supplementing lottery money's being credited to, we'd have a trace on all Pentecost's associates. And the added bonus would be that these files would also enable us to backtrack on previous payments, the dates of which might match up with the dates of the serial murders...'

I said rhetorically, 'So getting hold of these back-up files would kill two birds with one stone - it would provide evidence on the drug trafficking and money laundering and it could link Pentecost with The Phantom.'

'Exactly. So you see how important it is to get hold of it after Pentecost's acquired a lottery jackpot. Once we've analysed its data we can launch "Operation Starburst."' Nick saw my look of puzzlement. He explained that the NCA and a dozen or so other law enforcement agencies around the world had agreed on a series of co-ordinated swoops once the exact locations of all the drugs outposts were known. The raids had been named 'Operation Starburst.'

I looked at Nick thoughtfully and said, 'So getting hold of this back-up information is crucial. But only after a multi-million pound deposit's been made. Right?' Nick agreed. He said, 'We've been expecting Pentecost's man to claim last week's £17 million but, according to Venture, no-one's been in touch. But I'm sure that's why that old woman in Chiswick was killed. She was the winner but before she could alert anyone,

The Phantom got there first, killed her and walked off with the ticket.'

He said, 'But the damnable frustration is that no-one can prove a thing. That's why we need a break. And that's what I'm hoping we'll get from our trip to the Channel Islands.'

My head began to swim trying to understand the complexity of Allardyce's plan. 'Tell me if I've got this right. You're waiting for a Mr X to make a claim for the £17 million. When he does, and it ends up in Pentecost's bank, you expect it to be squirted – along with the now-laundered drugs money - to outposts around the globe. Outposts which you believe are linked with a narcotics and money-laundering enterprise. Once the money's been sent, the transactions would be faithfully recorded on his computer back-up system.

'Getting hold of this information, and deciphering account holders on it, would be the signal for an international police swoop. Also, by matching previous large deposits at Pentecost's bank with the dates and locations of the lottery murders, you might be able to link the drugs and money-laundering operations with the serial killings. Have I missed anything out?'

Impressed with my summarising, Nick said, 'Only one thing. Once we've got all this evidence, we stand a fair chance of sweating The Phantom's identity out of Pentecost.' I said nothing but it seemed to me the NCA had set itself an impossible task. But, as the Chinese say, journey of a thousand miles begins with first step. And first step here was someone had to claim the £17 million winnings. Which gave me an idea...

Fourteen

The next morning Nick and I left the cottage and went in separate directions - he to the NCA HQ in Tinworth Street to brief Allardyce on our trip, and me to my bank. There, I asked for my sealed envelope and a private room for five minutes.

Back at the office I told Theo more about how The Chief had made me an offer none of us could refuse. Theo agreed that I could take a few extra days off, which had been owing to me. My name had already been removed from the reporters' roster.

JJ was hunched over his glowing terminal, pecking at its keyboard. I asked him what the latest was on the London murders. He shrugged, 'Everyone's making up whatever they can to give their story a fresh feel. But the truth is the cops are clueless and we're all chasing each other's tails. I don't think The Phantom need lose any sleep.'

I said quizzically, 'There was a curious moment when I was interviewing Pentecost yesterday. He clammed up as soon as I asked him about his father. Any idea why?'

JJ looked at me strangely. 'No, haven't a clue. Not crucial to the profile, though is it?'

'No, but it's a tantalising gap.'

I gave JJ the phone number of The Breton Hotel in case he

needed to get in touch. I told him that Nick and I were mixing business with pleasure. He looked startled for a moment, then his face broke into a smile. He reached over and squeezed my hand. 'I'm really pleased for you, Emms. I dunno, some people have all the luck. I get stuck here chasing a vanishing story up a cul-de-sac and you get a romantic break, all expenses paid....' Then he looked serious for a moment. 'But, you're doing the best thing possible. It'll get you away from all the trauma of the last couple of days.'

The limousine, with blacked out privacy windows, arrived in mid-afternoon and drove us in style to City Airport where we were given VIP treatment before boarding Sir Hugo's Gulfstream-G650. With a range of 7,000 miles it could carry 8 passengers in luxury more than half way round the world. In this instance it would be taking just two people a short hop of 200 miles. Sir Hugo, unconcerned with the expense, had gone on ahead and had then sent the jet back to pick us up.

On the flight Nick was more than attentive - he was almost proprietorial, as though it was a foregone conclusion that I belonged to him again. I began to feel the first faint stirrings of the same resentment that had finally led to our splitting. My thoughts floated back to last night. I should have remembered that wine always had that effect on me. It only took a few glasses before I was viewing life through a romantic, rose-coloured magnifying glass.

But, the morning after, the practical side of my nature always asserted itself and sat on my shoulder tut-tutting over my alcoholic excesses. It was tutting now. Nick and I had parted for good reason, I thought. One candlelit dinner and two bottles of Sancerre had changed nothing. I put these musings out of my mind. I had enough to worry about for the time being. But, memo to self: it wouldn't be fair on Nick if I let him carry on thinking we were a couple again.

My introspection was interrupted by the 'ping' of the seatbelts sign as we swooped towards Guernsey Airport runway. Just an hour and a half after walking out of The Globe, we entered The Breton Hotel's reception. When we announced who we were, three receptionists with welcoming smiles vied to greet us. One, in a smart green suit and crisp white blouse explained that our room, and all other expenses, were with the compliments of the management for the duration of our stay.

On the top floor we were shown into the hotel's Royal Suite. I gasped as we walked in. The room was full of flowers. There were different arrangements on the coffee table, the writing desk and on the dining table in the corner of the room. The bedroom, off the sitting room, also had a display. The porter withdrew, bowing his head deferentially.

When he'd gone, Nick put his ear to the double doors and then raised his finger to his lips. He pulled me to the French doors, which led out onto a balcony overlooking the island's harbour and yachting marina. As we stood together, our hands on the guard-rails, looking out to sea, he leaned towards me and pretended to nibble my ear.

He whispered, 'Be very careful what you say and do in the room. It might sound paranoid but Hugo might not just be an old-fashioned romantic. It's far more likely that he's arranged this room because he's bugged it. There might even be the odd closed circuit camera about. So whatever we do it must chime in with us, the happy couple planning our future.'

Nick saw me staring at him and shaking my head. He said warily, 'Darling, what's the matter?' 'It's...it's...' I waved my hand round us.'...All this. Nothing seems real. And I can't help feeling that last night wasn't real either. I mean things haven't changed in us...What we found difficult to live with in each other six months ago is still there.'

'You mean you wished last night hadn't happened?'

'Oh Nick, I don't know. And while we're in the middle of all this how can we be sure? Let's just cool it for a while and concentrate on uncovering whatever Pentecost's up to. Then we can take stock of our own situation.' He looked disappointed. 'But we're supposed to be two lovers attempting a reconciliation. If this place is bugged, we're not going to be very convincing.'

I reasoned, 'We can still be affectionate and considerate. We don't have to be going at it like warthogs to be convincing, do we?' Nick smiled lopsidedly and said without rancour, 'OK, my love. We'll play the parts with no strings attached.' He held up his crossed fingers, 'Pax, eh?'

We showered and changed for dinner before going down to the restaurant. Nick ordered a bottle of Moet and I don't know how much of it was an act but we laughed and giggled like a honeymoon couple. Later that night I stamped on my romantic inclinations as they surfaced through the alcohol and, platonically, Nick and I slept the night away.

The next day, while I waited for the summons to visit Sir Hugo's offices in Lefebvre Street, in the capital St Peter Port. Nick and I just enjoyed each other's company. We slept in late, ate out and visited some of the island tourist attractions along the way. The most recent dramatic chapter in Guernsey's history was the occupation by Hitler's troops during World War 2.

All round the coastline the evidence was still there in the shape of stark concrete and steel bunkers. They were built by slave labour imported from Europe. The Fuhrer decreed that the British archipelago should be turned into an impregnable fortress. For five years those islanders who hadn't evacuated to

England lived under the Nazi jackboot.

We hired a car and drove round the coast road. I tried to see if anyone was following us, but if they were it wasn't obvious. We pulled in at a viewing point on the cliffs 200 feet up. Across the sea the island of Sark rose chunkily out of the spume and Jersey was a smudge on the horizon.

Nick stroked my hair and then caught himself. He adopted a business-like expression. 'Jim Allardyce has arranged for us to be linked to the NCA HQ's computer. We'll feed in our data and they'll analyse it and plot our next moves. Meanwhile, we try to get under the skin of Hugo's operations.'

I was puzzled. 'Where's the computer; not in the hotel room, surely?'

Nick said briskly, 'Tomorrow, we check out of the hotel. We can tell Pentecost that, while we're most grateful for his kindness, we felt we needed to be on our own. Then we move into a holiday let. At least that's what it's supposed to be. But, it's actually owned by the NCA and on the books of an agency in St Peter Port.'

Nick rubbed his hands. 'I think you're going to be impressed, Emms. We've been planning for this for some time and the IT boys have thrown everything into matching Sir Hugo's technology. Our new home's a temple of high tec. Not only will we be permanently patched into the NCA's server, but we'll also have the codes to access the National Police Computer, Interpol and Europol's records, ditto the FBI and CIA. Plus we have scrambled voice and visual contact with Tinworth Street.' His face creased with amusement, 'And, if we get bored, we can surf the Internet and play Grand Theft Auto, or chess if you feel like more intellectual stimulation.'

When we got back to the hotel there was an envelope waiting for me. It contained an invitation from Hugo to myself and my 'escort'. It said he would be delighted if we joined him and a few friends for dinner in a private room at L'Escalier Restaurant that evening. My 'escort' should wear black tie.

In our room I waited until Nick was in the shower before opening the wardrobe door to reveal the personal safe installed for the convenience of guests. It was open and ready to be fed a personal electronic code. I punched in mine and took an envelope out of my bag and put it inside, slamming the door. I listening to the whirr of the digits being fed into the memory and tried it to make sure it was securely shut. It was.

Fifteen

When I emerged from the bedroom at just after seven, Nick said I looked stunning, which made me feel good despite what Annie had said about a man loving what was on the inside, as well as what was visible to the eye. In all the time we'd known each other Nick had avoided mentioning 'Mark.' Perhaps he really didn't think it was important.

The outfit I'd chosen tonight showed off the tan I'd managed to acquire from what little sun there had been this year. The maxi-length, gold-coloured dress had a halter neck that flattered my figure. A deep split down both sides revealed, though I say it myself, attractive legs. Even the single-minded Sir Hugo might find his pulse quickening, I thought. On my feet I wore gold sandals and round my neck a gold cross on a gold chain. Just a dab of my favourite perfume, Obsession, completed the ensemble. I was ready to take on the world.

'You look good enough to eat,' Nick said taking me into his arms. I felt myself tense up and he must have sensed it too, because he released me with an apologetic, 'I know. Down boy.' He gave me a pleading look. I said sternly, 'Right now we have to win Hugo's confidence and size up any of his friends who might be useful. So, tuck your libido back into your trousers and let's go.'

While Nick checked to see if our car had arrived, I handed an envelope I'd just removed from the room's safe to the receptionist. I said, 'This is extremely important. Someone will be calling in later to collect this for a Mr Scarlett. Please make sure it's handed over. There'll something left for me in exchange.' Our association with Sir Hugo had its effect. The smart youth behind the desk practically snapped to attention. He said he'd make it his personal business to ensure my instructions were carried out to the letter.

When we were shown into Hugo's private room, his other guests were already there. They were sitting round a table under the window, which looked out across the harbour to the other islands, which were basking like whales reflected in the evening sun. Sir Hugo got to his feet and fixed his eyes on me as we walked across the floor. He clambered out from top place at the table and engulfed my outstretched hand between two pudgy fists. His jowly face split into a wide smile. 'I confess, Miss Holgate, that in the office I was impressed by your perspicacity. Now I'm captivated by your beauty. You're quite, quite exquisite.'

Flattery from some men can be nauseating. But from Sir Hugo it seemed natural and charming. 'Thank you, kind sir. And do please call me Emma.' I turned round and pulled Nick closer. 'May I introduce Nick Marlowe? Nick, Sir Hugo Pentecost, my boss's boss's boss's boss.' Sir Hugo chuckled and extended a hand. 'My dear sir, delighted to meet you. I trust you'll find your visit here condusive to the three "R's" - relaxation, recuperation and...ah...romance.' I shot a look at Nick and turned to bathe Hugo in one of my brightest smiles.

I said, 'We're so grateful to you for the marvellous room at the hotel. And for the film star welcome your staff gave us. It really is appreciated and it got our first day in the Channel

Ticket to a Killing

Islands off to a wonderful start. But...I hope you don't mind...we've decided to rent somewhere of our own for a few days...' I winked at The Chief hoping he would see himself as a fellow conspirator and not be offended at our rejection of his hospitality.

'Ah, I do understand. The most opulent hotel room can still seem so impersonal compared with one's own...what shall we say..? One's own little nest.' The other guests who were watching the encounter joined in the chortling and, after winking back, Sir Hugo sat us down, me on his left and Nick opposite. He surveyed those round the table and said, 'Emma Holgate is one of my top reporters on The Globe - you may have seen her recent series on National Lottery winners. And Nicholas is her...er...fiance. They're over here for a short break, away from the pressures of life in the big city.'

The others all murmured appropriate noises. Hugo made the introductions, starting with the man sitting on my left, 'Emma and Nicholas may I introduce Senator Matthew Le Page, president of Guernsey's Finance and General Purposes Committee. Knowing him he'll be too modest to admit he's one of the island's most powerful politicians. Indeed, if he held the same position in the UK he'd be the Chancellor of the Exchequer.'

Matthew Le Page looked faintly embarrassed but inclined his head in acknowledgement. I turned to look at him for the first time. He was about 38, dark-haired with an open, attractive face. His brown eyes were crinkled at the edges and I saw they were looking directly into mine. He wore an expensively-tailored dinner jacket which showed an athletic figure to advantage. Subconsciously something must be going on in the deepest recesses of my brain because Mark, the scar, woke up and began to itch.

Sir Hugo was continuing round the circle '...and next to Nick is Sophie Baxter, my PR chief. Sophie ensures that any publicity that Pentecost industries gets is always good publicity. She anticipates problems and is most adroit in transmogrifying them into PR triumphs...'

I watched Nick's face. By his expression he was impressed. Sophie was about 30, a natural blonde whose wavy tresses formed a perfect context for blue eyes, a neatly-proportioned nose and a full mouth set in a strong face. Nick saw me looking at him and tore his gaze away and smiled nonchalantly.

Sir Hugo had now reached the man sitting the other side of Sophie. He introduced him as Charles Manderson, Chief Executive of the Western Bank, with whom the Pentecost companies had their accounts. Manderson's features were florid beneath a receding hairline. An ingratiating smile hovered about his face, ready for instant use, while his eyes calculated the worth of everyone in the room. 'Charles is an enormous help in keeping the Pentecost wheels of commerce turning. Is that not so Manderson?' He replied unctuously: 'You might well say so, Sir Hugo, but of course I couldn't possibly...' Dutiful laughter all round at the ritual niceties.

'And last, but by no means least, may I introduce my colleague next to Matthew...?' All eyes turned in the direction of a stunning-looking woman with shoulder-length, dark hair, dusky skin and eyes that seemed almost black...' Francesca Botero...Guernsey represents the nerve-centre of my financial affairs and Francesca ensures they run smoothly. She also acts as my link with my South American holdings.' Francesca gave a controlled smile and responded politely in a throaty voice which had a slight accent.

Sir Hugo said warmly, 'I consider few people are indispensable in this world but to me Francesca is one of them.

She has an encyclopaedic mind and is better informed about international money markets than anyone I know. She has an instinct for investment and, if she worked on her own account, she could play the stock market and retire with a fortune.

'But, happily for me she finds her fulfilment in being my right hand, working closely with my other indispensable fellow traveller George Bixby. At the risk of sounding immodest, the Pentecost empire now encircles the Globe - from the Americas to the Russian Federation...And much of my success is due in no small measure to that dear lady sitting there.'

Francesca broke in, 'Please, Sir Hugo. Spare my blushes. All I have done is administer decisions you have already made. Any competent manager could have done the same.' Sir Hugo gave a small bow. 'Your modesty becomes you, my dear.'

The introductions completed, the meal was served. It was accompanied by bottles of Chablis and Nuits St George with which a waiter, lurking unobtrusively in a shadowy corner, regularly topped up our glasses.

As the first course of cream of cucumber and dill soup was laid before us, Sir Hugo held the stage. Inclining his glass of Chablis towards me before taking a sip he said, 'I believe you worked at one time on The Globe's financial desk, Emma? ' I nodded. 'So you'll be aware of the importance of Guernsey in the world of finance and banking?'

I said I knew billions of pounds were lodged at any one time in Channel Island banks and that Jersey and Guernsey's importance as finance centres were growing all the time. However, there was a shadow lurking in the shape of Brexit and how that would play out for the City of London and, inevitably, its offshore associates.

Sir Hugo nodded, 'Indeed this has become something of a distraction. But there are some who say that threats can be turned to opportunities and my spies tell me that, even as we speak, entrepreneurial minds are working out ways in which Guernsey can positively benefit. Indeed, yes, and most grateful we should all be too, to those inestimable colleagues who can see opportunity in change.'

Warming to his theme he went on, 'One of the reasons for the popularity in finance circles of these offshore jurisdictions is their political stability. While other nations - in Europe and the UK for instance - all grapple with continual upheavals Guernsey, for example, sails placidly on, providing stability in a sea of troubles. The markets love stability, so the markets love Guernsey.'

Nodding in the direction of Manderson he said, 'Bankers like Charles thrive on certainty, predictability, reliability. Guernsey and...' inclining his head towards Matthew '...politicians like Senator Le Page, are cognisant of this and do everything to foster a stable climate. Here there is no party politics, so there are no dramatic lurches to the left or right every five years. The result? We businessmen can bring our money to a safe environment and concentrate on making it work...'

Nick said, 'But is any environment safe for money these days? If reputable and old-established financial institutions like Lehmans and Barings can go to the wall, virtually overnight, who can we trust to look after our hard-earned cash?' Nick ticked off other examples of near-miss bankruptcies. 'Merrill Lynch, AIG, Freddie Mac, Fannie Mai, HBOS, Royal Bank of Scotland, Bradford and Bingley, Fortis, Alliance and Leicester...Who's next, Barclays? HSBC?'

Manderson interrupted smoothly, 'A lot was learned from the Banking crash. There are so many checks and balances, rules and regulations, stress tests etc that a repetition's unthinkable.' He laughed lugubriously, 'I think I can safely say that if you won the lottery, Nick, your millions would be safe in our hands.' I said provocatively, 'But it's not just banks going bust that's a hazard these days, is it? There's hacking, computer fraud, money-laundering, phantom cashpoint withdrawals...It seems to me that the criminals' technical ability is one step ahead of the banking industry's.'

I could see I held everyone's attention. 'When I was on the Finance Desk we were always hearing about millions being hijacked in some electronic heist which the banks always vehemently denied. And what about money laundering? Don't tell me that doesn't go on.' Sir Hugo said equably, 'My, my. We are getting serious. But, let me reassure you, my dear, that as far as Pentecost companies are concerned, there are strict safeguards in place across all my enterprises to ensure our reputation is never sullied by any suggestion of wrong-doing.'

Matthew said, 'I do agree to some extent with Emma's point, Sir Hugo. As you know I, and our Financial Services Authority, are closely concerned with ensuring the financial probity of all dealings in Guernsey: the island's economy depends on its impeccable reputation. So I guess I'm better-informed than the average man in the street about the problems facing the world's financial institutions. Emma's right in saying the challenges are enormous...'

As we moved onto the main course of grilled lobster or steak, Matthew got into his stride. 'For the sake of argument, Sir Hugo, how does a multi-national corporation like yours, with interests ranging from the media to shipping, ensure someone, somewhere in your organisation, isn't using your books to legitimise, say, drugs money?'

Francesca, who'd been silent up to this point, interjected. 'We realise the danger of such a possibility, Matthew. That is why Sir Hugo and I long ago adopted a policy of "know your enemy." We made it our business to learn as much as we could about just such things as money-laundering. And then we sat down and worked out systems to combat it.'

Sir Hugo ruminatively studied his glass of red wine before taking a sip. Then he said, 'I must say I found it fascinating. I had no idea what was going on until we started to enquire.' He gazed at me. 'We got most of our information from a fellow journalist of yours, Emma: One Ian Levy, now working in Canada. He'd gone under cover and did a thorough investigation of methods employed by drugs syndicates to legitimise their payoffs...'

'And what did this Levy discover?' Nick asked.

I watched to see if there was any concern on the faces of either Francesca or Sir Hugo at the trend of the conversation. Nothing. Sir Hugo seemed absorbed in something on the ceiling before saying, 'According to Levy there's more money spent in the world today on illegal drugs than on food. Currently, there's about three trillion dollars of drugs money in circulation and all of this has been introduced into the world's banking system.

'Levy's report said that money-laundering's done in three stages...' Sir Hugo squinted in concentration. 'Let me see...From memory he called these stages...Placement, Layering and...what was the other one..? Ah yes, Integration. Placement is the drug barons' biggest problem apparently - getting the cash into circulation. But once it's there it still has to be hidden from the authorities - that's the layering bit. It's transferred electronically round the world in and out of fake companies until it's impossible to trace back.

'The final stage is the integration of the money which, by now, has become so many blips on the screen. This is done by cementing it into assets like property, cars, yachts...Once they've done that the criminals can openly sell these assets as legitimate business transactions.'

Sophie said, 'Thank God I've never had to try to cover up anything shady in Sir Hugo's companies. Some of my PR colleagues, I can tell you, haven't been so fortunate though.' She turned to her boss, 'From what you say, Sir Hugo, you've been very diligent in avoiding contamination. But, what are the authorities doing about those who aren't so fastidious?'

As Sir Hugo went to answer, Matthew jumped in, 'Speaking as one of those authorities, I can tell you it's a never-ending battle of wits. In the US they've set up FINCEN--the Financial Crimes Enforcement Network and the law states that anyone receiving more than ten thousand dollars in cash in any one transaction has to disclose it.

'Last year ten million such deals were reported to FINCEN who've got state-of-the-art computers analysing the information. When they discern a pattern and identify something suspicious they pounce. But, as you can imagine, a lot of deals slip through the system.'

Nick decided to play the innocent abroad. He asked, 'What are the rules in the UK.'

Sir Hugo said, 'Nicholas, my dear sir, it grieves me to tell you that the poor old UK does not distinguish itself in this matter. Despite passing legislation like the Serious Crimes Act, the Proceeds of Crime Act, the Terrorism Act, the Money Laundering Directive and a plethora of other regulations, we still lag behind our American cousins. In 2013 they even establish a body called the National Crime Agency whose sole role is to investigate money laundering and terrorist financing. But still illegitimate money still manages to slip through the net.' I shot a look at Nick but he kept his face expressionless.

Sir Hugo then gave his audience a master class on the subject which shocked me and, glancing across at Nick, shocked him, too. Basically, Sir Hugo revealed so many holes in our regulatory system that billions of corrupt funds were pouring into the UK every year. He said it all came down to a simple human weakness which he summarised as 'Don't Look, Won't Find.'

'Last year 20 of the 22 relevant supervisory bodies failed to meet official enforcement standards and one third of all banks dismissed serious suspicion of laundering without adequate review. Oh dear Oh dear! What does that tell you, ladies and gents? Answer – that Blighty is open for business to every drugs cartel on the planet.'

I said, 'But what counts as suspicious?'

'Precisely, my dear Emma. Thereby lies the rub. It's all so subjective. Some officious bank clerk might regard an old lady's £500 retrieved from her mattress as suspicious, while another might not turn a hair at a £50,000 deposit to buy a dilapidated farmhouse. However, the system's being improved slowly. And throughout the financial world the screw is beginning to tighten...'

'...which presumably means,' said Nick, 'that the cartels are having to be more and more ingenious in finding ways around the supervisory regimes.'

'Manderson shook his head vehemently, 'There's no way that's yet been invented whereby drugs money can be transmuted into clean cash without leaving some sort of trace.' Matthew greeted this remark with a cynical grunt.

Over the passion fruit sorbet I decided to push this trend of the conversation further, to see where it led. 'Earlier Mr Manderson, you said all money-laundering leaves some trace. Well, I think I know a way that would be undetectable...' All eyes swivelled to me as I peered round the table with a neutral expression.

Francesca said huskily, 'Please do tell us. I thought we had thought of everything.' I noticed that Matthew had a slight smile on his face. It might have been my imagination but Manderson was running his finger round his collar as if it was suddenly too tight for him. Sophie looked genuinely interested, Nick apprehensive. Francesca was staring at me fixedly and Sir Hugo had one eyebrow raised.

I went on, 'It came to me while I was writing my articles on lottery winners. I thought to myself that if the drugs syndicates could only win the lottery they'd instantly have an alibi for their money. They could make huge deposits in legitimate banks and say, if questioned, that they'd just won the lottery. Once verified, the heat would be off. Every time the same person, or company, made a deposit, it would be assumed they were shifting their winnings about.'

Addressing Sir Hugo, I said, 'I mean it must be frustrating to any would-be money launderer to have, perhaps millions of dollars rotting away in some left-luggage locker for want of a way to get it legitimised. I believe that Pablo Escobar had to write off forty million dollars because he couldn't get it into the banking system quickly enough. Forty million in cash is quite an incentive.'

Sir Hugo laughed genially, 'My, my. I can add ingenuity to your many talents, Emma. But, there's just one slight flaw in your plan: How does the launderer arrange to win the lottery in the first place? And, if he could do that, why bother with his dubious lifestyle at all?'

'Oh, he doesn't actually win the lottery - he just acquires the ticket?'

Francesca said levelly, 'And how does he do that?'

Nick shot me a warning look. I shrugged. 'That, I'm afraid, is where my theory runs into the sand.'

Manderson said silkily, 'There you are, Miss Holgate, I told you there was no perfect system. I must say I'm relieved that you haven't found a weakness in our defences.' I had noticed that throughout our discourse Manderson had been eyeing me with lust in his eyes. The thought of it sent a shiver of revulsion down my spine.

The atmosphere lightened as the waiter brought coffee into the room and glided round the table serving it. When he'd gone, Sir Hugo asked his guests if they minded him indulging his very non-pc habit of an after-dinner cigar. No-one had the nerve to object so he removed one from its holder and lit it, puffing furiously to get it going. Waving away the clouds of smoke he said, 'A most stimulating and enjoyable conversation. Much food for thought..Hmmm...Much food for thought.'

Sixteen

Sophie and I left the table together for the powder room. As I washed my hands and she repaired her makeup I asked her what she knew about Matthew Le Page.

'Fancy him, do you?'

'He is an attractive man, yes. But what's his position here in Guernsey. I mean, what's all this stuff about Chancellor..?'

Sophie glanced at her watch, 'The Chief doesn't like me straying for too long. You're right, Matthew's an attractive man. All the more so because he's also a powerful one. To some people there's no greater aphrodisiac than power.

'Because this island's self-governing and because it's massively important as an offshore business centre, Matthew's position as "Mr Moneybags" makes him just about the most important politician in these islands. And, besides being the equivalent of the UK Chancellor, he's also the head of Guernsey's cabinet, so nothing happens here without him being in on it.'

'And where does Mrs Le Page fit into all this?'

'There isn't a Mrs Le Page. At least not any more. She was quite a woman by all accounts. Tragically she died competing in the Fastnet Yacht Race a few years ago. Since then a lot of females have lusted after Matthew but, as far as I know, he hasn't resumed a permanent relationship.'

Sophie continued, 'There are a couple of kids who're away at boarding school and, apart from them, politics and his job seem to be his whole life. He's an intelligent man with a degree in business management. And it's those attributes, as well as a natural instinct for politics, that's been responsible for his comparatively meteoric rise through the ranks of government here. He'd be a good friend to have but a dangerous enemy.'

Sophie gave me a sideways glance, 'While we're swopping info, is it true what Sir H says, that you and Nick are here for romance?' I remembered that Nick and I were supposed to be attempting a reconciliation. Yet, I could tell Nick was attracted to Sophie and she obviously was to him. And, if I was honest with myself, Matthew's warm thigh against mine all evening had done strange things to my emotions. Or was the Chablis up to its old tricks?

I shot a sister's-against-the-world smile at Sophie. 'You know how it is. Nick and I did have something serious going, then we split up. When that happens you get lonely and wonder if you've done the right thing. Well, when we met up by accident not long ago, we found we'd both been thinking the same way so decided to dip our toes in the water again...'

'...And how's it going?'

'It's early days yet, but we're both finding the old incompatibilities coming back. So, we'll have to see.' Sophie asked me what Nick did for a living. I said the first thing that popped into my brain. 'Oh, something boring, I'm afraid. He's an estate agent'.

When we returned to the dining room everyone was talking animatedly together. Francesca was leaning towards Manderson and his face was suffused with pleasure. Nick and

Matthew were in intense discussion and Hugo was leaning back, beaming benevolently at the assembled company. They all looked up as Sophie and I resumed our seats.

Sir Hugo tapped the side of his coffee cup with his spoon and the conversation subsided. He surveyed us all waiting expectantly round the table. He said, 'I'd like to make a little announcement. I feel I can't allow this gathering of friends break up without telling you something which excites me more than anything since I took over my first newspaper...'

He stared at me, his face flushed from the heat and the wine. 'The delightful Emma has already heard my secret but I asked her to be discreet as I am now asking you all. I will be making it public when the time is right. Until then, please treat this with the confidentiality of the confessional.'

Matthew said, 'This all sounds very intriguing, Hugo. Don't keep us in suspense.'

'Of course. I'll come straight to the point.' He pulled his frame up to its full height and said with a flourish, 'My tame genius, dear George Bixby, has invented a new kind of rainbow...' He gurgled happily...'That's what we've decided to call it - our Rainbow Defence System. But, instead of containing all the colours in the spectrum, our rainbow bestows immunity across the entire range of computer viruses, Trojan horses, file infections, logic bombs and all the other attacks which bedevil our interconnected world. In short, we have invented a computer protection mechanism which will revolutionise the IT industry…'

All our faces gazed up at him as he went on to recount the same story he'd told me in his office two days ago. When he'd finished, Manderson was the first to speak. 'By God, Hugo, with an invention like that you could take over the world. You could name your price. Microsoft would sell their souls to get their hands on it...' The implications are...are...mindblowing...' He spluttered to a halt.

Sir Hugo said triumphantly, 'But, that's only the half of it. As we speak my miniature Einstein is perfecting part two of our grand plan. When he's finished we really will be able to take over the world.' He noticed Sophie was staring at him in puzzlement, 'But not this week, my dear, have no fear. I shall brief you fully when the time comes.'

He coughed. 'Forgive me, everyone, if I seem a touch elated, but I have waited a lifetime for this.' He held up his hand, 'I regret I cannot answer any more questions. But just remember, you were the first to hear about something which will fairly stagger mankind...But, enough shoptalk. Please order whatever liqueurs you wish...' He signalled for the waiter...'and some more coffee.'

Reluctantly, we reverted to talking among ourselves. While Manderson switched back his attention to Francesca and Sir Hugo and Nick had their heads close together, I turned to Matthew and said quietly enough not to be overheard, 'I wonder if I might ask your advice about something.' He smiled and quirked an eyebrow. I continued, 'If I wished to deposit a rather large sum of money in an offshore account in Guernsey what bank would you recommend?' I jerked my head towards Manderson, 'Somewhere other than The Western.'

He looked at me seriously, 'All the banks here are reputable.' Then, relaxing into a smile again he said, 'But, if you wanted to keep your affairs separate from Hugo's and The Western then I'd recommend the Royal Bank. It's run by a long-standing aquaintance of mine. He's a bit stuffy but straight. And the bank has a long tradition of rivalry with The Western. His name's Francis Le Boutillier, by the way. I'll give him a call and mention you might be in touch if you like...'

He held my gaze for a moment, 'And, if you want to contact me you'll find me listed in the front of the telephone directory under MP's.' As he spoke, I felt something like an electric current shoot from my chest down into my stomach. His eyes continued to look into mine for a few seconds more and then he turned away. He stood up and leaned towards his host. 'A most enjoyable evening, Hugo. I hope you don't mind if I leave now, but I've an early start in the morning.'

A waiter appeared with Matthew's coat and with a last wave to everyone and a glance in my direction he was gone.

Seventeen

As the party broke up, Manderson reluctantly tore himself away from Francesca and ditto Nick from Sophie. Sir Hugo flashed a wide smile at me. 'Thank you, dear Emma, for the pleasure of your company tonight. Perhaps you'll be good enough to let my secretary know your mobile phone number and we can arrange to continue our interview.'

It was a warm evening and Nick and I decided to walk the half a mile or so to the hotel. By this time it was dark and as we skirted the harbour wall the lights of a thousand yachts shimmered in the waters of the most modern marina in Europe. Nick broke the silence first, 'I thought you were sailing very close to the edge when you started talking about your perfect system of laundering money.'

'Perhaps. But I wanted to see what effect it had.'

'Well, apart from looking suitably surprised I didn't notice anyone suddenly throwing down their napkin and declaring "OK guv, it's a fair cop. We've been rumbled."'

'Sarcasm, lowest form of wit and all that. Didn't you notice Manderson looking distinctly uneasy?'

'I noticed him looking hot. But so was I. Emma, please don't be reckless. Remember, I'm in the middle of a major case here and everything's got to be handled with kid gloves.'

I said casually, 'What? An estate agent involved in a money-laundering investigation?'

'Sorry, you've lost me.'

'Your dinner companion - the one whose ample bosom you seemed so fascinated by - asked me in the loo what you did for a living. Well, I couldn't say ex-Special Branch now working under cover for the National Crime Agency could I? So I said the first thing that came into my head.'

'So you said estate agent? But, I don't know anything about selling houses.'

'I'm sure you can busk your way out of it should Sophie press you more on the ins and outs...' Nick looked at me with a mock scowl. 'And you seemed to get along remarkably well with our Senator Le Page.'

'I admit I do find him attractive,' I said.

Nick grinned. 'Well that just about puts us on an even footing then. 'OK, let's change the subject. What do you make of tonight?'

'Well, the meal and the wine were excellent - as you'd expect from dinner with any average billionaire media magnate...' Nick gave me a friendly push of exasperation. I said, 'But, seriously, underneath I got the feeling there was some sort of hidden agenda. It reminded me of what you were saying the other day about powerful people needing the thrill of living close to the edge. Tonight, it was almost as if Sir H wanted to boast of something, but he allowed himself only to go just far enough to tantalise us.'

Instead of turning right to cross The Esplanade and up the steps towards the hotel, Nick steered me in the other direction and we began strolling towards the end of the Crown Pier. The other side of the harbour above a swirl of mist, and lit up like something out of a Walt Disney theme park, was Castle

Cornet. It floated sedately, seemingly in mid-air.

I'd read in the hotel's potted history of Guernsey that, at the time of the English Civil War, Castle Cornet had no causeway and was cut off from the island. Supplied from the sea by the Royalist Jersey, it spent years amusing itself lobbing cannonballs into Parliamentarian St Peter Port. Nick broke into my thoughts. 'What do you know about this Rainbow thing? '

'Only what Sir H told us tonight. He mentioned it when I went to interview him in London. If it's as good as he says, he's set to make billions.'

'Which makes it more difficult to believe he's up to anything shady.' We stopped at the pier railings and looked out to sea. The stars pricked glittering holes in the velvet canopy above us. For some strange reason images of Matthew Le Page kept impinging. The press of his thigh against mine tonight and the way he looked into my eyes hovered warmly in my thoughts.

Nick went on, 'Your question keeps going round and round in my mind: Why would someone as eminent as Pentecost - and now from all accounts about to quadruple his fortune - risk everything for something as squalid as money-laundering and, possibly, murder?'

I said, 'Contrarily, the answer you gave me then made more sense the more I thought about it. Look, let's see if we can fit anything logical together from what we know so far.' I ticked off on my fingers as I spoke. 'First of all there's The Phantom. We believe he's a contract killer targeting National Lottery winners for organised crime. The criminals acquire the murdered person's ticket and use the squeaky clean proceeds to launder drugs money. So far they've got away with it because no-one's connected the serial killings with the lottery.

'Whoever cashes in the stolen ticket is one of Mr Big's team

Ticket to a Killing

of Joe Publics all of whom remain anonymous and pass on their takings in exchange for a cut. Up till now, the scheme's worked perfectly allowing Mr Big to launder massive amounts of illicit cash. OK so far?'

Nick nodded and said, 'And, the huge amounts of money involved in lottery wins would routinely be enough to justify interest from a lot of very nasty characters. That's understood. But what I'm reluctantly coming to realise more and more is that it just doesn't make sense why someone of Sir Hugo's reputation should be up to his neck in it. Why should the man who's got everything risk losing the lot?' The silence hung heavily between us as we both pondered. There was no logic at all in Pentecost's involvement.

Eventually I said, 'Perhaps we're looking at this from the wrong angle. Let's try a bit of lateral thinking. Leave money out of it. What else might Pentecost gain from being mixed up with The Phantom? Thrills?

'And the money-laundering? With his network of companies world-wide, he's got a guaranteed way of increasing his fortune with little risk. You heard him yourself tonight: money reduced to electronic blips zapping round the world and becoming almost impossible to detect.'

Nick said doubtfully, 'No, that's still not a convincing enough reason for the risk, miniscule though it might be.'

'Well, let's try another motivator, then. Power. The more money he has the more power he gains. Power across borders, across continents, throughout the world. His satellite TV, radio and on-line operations are global and supply him with an unrivalled platform for disseminating his own politics or philosophy.'

Nick began to get excited. 'Yes, and if you throw in motives like hatred, revenge, driving ambition and stir them together with a lust for power you come up with the classic ingredients for megalomania.'

I sighed, 'Very convenient for us. But it sounds too much like something out of a James Bond movie. Goldfinger, Blofeld and all that. It just doesn't seem to fit with an urbane, self-made man like Hugo Pentecost. Although, come to think of it, JJ reckons that underneath the outward charm, Sir H is as ruthless and egocentric as Genghis Khan.'

Nick blew out his cheeks in exasperation, 'Yeah, but all that aside, we're no further forward. We've got our suspicions but nothing more.'

I said, 'Don't forget your master plan - tracing a lottery payout from its first arrival in a Pentecost bank account through to its destinations.'

'Yes, but the flaw in that idea is we could wait weeks, or months, before it happened.'

I said encouragingly, 'Or one of his agents could be about to collect a cheque any time now...'

Back at the hotel, while Nick went off to the porter's desk to order a Times for the morning, the same receptionist on duty earlier lowered his voice discreetly. He said a peculiar-looking schoolboy had collected my envelope on behalf of Mr Scarlett.

He added uncertainly, 'At first I didn't want to give it to someone so...so...dubious. But when, in return, he offered this addressed to you, I thought it must be in order. I hope that was alright.' The young man handed me a single sheet of folded paper.

I asked him what the boy had looked like and he screwed up his expression. 'He was the same size and shape as a schoolboy, and was dressed like one, but he had a strangely mature appearance, like...like...a...dwarf. The young man's face cleared. That's it, he was a midget.'

Mark began to itch furiously. Involuntarily I touched my face. Could it have been Sir H's genius, Bixby? If it was, at a stroke I'd been given proof of a link between The Phantom and Sir Hugo. But, I mustn't get too excited. It could be a simple co-incidence. Just because the go-between had been a short, male individual didn't mean it definitely was Bixby. But, if it had been…I unfolded the note and glanced quickly at a message in scrawled capitals: 'PHONE BANK ACCOUNT DETAILS TO...' There followed digits which I recognised as the number of a mobile phone.

Phase one of my plan was almost complete.

Eighteen

A balmy breeze was blowing up from the Canary Islands and it was warm enough to sit out on the balcony, wrapped in bathrobes supplied with the compliments of the hotel.

Beyond St Peter Port harbour, I could see the streetlamps of the other Channel Islands. Through binoculars, also Hotel-supplied, It was even clear enough to distinguish a set of traffic lights on the coast of Jersey, mechanically going through its cycle from red to amber to green. Then from amber to red again.

While I waited for Nick to come out of the shower, I poured us both a drink and reviewed where I was with my own private plan of campaign. As instructed by The Phantom when he'd rung me at my flat, I'd left Annie's winning lottery ticket at reception tonight. That was the envelope the "schoolboy" had collected. In exchange The Phantom had promised to pay one million pounds into any bank account I cared to name. It was twice what Annie had offered me to administer her money. But I thought, in the circumstances, she'd approve of what I was doing. I wasn't going to risk involving my bank in London. That was why I needed a discreet account here in Guernsey.

And that's what I'd be arranging as soon as I could at the Royal Bank - as recommended by Matthew Le Page. Once I'd

Ticket to a Killing

done that, I'd pass the account details on via the mobile phone number left for me tonight. So far, so good. But, there was a snag. I didn't trust The Phantom and he didn't trust me. That was why I'd torn the ticket down the middle. In due course The Phantom would discover the half he had was worthless without its twin, which was in the hotel safe, protected by my own combination.

So, it was a stand off. And at the moment I held the initiative. When The Phantom next rang me I'd tell him he'd get the other half, after he transferred TWO million pounds into my offshore account. He had a choice: all or nothing. The halves were no value to either of us, so he'd be forced to trust me.

I'd give him the missing piece when I had my two million. And then, as soon as the £17 million prize money was claimed and the cheque paid in, the NCA operation would begin. After that I'd just have to make sure I didn't walk up any dark alleys until The Phantom was behind bars.

Nick came out on the balcony still rubbing his hair. He slumped in one of the plastic chairs and sipped his Southern Comfort. He whispered lasciviously, 'If someone is spying on us why don't we give them something convincing to report back.' I gave him a baleful look. I said, 'How about tearing your mind away from sex for a minute and help me sort out something that's been nagging me...'

Nick groaned, 'I thought with all the alcohol we'd consumed tonight, you might be persuaded to relax a bit.' I said, 'In all that talk earlier about Pentecost and his motives we never did think through what he might be up to if he is a megalomaniac. It could have something to do with the strange way he reacted over something I said during our interview session.'

'In what way stramge?'

'When I innocently suggested he seemed to be following in his father's footsteps, Sir H nearly jumped down my throat. He's obviously very hung up about something that happened in his early days. But he told me to drop the subject.'

'Which, presumably, you did?'

'What else could I do? The Globe's his paper and I'm his employee. I did what I was told. But, it might be worth checking the NCA database and see what it comes up with.' Nick said, 'Meanwhile, back to his behaviour tonight.'

I said, 'Did you notice he talked about world domination?'

'Yes, but as a joke.'

'I'm not so sure. I got the feeling it was a sort of double bluff. We'd take it in jest but he meant it for real. It's just the sort of thing a megalomaniac would do. They'd enjoy playing with words knowing that later, when the truth was out, we'd all look back on the conversation and feel stupid. As though we'd been outwitted.'

Nick said, 'But all this is speculation.'

'Let's brainstorm a minute. Just suppose that underneath that urbane front he is mad. Suppose he actually does believe he can take over the world. He can't mean literally can he?'

Nick looked at me thoughtfully. 'Not in the conventional sense, maybe. Not with guns and bombs. But what if it's something to do with computers? Everything relies on computer systems these days. He did say his midget Einstein was working on something even more exciting than his Rainbow anti-virus system.'

As Nick followed his own logic, his adrenalin began to flow. 'Suppose, phase two of Bixby's invention was "offensive rather than defensive?" Suppose he's come up with some kind of bug...'

'...Virus'

'OK, virus. But what if Bixby's invented an incurable virus. That would give him immense power over the whole industrialised world. He'd have his Rainbow in place but everyone else would be vulnerable. You know yourself what happens in an organisation if a computer crashes for just an hour. The whole place grinds to a standstill. If Pentecost had some way of infecting the world's computer systems while protecting his own, he'd be the one-eyed king in the country of the blind.'

In a crazy way, I thought, it made sense. I whispered, 'So, if he's about to take over the world, why has he been grubbing about with money-laundering, drugs and murder?'

Nick looked at me, a pained expression on his face. He said, indignantly, 'If I knew all the answers, we wouldn't need the benefit of your brainpower would we?'

'Alright, Holmes,' I grinned, 'Let's talk about The Phantom. What had the NCA managed to put together?'

'Strictly speaking, individual police forces are still conducting their own inquiries and we're in a co-ordinating role. That's been useful in giving us an overview. It's obvious the guy's a cold-blooded psychopath - at least that's the psychological profile the experts have come up with.'

'So we're sure The Phantom is male?'

'Almost certainly. Apparently, women murderers prefer poison or a knife. And they rarely mutilate their victims.'

'So The Phantom's a man - what else?'

'The psychologists reckon he's young to middle-aged, very cool under pressure, probably a master of disguise. Or completely ordinary in appearance, so no-one gives him a second glance.'

'Why does he always use the same bizarre way of killing his victims? At least Jack the Ripper had some sort of rationale for mutilating prostitutes. But why does our man shove the muzzle of a pistol into someone's stomach and shoot a bullet into their organs? It's macabre.'

Nick shrugged, 'Who knows what motivates a madman. But, the method does have a practical advantage. The sound of the shot's muffled by the body so the murder's more or less silent. And the victim's dead in seconds.

'We've gone round and round on this for hours and the best we've come up with so far is he's a sociopath, of completely innocent appearance, who kills to order with professional precision. To him a human being's life is no more significant than a worm's.'

I said, 'What puzzles me is how a stranger, even someone completely ordinary-looking, can get close enough to push a gun into their belly button, without them becoming suspicious or alarmed.'

'We've thought about this too. Who would you allow into your home without asking to see any form of identity? I'll tell you, a priest with a dog-collar...or maybe someone in obvious distress...Or, of course, someone claiming to be from Venture.'

I suddenly noticed that Nick was staring at me with a wistful expression. He said, 'Don't you think we've done enough brain-bashing for one night?' After hesitating he went on, 'Look, Emms, I'm sorry if I got the wrong end of the stick after we made love. But, it was so...so...special that I thought everything was alright again between us...'

'Nick, you're right, it was special. But you can't just pretend we haven't been living our own, independent lives for six months. To be honest, Nick, I found your bland assumption that I belonged to you again insulting. I enjoyed making love as much as you. But, I don't see it as proof that I've subjugated my independence to your masculine domination. I'm sorry, I'm not explaining myself very well...'

Nick's eyebrows knitted. 'If I gave you the wrong impression it's me who should apologise. Look, how about we start again as equal partners? I promise I won't draw any wrong conclusions if we make love again.' I gave him an old-fashioned look and then the tension drained out of me. OK, I reflected, we both knew where we stood now. And sex between us had been so good.

My feelings must have shown in my face because the next thing I knew Nick was behind me and his hands had slipped beneath my bathrobe and were cupping my breasts. Expertly, he was tweaking my nipples between fingers and thumbs. An exquisite jolt stabbed groinwards and suddenly we were kissing passionately. Nick led me through the French doors into the sitting room where he turned down the lights and pulled the curtains. As he did so his towelling fell open to reveal a pulsing erection. He swept open my bathrobe and began rubbing his body against mine.

Thoughts of the wine I'd consumed tonight and the regrets I might feel in the morning flitted through my mind. But this was now. I wanted Nick to make love to me. Ripples of desire rose inside me, swamping all the warning voices. As it always did.

Nick's lips were crushing mine now and our tongues were exploring frantically. Our breathing came in stertorous gasps. I slipped Nick's robe off his shoulders and it dropped in a heap. I began kissing and licking his shoulder, chest and abdomen, stabbing and swirling my tongue around his belly-button.

Nick's hands cupped the full weight of my breasts and his fingers continued to squeeze my tips with a metronomic rhythm. Nick gave a gasp of pleasure as I grasped him in my right hand.

Nick pulled me to my feet and slipped off my bathrobe and, for a moment, we stood inches apart panting and trembling. I wanted him so badly. My head was whirling and my heart was trying to pound its way out of my chest. I kissed his nipples and I felt them harden at the touch of my tongue.

He dropped his right hand to my thigh and his fingers slid upwards and a delicious sensation surged through me. I shuddered as he slid back and forth. As he looked down at me he said, 'You've got the most beautiful body I've ever seen.' I smiled lazily. 'You're not so bad yourself...' I said huskily, 'I want to feel you inside me, now.' With a triumphant grunt Nick removed his fingers, lifted my buttocks and thrust into me.

Exquisite sensations exploded in all parts of my body as he pounded and rammed into me. Seas began to roar in my ears and paroxysms of divine heat swelled through my groin. Nick's tempo increased as the primitive call of his body became unstoppable. As we thrust and jerked in rhythm, our breathing came in increasingly ragged gasps. Our moans and cries became a frenzied duet until, with a final, explosive spasm, our beings merged into a heavenly bliss.

Nineteen

The following morning we checked out of the Breton Hotel and moved into our holiday let on the fringe of the town. In his role as an estate agent, Nick might have described our new home as 'bijou'. It was a converted fisherman's cottage and wasn't a lot bigger than a Wendy house. There was a kitchen and workroom/sitting room on the ground floor and a bathroom and bedroom upstairs.

There was no hall. You opened the front door and it led straight into what would have been the family's living room. For the benefit of the NCA's operatives it had become a repository of state-of-the-art digital technology.

Almost the entire floor area was taken up with two L-shaped desks on which sat two computers, keyboards and a wireless router. One wall contained shelves of reference books of every kind from Who's Who to Crockford's Clerical Directory. In the corner was a 40-inch flat screen television with a remote control covered in an array of buttons, which I took to be the link with secure, private satellite channels.

The kitchen was small but fitted with every modern device, from a washer-dryer to a space-age microwave oven capable of producing a Sunday lunch with all the trimmings. Up a steep flight of stairs was one room, containing twin beds and another

TV in the corner. The only window overlooked a park. Opposite, across a small landing, was the bathroom with shower, washbasin and bidet.

When I came downstairs after unpacking, Nick was sitting at a glowing computer terminal. He looked up, 'Ah, just in time for me to run through the basics of the NCA's wizardry.' I groaned. It had taken me months to master The Globe's electronic newsroom. For the next 10 minutes Nick demonstrated how to switch on, log on, enter my own secret passcode, select my menu, call up data or send information via the specially-encrypted router.

'You can even surf the Internet,' he said drolly.

I said, 'Look Nick, you know I'm a bit of a technophobe, so you'll have to be gentle with me.'

Nick snorted, 'Where have you been, on another planet? Everyone's internet-savvy aren't they.'

'Well I'm not,' I said glacially. Nick plunged on, with his tongue firmly in his cheek, I think. . .'Right. Well, I'd better explain the basics. The Internet is a world-wide electronic spider's web linking billions of computers. You can send, or receive, anything from anyone on the Net. And not just words, but pictures, music, spreadsheets, videos. You name it, if it can be digitalised it can be squirted from one side of the world to the other in seconds.' I said, 'Yes, yes, I know - it's a miracle of modern science.' And, just in case he truly thought I was a Luddite I added, 'How do you think a journalist gets her research done and copy filed? Why, via this modern miracle, you berk!'

For the rest of the morning we practised getting around the system. After a salad lunch we pushed the two single beds together, remade them as one and spent the next two hours making love again.

Twenty

'Emms, I've been summoned back to London. Allardyce wants a briefing on Pentecost's dinner and he wants to bring me up to date on a few developments.' We were lying in post-coital euphoria that Friday afternoon when Nick made his announcement.

'The Commander seems to think there might be a nugget in Pentecost's dinner party which could give us a lead...' I said, 'I thought the whole idea of this subterfuge was so that you can stay close to me to protect me.'

'That's true. But we don't think there's much likelihood of The Phantom getting through our defences here. We've got a round-the-clock watch organised at the air and seaports which makes this little dot on the map tight as a drum. And, before you know it, I'll be back by your side...' Playfully, Nick pulled me closer.

I thought that if my theory about the dwarf Bixby being my mystery delivery boy proved correct, Nick was leaving me in the lion's den. And, that reminded me. I'd been waiting all day for a summons from Sir Hugo, to conduct part 2 of our interview, but I'd heard nothing. ' But tomorrow's Saturday,' I protested. 'Can't you brief Allardyce on one of your secure satellite links. Or use something else in all that hi-teckerry downstairs?'

'The forces of law and order never sleep! Seriously, though, I could, but I've got to pick up some new software to give us the interface with all the ports we need.' Before Nick could lapse into any more Swahili I said, 'So, apart from monitoring my boss's behaviour, what else do I do while you're away?'

'How about contacting that nice Senator Le Page? I'm sure he'd love to hear from you...' I hit Nick playfully with a pillow. 'And in the meantime,' I said, 'I suppose I keep up the pretence about you and me cosily here in Guernsey attempting a reconciliation...'

Nick looked hurt. 'I'd hardly call it a pretence. Yesterday I thought we gave a pretty convincing impression of two people in love.'

I groaned under my breath. 'Don't let's go over all that again, Nick. I thought you understood. I've told you that in the time we were apart I found a new independence. And a confidence in myself. Now, I'm not ready just to go back to where we were before.'

I added gently, 'You're a marvellous lover, and while neither of us is attached I don't see why we shouldn't enjoy each other's company and...well...the sex.' I added with brutal frankness, 'But, I don't want you thinking that every time we make love we're a step closer to becoming engaged again. Anyway, I want to get back to normality before thinking about long-term relationships.'

Nick said casually, 'So you wouldn't be too upset if I happened to bump into someone else...say Sophie...on the plane to Gatwick tomorrow?' I stared at him and then couldn't help a smile. 'You bastard. You've planned to meet that blonde Jezebel all along, haven't you? I suppose poor old Allardyce is just a handy alibi.'

Nick sat up, turned, and put both his hands on my shoulders. 'Now, be fair darling. What have you just said? You're happy to share a bed for our mutual convenience but you're not ready for a deeper commitment. So, fair do's. I'm free to engage an attractive female in meaningful conversation, no strings attached.'

I said, 'Meaningful conversation's about the limit, though. I'm not sharing my bed with you if you're sharing hers.' Nick suddenly looked serious. 'But, you're wrong. I hadn't planned it. It's a co-incidence that she's on the same flight as me.' He added hurriedly, 'But we have agreed to meet up for a drink - and that'll be all, I promise.'

I was puzzled how they could have made those arrangements if they really hadn't planned it over dinner. They hadn't met since and Allardyce's summons must have come by text or email some time today. I pushed it to the back of my mind. I was more interested in noticing that I didn't feel a twinge of jealousy.

I let out my breath in a long sigh. 'I've no right to dictate to you. All I ask is that you're honest with me. We're going to have to work together and I can cope with anything if I know you're being truthful.'

'Fair enough.' Looking at his watch, he added cheerfully, 'We can just about squeeze in a leisurely dinner before it's bedtime again!'

Twenty-one

Nick left by taxi early the next morning to catch the 07.30 flight to LGW, leaving our hire car for me. Two hours later I was waiting outside the Royal Bank. Thank God for Saturday morning opening. I asked to see the manager and said I was expected. Half a minute later I was being ushered into Mr Francis Le Boutillier's inner sanctum.

He rose slowly to his feet to shake hands. He was tall, thin and middle-aged, with slicked down dark hair, like a cat's. 'I believe Mr Le Page has been in touch?' I said. He regarded me neutrally. 'Indeed, he has. He's explained that you're a business colleague of Sir Hugo's and would like to open a private account with us?' I nodded.

His eyebrows furrowed. 'Well, you know, strictly speaking the island laws require us to take up references before we accept any deposits from unauthenticated sources - money-laundering you know. It's the modern scourge.' He added pompously, 'But since Mr Le Page has vouched for you personally, I'm prepared to forgo that particular requirement.'

I looked suitably grateful as he slid some forms across his desk. A few minutes later I handed him the completed documents, plus my passport for ID purposes. He furnished me with a welcome pack from the bank. I flicked the folder

Ticket to a Killing

open and inside was a 10-digit number.

Le Boutillier pointed a bony finger at the figures. 'To make any deposits, all that's needed is the number. Once the money's in the account only you, personally, can authorise any withdrawals or transfers. And, even then we do insist on a signature.'

'That seems very satisfactory to me, Mr Le Boutillier. I must say, it makes life a lot easier knowing the right people.'

'Oh, I wouldn't normally have waived the rules however well I knew someone. But, Mr Le Page is rather an exception. Since he's the island's own Chancellor and could be said to be responsible for the £200 billion or so invested in Guernsey's finance industry, his word's as solid as the Governor of the Bank of England's.'

'Which reminds me Mr Le Boutillier. I'm expecting a rather large deposit in the very near future. Will you ensure, personally, that the transaction goes smoothly. It wouldn't do if a million pounds ended up in the wrong account would it?'

Le Boutillier dropped his superior air. 'A million, Eh? I think I can guarantee total satisfaction Ms Holgate. And please do call me Francis.' I pressed on. 'And there could be a further million shortly after that. Any problem? ' He bowed practically to his waist assuring me there wouldn't be.

I asked if I might use his phone and he found me an outside line before leaving me in private. I dialled the number left at the hotel in exchange for the half lottery ticket. I'd been surprised at not hearing anything from The Phantom. At the very least I'd expected an abusive call. But nothing. Eventually the ringing stopped. It was an answerphone. I decided to text the number instead, that way I could be sure it wasn't garbled. I put the bank's phone down and keyed the same number into my mobile. Then I tapped out the number of my account, reading it back to myself carefully to make sure I'd got it right and then added: EXPCT CSH DPOSIT MON. I pressed 'send' and watched the whirling circle until it confirmed the message had gone.

When I got back to the cottage, I accessed my NCA emails. Strangely, the senders seemed unaware that I existed as all the instructions were for Nick. Later, I was Googling some background research when the screen bleeped and the word 'message' appeared at the top right-hand corner. I pressed the key marked 'M' followed by 'Go' and flicked to my own personal mailbox.

It was from Nick. 'Emma,' he wrote, 'sorry but I'll been delayed. Commander insists I master new software and attend tutorial on latest gizmos. Hope to be on 1930 flight from LGW arriving Gsy 2030 tomorrow (Sun). Luv N.'

I selected reply and rather unimaginatively, typed, 'Message received and understood.' I clicked 'Send'. There was a 'Whoosh' and 'message received' flashed at the top left of the screen. As I was silently congratulating myself on my small mastery of the technology, my mobile phone chirruped. 'Hello Emma, it's Matthew.' At the sound of his voice my heart began to thump wildly. He said, 'I've just been onto your hotel and they said you'd already checked out. Then I remember you saying something about a holiday let and I got your mobile number from Sir Hugo's secretary. I hope you don't mind. I'm just ringing to see if all went well with Francis this morning.'

A mischievous demon squeezed my throat but I managed to say, 'Hello Matthew. Yes, everything's fine - thanks to your smoothing the way.'

'Good. Look, I wondered if you and Nick might like a trip out in my boat tomorrow. The forecast's ideal and a friend and I are planning to sail round the island. It really can be beautiful this time of the year.'

'That's a shame...' I said, 'Nick's in London and won't be back until tomorrow evening...' There was a brief silence. Then Matthew spoke again. 'Why don't you come on your own? I did take the liberty of mentioning my idea to Sir Hugo's secretary just now, in case he'd fixed an appointment for you for tomorrow, and she said he had a full diary and for me to go ahead.

'So, you've even got the approval of your boss's secretary and I'd say that practically constitutes a three-line whip.' He laughed. I said what about his friend who was expecting a foursome. 'Jack won't mind. And I know you two will get on fine. What do you say?' I didn't need any more persuasion. 'Ok, I'd love to.' He said his boat was moored at number four pontoon in the Queen Elizabeth Marina and that it was called *Multum in Parvo*. I said I'd see him at 10 o'clock.

For the rest of Saturday morning I was filled with a new cheerfulness as I tested my new Ultra security rating and the versatility of the NCA's own information databank. Humming to myself, I started by inserting into the search field a general keyword "drugs" and clicked my mouse twice. Suddenly the screen was filled with references ranging from "alcohol" and "amphetamines" to "solvents" and "XTX".

As most money-laundering involved the proceeds from illegal substances I thought I'd familiarise myself with some background on the biggest selling products. I clicked on 'cocaine'. The screen told me: 'A powerful stimulant derived from the Andean coca shrub. It comes as a white powder and users inject it, or more commonly, grind it finely with a knife or razor blade and sniff it through a tube.

'Effects tend to peak and ebb very quickly, in about 20 minutes, so to get more highs more frequent doses are required.' The data went on: 'Smokable cocaine is known as "crack". A "rock" of crack is about the size of a raisin and is either smoked in a pipe or heated on tinfoil. The "high" from a single dose will last only 10-12 minutes. Effects and consequences similar to amphetamines except greater respiratory problems. Crack has potentially fatal toxic action on heart.'

It went on, 'Effects: excitability, alertness, exhilaration, indifference to pain, illusions of physical and mental strength, aggressive behaviour, sensitivity to light, depression, sleeplessness. Dangers: convulsions, nose ulcers, depression, weight loss, HIV and hepatitis risk, dependence.'

I looked up similar detailed breakdowns on heroin, ecstasy, cannabis and amphetamines. Suppliers' inventiveness knew no bounds and the latest street drugs included derivatives of synthetic substances with names like krokodil, 2C-P, molly and suboxone. It made depressing reading. It seemed like half the world was poisoning itself looking for kicks; the other half was living in fear caused by the spin-offs from a burgeoning narcotics industry. The authorities were doing all they could but they were fighting a losing battle. Civilisation was going to hell chasing dreams and illusions.

I clicked on 'cartels' and again a long list of choices scrolled onto the screen. My eye flicked down the list passing 'oil' and 'OPEC' and stopped at 'Hell's Angels'. A mistake, surely? What had leather-jacketed motor-cycle gangs got to do with cartels? I wondered.

Out of curiosity I clicked twice and was astonished at what flickered up in front of me. Under a picture of a man of Latinate appearance it said: 'Rafael Sevilla: known as Angel because of his association with a prominent chapter of the Hell's Angels motorcycle fraternity.

'Came to the attention of law enforcement agencies as the brains behind the reformation of the HA's infrastructure into worldwide network of crime syndicates. Now in league with Colombian drugs CARTELS and poised to flood Britain and Europe with cocaine.'

An annotation off the US Drugs Enforcement Agency computer was included in brackets: ('Yes, you had better believe it. These dudes have swopped their leather jackets, long hair, brawls, biking and wild parties for smart haircuts, sharp suits and stretch limos...now read on').

The notes continued: 'They are organised like a cross between the most exclusive masonic lodge and the Mafia. They used to bite the heads off chickens as part of their initiation ceremonies. Now, every member attends a three-year 'graduate' training programme emerging with a sophisticated array of business management skills. Across the globe they have 130,000 members in 55 countries, including lawyers, accountants, bankers.

'Years ago they realised their most precious asset was their international contacts. Now they have infiltrated every echelon of society. In Britain they have 40 chapters and 10,000 members. British HA's now have vast resources including a 'fishing fleet' of trawlers made redundant by the EU fishing quotas.

'Two were recently seized by customs and police and were found to contain three tons of cocaine. It is believed that this seizure represents a small fraction of the cargoes that get through. Their ships are being equipped with the latest technology and are becoming harder to apprehend. (For further information on this, Ultra-Ultra security passwords now required).'

But the details on 'Angel' were still on the file. I looked again at his photograph. There was something familiar about the challenging way the eyes stared at the camera. I'd seen that look before, but where? I continued scrolling the information.

'Rafael Sevilla, aged 52, under police observation for years but never charged with any offence. Implicated in the torture and murder of four people in UK. Born in Colombia but came to UK in early 2000s. Later member of Bristol Chapter of Hell's Angels.

'Made regular visits to native country. First known contact with drugs cartels made in Santa Marta, northeast Colombia, through HA members there. Invested £2 million and smuggled 1000 kilos into Britain. Operations have grown in significance until now on the edge of a takeover of Britain's £15 billion drugs market via fleet of trawlers (see above)...'

What I read next made me jerk upright in my seat. It said: 'Known associate of UK and Channel Isles businessman Hugo Pentecost.'

I keyed the word "Pentecost" into the system. The screen went blank and the computer took time to think about it before flashing on the screen: 'Pentecost, Sir Hugo. Born Hugo Jazinski. (Further access restricted to Ultra-Ultra security rating).' So, I thought, whatever they had on Hugo wasn't available to be trawled through by the likes of me. Fascinating.

Twenty-two

I'd just finished a sandwich and a cup of coffee when my mobile rang again. It was JJ. 'Hi, honey. How's life in the stratosphere?' I told him that, apart from dinner with The Chief the night before last, I hadn't had a chance to talk to him at all. It was almost as if the boss had forgotten I was there. Or, I thought, maybe this profile for the paper was just an excuse and that he really wanted me in Guernsey to keep me under observation.

'What's going on at your end, JJ? I've been Googling and keeping up with what the nationals are running but they don't seem to have anything new on The Phantom killings. Have the police had any breakthroughs?' I could picture JJ at his desk, making a small space for himself among his notes and cuttings. 'Not a thing Emms. The cops are holding two Press conferences a day and just regurgitating what they've already told us. They're clueless and desperate. It's almost pathetic watching them running round in circles getting nowhere.'

'So the story's going off the boil?'

He snorted. 'You could say that. If you ask me it's practically a kettle-full of ice.' What a pity, I thought, that I couldn't tell JJ what was really going on. What an exclusive he'd have! How on the one hand I was working with the British FBI to nail our own boss. And on the other was pursuing my own private deal with a murderer sought by police and the media throughout the land.

I knew I was being what Sir Hugo might call a 'funambulist'. I was dancing on a tightrope. I was supping with the devil and my spoon wasn't that long. I'd persuaded myself I was pretty safe so long as I had the whip hand over possession of the ticket. But, once The Phantom and whoever was behind him, had that scrap of paper, I was no use to them any more. I had to keep one jump ahead.

The suspicion growing in my mind, about the identity of The Phantom, was the one thing giving me an edge. If I could unmask him in time, I'd be safe. And I'd have a two million bonus. If Nick and the NCA could find enough evidence against Pentecost, they'd wrap up the money-laundering network and I'd have the story of the century. Correction, JJ and I would have the story of the century. When it was all over, we'd sit down together and write it as a collaborative effort.

'JJ, could you do me a favour?'

'Anything, Emms, if it gets me away from the paperwork. Poor old Theo. He wanted The Gorgon's job but he didn't realise he'd need a Master of Business Administration degree to do it. The mere fact that the editor gets killed doesn't even seem to have broken the accountants' stride.

'They're now on Theo's back for statistics and he's flipped into manic mode. He's become a man possessed. He keeps sending out emails in Gorgon-speak going on about costs per hour of the newsroom, costs per reporter, per terminal, per paperclip, per lightswitch. He's now into benchmark-standards, overheads reviews, zero-budgeting, performance indicators and God knows what other Harvard guru-babble...'

Ticket to a Killing

I sympathised and brought the conversation back to Pentecost Industries. 'What do you know about a guy called Bixby, George Bixby?' I asked. JJ Hummed. 'Name rings a bell. Isn't he some kind of computer nerd with Pentecost?'

'Not just a nerd. By all accounts he's got an IQ in the thousands and masterminds all The Chief's computer systems.'

JJ's recognition dawned. 'Got it. He's a shadowy figure. Rarely seen in public. But spoken of with awe around the Pentecost bazaars.'

I said, 'I know this is a tall order. But, any chance of you seeing if Bixby was in any of the areas of The Phantom murders when they happened.' There was a pause on the line. Then JJ said incredulously, 'You're not seriously suggesting that Bixby could be our serial killer...I mean, isn't he a dwarf or something?'

I said drily, 'Are dwarves incapable of homicide?'

'No, but you don't tend to associate the little chaps with murder and mayhem. I admit Snow White had a grumpy one but...'

'...Look, JJ. I know it sounds far-fetched. But think about it for a minute. Bixby's close to Pentecost, in fact devoted to him by all accounts. A diminutive figure like that would lull his victims into a false sense of security when they open the door to him. By the time they find out he's not all he seems, they're dead.'

'Well...Ok. As it happens I do know Pentecost's secretary and she owes me a favour. I'll say I'm working on some background for you on Sir Hugo's profile. I'll ask how often Bixby travels to the Channel Islands. Then, I'll steer the conversation round to the dates of the murders. With luck she'll at least tell me if he was in the office on those days. If he was, that blows your theory and it's back to the drawing board.'

I said that would be fine. But, something that JJ had just mentioned nagged at me. But, I couldn't focus it. Something odd. What was it? Before I could pin the thought down he was moving on. 'I know you don't back the horses, Emms. But how about the stock market?'

'When I was on the City Desk, JJ, I saw too many investments go wrong to chance my arm. Why?'

'Geoff Travis has been blabbing his mouth off here about how he intends to make his fortune and tell The Globe where to put its job. I thought you might be interested, you being there at the hub of the international finance industry.'

' Sorry JJ, count me out.' I could mentally picture him shrugging and grinning into the phone. He said, 'Ok, but if you want to make a quick killing, insider trading's the only way to do it. And according to Travis one particular stock's about to go through the roof. He might be a bit of an old woman, but in all the years I've known him he's never seemed so sure about his information.

'And he's planning to put 10k where his mouth is, so he must be pretty confident.'

'Ok, for curiosity's sake what's he saying...'

'Well he reckons an outfit called Pronova Pharmaceuticals is about to go into orbit. Apparently, it's a small, British company that's been trying to get a foothold in America. They specialise in acquiring kindred firms who might be floundering after they've over-reached themselves in R and D.

'According to Travis's sources, Pronova's latest acquisition have just successfully completed tests on an AIDS vaccine. Apparently, there have been false starts on vaccines before but this one's the real deal. When this gets out the market price of Pronova will go through the roof.

'He reckons Glaxo have sniffed this one out and are about

to make a bid for Pronova. Which makes it a double copper-bottomed investment. Up until now GSK have looked on Pronova as a minnow not worth bothering with.'

JJ said enthusiastically, 'Sceptical though I am, Travis might be onto something here. I'm going to put a few hundred on it as soon as the market opens on Monday. I just thought as an old mate you'd like at least to know about it.'

I said with mock severity, 'Don't you know that insider trading's against the law?'

In a passable impression of The Chief JJ replied, 'I do...Indeed I do. But name me anyone who's been caught, tried and convicted. No, my dear Miss Holgate, the law is a mere palliative to wounded sensibilities. One is simply obliged to make a killing...'

I asked JJ what sort of killing he was referring to and we both laughed. I said I'd think about it. In the meantime, I happened to know Pentecost's London office was open on Saturday so could JJ get started.

He put the phone down grumbling about never having a weekend free, which wasn't true because it was a bone of contention around the newsroom that he always seemed to have Sundays off. Some reporters reckoned he must have had something on The Gorgon to get away with it.

With JJ's excitement about Pronova still ringing in my ears I thought I'd test the NCA computer's versatility. I accessed the stock market info and scanned it for any sign of bid fever. Nothing. Pronova's share price was steady at 110 pence.

Twenty-three

Wisps of mist, which the sun still hadn't burned off, played hide and seek among the yachts and motor launches as I walked along number four pontoon the next morning.

Multum in Parvo was a 34ft cruiser which, I was proudly told by Matthew later, was driven by twin 200hp turbo diesel inboard engines which made it easily capable of 20 knots.

The gleaming white superstructure spoke of a loving owner. As I started across the gangplank a voice that sent a warm wave of pleasure through me called out. 'Emma, welcome aboard.' If a man can look stunning in denim shorts and a sleeveless, blue cotton jerkin, he did.

He walked towards me holding out both hands. There it goes again, Mark the scar was itching furiously. I responded to Matthew and for a moment we stood there, looking into each other's eyes like young lovers. He pulled me towards some stairs and ducked as he went below. I followed him into a spacious cabin dominated by a dining table flanked by bench seats.

Beyond was an open door. It led to a small corridor at the end of which I could see the sleeping quarters. To one side was a petitioned-off area with toilet and showers. Towards the stern was another opening which, I imagined, contained another bedroom. 'Well, what do you think of her?' Matthew's eyes glowed with pride.

'Very nice,' I said.

'Nice? Nice? Where's your soul my good woman? She's beautiful and full of grace. And when we're out there together,' he gestured exaggeratedly at the sea beyond the harbour breakwater, 'we are in tune with the infinite.'

'I'm sorry, Matthew. Being a Londoner I haven't had much of an opportunity to splice the mainbrace, or whatever it is you sailors do. ' I looked around again. 'But, on second thoughts, she does have a certain Je ne sais quoi...'

'I'm only joshing, Emma. In truth I'm a late convert when it comes to matters nautical. You see...' His face clouded over...' I bought this boat for the family. My wife was the expert sailor. To be honest she was a bit contemptuous of those weekend poseurs who bought themselves floating gin palaces and relied on powerful engines and satnavs to keep them out of trouble.

'But, when Melissa and Tom came along we decided a sensible compromise would be a cruiser with sails. Then, we could take the children out in reasonable comfort and safety. Laura hoped they'd get to love the sea as she did and when they got older they'd take up proper sailing themselves.'

He said, 'It's ironic really. If she'd stuck to engines she'd still be alive...' He hesitated and looked at me sadly. 'You may have heard that she was drowned crewing in the Fastnet.'

I said awkwardly, 'I'm sorry. Yes, I had heard...' I decided to change the subject, 'How old are the children now?' Matthew's face brightened. 'Melissa's eleven and Tom's nine. They're both in England at boarding school. They're doing well and seem to be coping with the emotional trauma of losing their mother.'

I was conscious in the brief silence that followed of the fenders squeaking and groaning as the hull was pushed by the rising tide against the pontoon. I had a sudden fantasy of taking Matthew into my arms and soothing away the hurt. For a moment we just stood looking at each other. To break the pause, I said, 'It's a strange name, Multum in Parvo. What does it mean?'

Matthew smiled and again a sad look flickered across his features. 'It's what I used to call Laura. It's Latin for "much in little". That's what I thought she was. She was quite tiny but packed with amazing qualities. It became a joke between us and I named the boat after her...'

'Ahoy, anyone there?' A man's voice interrupted from the hatchway.

Matthew snapped out of his introspection and called up the steps, 'Come on down, Jack.' A pair of size 13 shoes, followed by a thick-set, solid-looking man, descended. He had a friendly, grizzled face. The lines round his eyes showed he had a sense of humour. I liked him instantly.

'Emma, I'd like you to meet a very old friend of mine, Jack Gideon. Jack this is Emma, of whom you've told me so much.' Matthew smiled at my puzzlement. 'Emma, I must apologise. My invitation to you today was genuine but I also have an ulterior motive.

'If we had made up a foursome, Jack would have been my partner. But he would have spent the day professionally sizing you and Nick up. It's the truth when I say Jack's a chum. He is. In fact he and his wife, Joan, had been friends of Laura's and mine for years. Now Laura's gone, Jack's the best mate I've got.' He saw I still had a puzzled look on my face. 'But, he is something else as well. And this is where I'll hand over to him to explain.' We all sat round the dining table, Gideon opposite me and Matthew by my side. I could feel the warmth of Matthew's leg against mine. At his touch I felt the faint stirrings of desire pool in my abdomen.

Gideon said, 'I'm a Detective Superintendent in Guernsey's Special Branch but I'm on temporary attachment to the NCA.' He nodded towards Matthew. 'Matt's in on everything because of his position in Guernsey's government.'

So, I thought, another tangled web. Matthew was a guest of Sir Hugo's at dinner on Thursday but could have been briefed by Gideon and could have been watching for clues. And he probably knew Nick and I were there with ulterior motives, too.

Jack explained, 'As the island's Chancellor, he's obviously got an interest in anything that threatens the stability of the finance industry here. But, he's also the political link between Guernsey and the UK Home Office. He knows everything that we're working on and is helping us where he can.' I swivelled in my seat and looked at Matthew. 'Is that why you were at Hugo Pentecost's dinner party the other night?'

'I was there because he'd invited me. Hugo obviously doesn't know he's under suspicion and his invitation to me was by way of a courtesy to my position rather than his liking for me, personally. But, it was an ideal opportunity for me to meet you and Nick and watch the interaction between you all.'

He went on, 'Both the Home Office and Allardyce usually take it in turns to keep me up to date with developments. And I got the latest via Jack. So, by the time you and I met at Hugo's dinner I knew why you were involved and what your part in all this is.' His face split in a smile. 'Hence my introduction of you to Jack, who probably knows far more about you than me.'

Gideon broke in, 'For my own satisfaction, Emma, I'd like to summarise the current situation as I see it. Then we can look ahead at where we go from here.' He closed his eyes momentarily collecting his thoughts. Then he took a deep breath. He said, 'We suspect Hugo Pentecost is using his global business interests to launder huge amounts of money.

'This money's the proceeds of a growing drugs empire linked directly to the Cali Cartel in Colombia, which the US believes is responsible for 80 per cent of the world's cocaine production. Now, imagine what a blow to the drugs barons it would be if we could close that operation down...'

I raised my hand. 'I thought the Cali organisation had been broken up years ago. I remember seeing on the wires at work that five of the six ringleaders had apparently given themselves up to the Colombian authorities.'

Gideon grunted. 'That was a feint. The whole thing was an elaborate attempt to fool the US into thinking they were winning the drugs war. All the time it was being shifted to the control of one Amado Carrillo, known as "The Lord of the Heavens", who's now trafficking merrily through Ciudad Juarez on the US border, and through the Caribbean.'

I said, 'But, if it's like the NCA says, six heads growing in the place of every one you chop off, what's the point of any of this?' Matthew laid his hand on my shoulder. 'That's exactly what I said to the Home Secretary. But, he assured me that if we can get hold of the information on Hugo's computer immediately after a sizable payment's been made into his main account, we can trace links back to all the companies here and abroad that he feeds cash to.

'Then the authorities will organise synchronised raids on all the offices, and arrest all those associated with them. It would be the biggest operation against the drug syndicates ever mounted. A lot of top people would be caught in the net and they'd implicate others. If the operation's a success the narcotics business will be set back years. And that's about the most anyone can hope for.'

I said to Gideon, 'But I was sucked into all this because, for some weird reason, The Phantom serial killer seems to be interested in me. What's my involvement got to do with drugs money and Cali cartels?'

'It's a starting point for us. The killer's a professional, hired by organised crime, to swoop on lottery winners and steal their tickets. The link comes when the money's claimed from Venture. The clean cash is used to launder massive bundles of notes waiting in someone's cellar somewhere.

'If we can find the so-called Phantom, thanks to you, we have another piece of the jigsaw which could give us a different route to the brains behind it all – we believe Sir Hugo Pentecost. But, in the meantime, the serendipity of your professional association with the man, gives us someone on the inside.'

I said, 'And how do you plan to get hold of this hard disk information? He's bound to have an impenetrable system making it impossible for anyone to break in and access it?'

Gideon shifted uncomfortably in his seat. 'We have reckoned on this. Nick's brief is to enlist the help of someone on the inside...'

'I said evenly, 'You don't mean Sophie Baxter, Hugo's PR woman, by any chance?' Gideon looked at Matthew and then back to me, 'Er...From what Matthew tells me about the dinner, they did seem to get on pretty well.'

I said explosively, 'Do you mean Nick was charming that poor girl solely in the line of duty?'

Gideon replied casually, 'I would have thought, in the...um...circumstances, you'd have been pleased to hear that.' It suddenly dawned on me that both Matthew and Gideon knew that Nick and I were acting out a subterfuge for appearance sake. I looked sideways at Matthew. He was grinning openly. Gideon was managing to remain po-faced.

'Seriously though,' I said eventually, 'I hate all this duplicity. I don't know who to trust.'

Gideon said. 'Take my advice, Emma. Hold onto a few simple facts. For a start, all you're required to do is be yourself with Pentecost. Interview him and keep your ears and eyes open for anything that could be useful. The only pretence with him is that you're supposed to be combining business with pleasure.

'That's our excuse to have Nick close to you...And that reminds me. I take it you haven't had any further reason for anxiety on a personal level about The Phantom?' Mark the scar reddened as I lied and said that I hadn't. I wondered if he'd try ringing me today.

I said, 'Could I ask you a couple of questions about something I saw yesterday on the the NCA computer?'

'Go ahead.'

'Well, I was accessing information on cartels and I came upon an extraordinary file on Hell's Angels. Is it really true that they've changed from being leather-jacketed motorcycle thugs into entrepreneurs in sharp suits?'

Gideon ran his fingers through wavy hair streaked with grey. He said, 'Yes, it's true. You probably also saw from the files that a known associate of Pentecost's is Rafael Sevilla. We believe it was him who conceived the brilliant idea of using the overseas chapters of the Hell's Angels to set up a drugs distribution network.

'They already had the brotherhood ethos, plus the antipathy towards any form of authority. They just built on this to create an international business and criminal empire. Along the way Savilla gyrated towards the South America operation and

Pentecost became the respectable captain of industry here – the dream combination for both of them.'

' And they still have a business relationship?' I asked.

'Very much so. In fact I understand you met Sevilla's daughter at Hugo's dinner.' I looked at him searchingly. 'You don't mean Francesca? But her second name was Bolero or something.'

'Botero. She was married briefly to a Colombian by the name of Hector Botero but it didn't work out. She kept his name because it gave her a separate identity from her father, who'd rather overshadowed her when she was younger.'

I said, 'So now she runs Hugo's offshore interests and obviously keeps in close touch with her father and his South American enterprises. How convenient. No wonder Hugo said she was invaluable to him.' I pressed on, 'The computer also said something about the Hell's Angels having a fishing fleet which they use to smuggle the cocaine...But, surely these ships are being tracked by border agencies and the police. Can't they just be arrested when they get into territorial waters?'

Matthew interjected, 'If only it was that simple. What happens is: tons of drugs are loaded onto what are often legitimate vessels. The cargo's then brought within easy reach of, say, the Channel Islands coastline. Still in international waters the ships drop their consignments over the side attached to weights, a buoy and a tracking device. If we pounce on that legitimate ship when it arrives in port we find nothing.

'Meanwhile, perhaps weeks later, a second boat arrives - the Angels' trawler - and activates the tracking device which releases the weight. The buoys float to the surface bringing with them their waterproof containers which are then picked up. The fleet then later offload the stuff into a cluster of launches which fetch up at various isolated landing places in the UK or France.'

Gideon said, 'However good our intelligence is we can't track every ship and can't watch every inch of coastline. We just haven't got the resources.' He added ruefully, 'The Hell's Angels have developed such a sophisticated intelligence-gathering network that we can't penetrate any of their chapters. And, on top of that, they seem to know our every move. That's why we're desperate for this "Operation Starburst" to succeed. Because if it doesn't we might as well admit defeat.'

I said, 'It really is that important? Despite the fact that it'll only gain you a few years?'

'Well, it could be longer. But, we've been months planning this. And we've only just managed to get our own computer technology brought up to spec and in place. But now we're ready. Once the next major deposit is paid into Pentecost's bank, his central computer will be triggered to transfer a tranche to all outposts of the Pentecost empire. If we're right, these outposts are implicated in the drugs operations.

'Once the blips are speeding round the globe and reach their destinations, we'll have as good as an AA route map to every one. That's the stunning simplicity of it: As the transfers are sent out over the Pentecost computer network, the hard disk on his master computer faithfully records that it has done its job.

'And in the process logs every "end receiver" in its memory. If we can get access to that disk, after the next transaction, we'll have a complete list of names, addresses, companies and bank accounts in the Angels' network. And, as we've said, we then organise a co-ordinated police swoop in a dozen or so countries and the syndicates are wiped out overnight.'

Gideon looked at his watch and grinned. 'Much as I'd like to join you for a relaxed day of sailing, three's a crowd and all that. And, in any case, my wife and kids would like to be reminded of what their husband and father looks like. So, I'll love you and leave you.'

He eased himself out from behind the table and climbed carefully up the steps, turning to give a half salute. In the silence that followed we could hear his size thirteens clumping their way down the pontoon.

Matthew said...'And then there were two. Now, let's forget all this for a few hours and enjoy a wet sheet and a flowing sea and a wind that follows fast...'

Twenty-four

I joined Matthew in the cockpit and, within minutes, we were heading out to sea. Shimmering in their own heat haze on the horizon was Sark and beyond that Jersey. 'What can I do to help? I said. Matthew looked round smiling. 'Nothing. As you can see I'm cheating. I'm leaving the sails. We'll use the engines to get us across the Little Russell - that's this stretch of water between Guernsey and Herm - and then we'll go through the Percee Passage to Sark.'

I sat on the bench seat, my attention alternating between the view and Matthew. He really was an attractive man, I thought. Almost six foot tall, rangy and muscular but with a self-deprecating air. In moments of repose, his expression betrayed an inner sadness.

Occasionally, he would look at the echo-sounder and check the co-ordinates on the satnav. He turned and caught me watching him. 'I could claim to know these waters like the back of my hand, but Laura taught me never to take the sea for granted. This area is full of rocky outcrops which are just below the surface at high tide.'

The events of the past week seemed unreal as we plunged through the choppier waters beyond the tiny island of Herm. I

Ticket to a Killing

could taste the salt in the wind as Matthew opened the throttle and *Multum in Parvo* plunged joyfully through the waves. Forty minutes later the growl of the engines subsided to a low burble as Matthew steered us into a natural harbour in Sark about the size of six football pitches.

Behind us were the sides of a small island rising out of the sea like a 200-ft high craggy, humpback whale. Matthew jerked his head in its direction. 'That's Brecqhou. It's one of 40 tenements, or holdings, that Sark's divided into. At one time every tenement-owner had the right to sit in the island's parliament. And if that sounds feudal that's because it was. Until early this century, Sark was the last feudal outpost in Europe. Now, it's been dragged kicking and screaming into the 21st Century and there's universal suffrage for its 600 residents.'

I must have had a look of rapt attention on my face because Matthew's voice assumed the tone of a tour guide. He said, 'Brecqhou's become the focus of a lot of media attention recently since its the home of two of the richest men in the UK, the billionaire Barclay twins. You can't see it from here, but on the other side of the islet there's what looks like a Gothic castle. But it's not medieval. It was built at vast expense in 1995 by the brothers as their dream pied a terre.'

Our heads swivelled back again. In front of us were the sheer cliffs of Sark, topped by a broad plateau. We glided to about 100 yards offshore. Matthew pressed a button, an electric motor whirred and the anchor rattled into the calm surface. He switched off the engine and turned. 'Alone at last,' he said, his eyes glimmering with amusement.

I looked around and noticed there wasn't another boat or human being in sight. The only sign of habitation was a small jetty which led to a path zig-zagging upwards to disappear behind some gorse, which dotted the sides of the cliff. The sun shimmered off an aquamarine sea.

Matthew said, 'It's breathtaking, isn't it? It's called Havre Gosselin, which is on Sark's quietest coast.' He pointed over the plateau. 'About a mile and a half away is the commercial side of the island where all the day trippers arrive and where the cargo's loaded. About this time of day it'll be seething. But, here, as you can see, we could be in our own private bay.'

I said, 'The only thing I know about Sark is that no vehicles are allowed.' Matthew laughed. 'If you don't count the hundreds of tractors which zoom about the island terrifying the life out of trippers.' He looked at his watch. 'Time for some lunch, I think.'

I said, 'I'm sorry. I didn't give it a thought. I didn't even bring a bottle of wine.'

'Have no fear, Matthew's here...' With that he went below and emerged with a red coolbox. 'I think I've brought everything we need. There's some lobster and salad, rolls, fruit and, not to forget...' He plunged his hand into the container and pulled it out in triumph...'some champagne...'

Three glasses and a lobster salad later I was suffused by a warm, romantic glow. As we shared the washing up in the tiny galley, I suddenly realised I was falling in love with Matthew. Or was it the champagne talking? I wanted to wrap myself in the warmth of his smile and sooth away his hurt. We looked into each other's eyes and Matthew seemed to be reading my mind. Throwing down the tea towel he took a hesitant step towards me. He placed both his hands on my shoulders and slowly drew me into his arms.

'Emma, I don't know what's happening to me, but whatever it is, it feels wonderful...' We stood there, holding each other fiercely, feeling the pounding of our hearts. I don't know how long we remained like it, the silence broken only by the gentle lapping of the sea against the hull. Matthew's aftershave and my perfume mingled intoxicatingly and we were enfolded by a blissful warmth that seemed to melt away all our past hurts.

Matthew eased my face from his shoulder and gazed gravely into my eyes, as if trying to read something deep inside me. Then, he leaned towards me, his lips meeting mine with a melting tenderness. We kissed, softly at first and then with increasing urgency. I could feel his hardness swelling against my groin.

Damn the champagne! I didn't want to behave like a slut but the alcohol was taking over. Would Matthew think I was an easy lay? Would he be disappointed in my lack of self control? 'Matthew, I...'

'Shhh, my darling. I know we've hardly met but I want you so badly. Don't be offended.' Offended? Reassuringly, I pulled his mouth down to mine and kissed him hungrily. He said between gasps, 'Well, if I am going to make a fool of myself I'd rather do it in the comfort of my cabin...' He took my hand and steered me through the little corridor to the accommodation in the bow.

He pushed open the door to reveal a double bed positioned diagonally, which left adequate floor space for dressing - or undressing. The bed was covered by a duvet patterned with black and red stripes. As we stepped across the threshold, we could see ourselves in a full-length mirror attached to the fitted wardrobe. We stood there holding hands, like a couple of teenagers. Matthew took both my hands in his and smiled shyly. 'Emma, sweetheart, I want you to know that I don't make a habit of this...'

I placed a finger across his lips but he removed it. 'I'm serious, Emma. Multum has always been very special to me.

Sort of sacred to the memory of Laura, if that doesn't sound too mawkish. But, you're the first woman that seems so...I don't know...so right, I suppose.'

'Make love to me Matthew...please.'

Twenty-five

I could feel my heart pumping as he undid my zip and my denim skirt dropped to my ankles. Slowly, his eyes never leaving mine, Matthew eased my tee shirt over my head and dropped it beside us. I stood before him in a white bra and briefs.

I slid my hand down to stroke Matthew's thigh. For a second he tensed and then relaxed as I massaged my palm towards his swollen trousers until it covered the throbbing hardness. His eyes closed and a gutteral moan escaped from his throat. He grasped both cheeks of my buttocks and pulled me fiercely against him, gyrating his hips against my pubic bone.

He wrenched his shirt over his head while I knelt and fumbled to undo his belt and the top button of his jeans. He cupped my bra in his hands as I undid his zip and eased his trousers down to his ankles. Dexterously, he stepped out of them while continuing to support the pendulous weight of my breasts. My eyes were six inches from the sensual bulge in his shorts.

As I eased the elasticated waist downwards Matthew gave a long, drawn-out sigh and began moving his hips slowly in and out. It was beautiful, feeling his excitement rising. We were opposite the wardrobe's full-length mirror and I could see myself on my knees. He was watching, too, and the sight was driving him to a frenzy. He began to make eager moans as his pelvis picked up a faster tempo.

I turned my head and crawled onto the bed. Shrugging out of my bra, I stretched luxuriously on my back and lifted my arms lazily above my head with my legs dangling over the edge. Matthew opened his eyes and smiled understandingly. He sank to his knees, slid my briefs down and tossed them aside. He seemed hypnotised by what he saw. A blissful, liquid spasm coursed through me. I humped my hips higher and drove hard against him. My perfume mingled with his aftershave to heighten the senses. Matthew's attentions were punctuated by ragged gasps as the tempo increased.

'Come inside me, darling, now,' I begged. Matthew climbed onto the bed and on all fours he positioned himself over me before easing himself between my thighs. Gently at first we rocked together, our spirits at one as our bodies met in intimate embrace.

Then I locked my legs behind Matthew's back in a scissors grip. Slowly at first, but with increasing urgency, we undulated together. Gradually, the mattress began to protest louder and louder as our bouncing became a frenzy. Ripples of pleasure gathered in my loins and seemed to reach out to touch every nerve end in my body. Both our faces contorted into a rictus of ecstasy as with one, final, triumphant cry we spasmed together in perfect harmony.

Twenty-six

We sailed all the way back to St Peter Port sitting side by side on the helmsman's seat like two young lovers and nosed into *Multum in Parvo's* berth at five o'clock.

'Matthew, before we go I need your advice. Do you know any stockbrokers in Guernsey who you can trust?'

'Why?'

'Because I want to make a rather large investment, but I want it done discreetly so no-one will know.'

Matthew laughed, taking off one imaginary hat and replacing it with another.'...You've met Matthew Le Page, Guernsey's Chancellor. Now may I introduce Matthew Le Page, Managing Director of MLP (Guernsey) Ltd, dealers in all recognised markets. Personal and corporate investment advice and portfolio management a speciality...'

My mouth gaped open. 'Do you mean, you're a stockbroker?'

'Well, more than that actually. Stockbroking is just part of the services we offer. However, madam, how may I help you?'

'But I thought you were a full-time politician.'

'Not full-time, no. Most politicians in the island have other jobs. In fact that's been a controversy for years. It's felt that the increasing complexity of government requires full-time MP's.

But no-one will grasp the nettle and make it mandatory. We do get paid but it's a notional amount just to come in line with other jurisdictions.

'You see, traditionally, being in the States, which is what our parliament's called, was a way of serving your community and it was totally voluntary. And, even these days, it's hard to shake off that mind-set. So we stagger on, running what amounts to an independent country, while trying to earn a living at the same time.'

I shook my head in disbelief. 'Oh well, mine's not to reason why. And it does give me someone on the inside I can trust.' He said, 'So what's this investment?' I took Matthew's hand and sat him opposite me where Gideon had been a few hours before. 'By this time tomorrow I hope to have a million pounds in that account I opened with the Royal Bank.'

Matthew's eyebrows shot up. 'I won't ask you how you've acquired a million. But, I assume it's all above board?'

I said, 'Trust me.' He looked searchingly at me for a moment and then nodded. I said, 'I've asked Le Boutillier - he insisted I call him Francis when he knew the size of my deposit - to let me know as soon as it arrives in the account. When it does, I'll ring you. If you'll accept that as adequate collateral I'd like you to buy, through nominee holdings, £500,000-worth of shares in a company called Pronova Pharmaceuticals.'

'That's one hell of an investment. Are you sure you know what you're doing? As far as I can recall, Pronova's a minnow. It's got a good management team, yes, but it's not in the major league.'

'Do you always quiz your clients like this when they want to make you a lot of commission?'

'Only when they're as attractive as you and I've just made love to them.'

I ignored the diversion. 'But will you do it?'

He took my hand and looked into my face. 'Of course I will, darling.'

'Marvellous. Start as soon as you get my call and have it wrapped up by the end of the day.'

'You know that size of acquisition's not going to go unnoticed in the City. And everyone will be trying to trace who the buyer is.'

'I know. But I want to remain strictly anonymous. Anyway, it'll be a nine-hour wonder because I've a hunch Pronova's price is going to go up like a rocket. When it does, everyone'll be too busy trying to buy a piece of the action to bother about me...'

There were footsteps above and a heel stamped twice on the deck. 'Come on down, Jack,' Matthew called.

Gideon ducked his head sideways and eased his way down the steps. He looked from Matthew to me and then back again, as if trying to work out what was different about us. Then he spoke. 'I have to say, the wife and kids are not at all impressed. As I told you this morning, I was intending to spend the day en famille but as soon as I got back, Allardyce was on the phone.

'He wanted to know where you were, Emma. When I told him, he said I should meet you on your return and tell you what they've found out about Pentecost.' He grumbled, 'I might just as well have been at the office. No peace for the wicked.'

'So what's the news?' I queried.

'Well, apparently, you and Nick have been trying to work out Pentecost's motives for putting everything he's got in jeopardy. For what? For money that he's already got enough of? Or power which he already has? You were right. It didn't make sense. And all the time it didn't, it cast doubt on what we were trying to prove.

'So Nick got an the NCA team digging into Pentecost's background more thoroughly than ever before and it's fascinating what they've uncovered. And it provides Pentecost with the motive we've been looking for.'

Matthew said in exasperation, 'Jack, we're on the edge of our seats here.'

'Well, it's like this. When Pentecost's father, Wladyslaw Jazinski, fled Poland during the war he brought back with him a document containing the names of all the Nazi sympathisers in the English Establishment. God knows how he got hold of it. At the end of the war, he decided not to open old wounds and filed it away with other papers at his bank. There the names stayed until Hugo qualified as a journalist.

'In the course of conversation Jazinski senior told Hugo what was lodged at his bank. The ambitious Hugo saw his chance to make a name for himself by selling a story about traitors in high places to Fleet Street. Even though at that time the war was well in the past, the names would have caused a sensation. Although many of them were dead, their families were scions of society and pillars of the community. He persuaded his father to hand over the document, which he took to the Daily Mirror.'

I said, 'But the story never appeared, did it?'

'No, that was where it all went wrong for young Hugo. A "D" notice was slapped on the story and the next thing Hugo knew was his aging father had been arrested on a trumped up charge of historic child rape. It was a device by the Government's dirty-tricks department to silence both the Jazinskis.'

I began to have a sneaking sympathy for Sir Hugo. What a terrible ordeal for him and his family.

Gideon continued, 'Unfortunately, that's where it took an even more tragic turn. Wladyslaw was overcome by the shame and hanged himself while on remand and Mrs Jazinski died a few months later of a broken heart.

'As you can imagine, this left an exceedingly bitter Hugo Pentecost in its wake. Later he changed his name and, as he became a tycoon, he expunged all evidence from the files of his own media empire. Gradually, the truth faded into history.'

Matthew said reflectively, 'But the bitterness didn't fade. In fact over the years it probably grew.'

'Quite so,' said Gideon. 'Running in parallel to all this was Hugo's association with Rafael Sevilla. From then on he ruthlessly used the Hell's Angels network and drugs money to fund his burgeoning legitimate business. In fact so much so that they're indivisible now. Hence the money-laundering through Pentecost Industries.'

I said, 'Was he so bitter that he didn't care about innocent people being murdered?'

'The NCA reckons that Hugo swore revenge on the people he saw as responsible for the deaths of the two innocent people closest to him - his father and mother. Hugo believed society had rejected them so he rejected society.'

Gideon went on, 'And the tame "ologists" reckon Hugo comes into the category of what's called these days "moral insanity." It used to be psychopath then sociopath but these labels were dropped because they implied psychiatric illness, which isn't always the case.

'So, he's morally insane. Needless to say, Hugo's not interested in any of this psycho-babble. He just decided to continue masterminding the drug-smuggling and money-laundering as his way of getting revenge on the Establishment.'

He concluded heavily, 'So, if he's not actually mad, Hugo's experiences have turned him into a cold-blooded, ruthless avenger.'

Twenty-seven

At the cottage I had two hours before Nick would be back, so I logged into the computer to see if there were any messages. There was one. It was from Nick. It said simply: 'Add to data on HP. Steady acquisition of gold confirmed. More follows later.'

I checked the financial pages and could see gold's value had been steadily rising as someone bought heavily. But, it still hadn't got to critical mass point where its price would be off the scale. If it was Sir Hugo, he was stockpiling massive amounts of the stuff. But why? It was more profitable these days to deal in currency.

I decided to check with Geoff Travis. He picked up the phone on the third ring with a gruff, 'City Desk.'

'Geoff, it's Emma.'

His tone lightened. 'How are you dear girl? And how is the centre for offshore bonking?' He chuckled at his own wit. 'Very droll, Geoff. But, it is your expertise on matters financial I'm ringing about.' He sensed my seriousness and cut the banter.

I asked, 'What's happening at the moment to gold prices?' I heard him tapping a few keys on his computer terminal.

'Thirteen hundred dollars an ounce - up five on the day and

10 on the week. It looks as though someone's buying.'

'Why would someone be salting gold away like that?' I asked.

'Could be a number of reasons. It's a classic hedge against inflation. So, if an investor thought the CPI was going up, he might buy into gold.'

'Does that incentive apply now?'

'Not really. There are other reasons for stocking up on gold though. For instance, as Far Eastern economies start to boom, the demand for gold goes up. We are in that cycle now.'

'But,' I said, 'enough for an investor to start to corner the market?'

'No, I wouldn't have thought so.'

'So why else would some financier decide to spend millions on hoarding gold now?'

I could visualise Geoff rubbing the side of his jaw as he ran through the options in his mind. Eventually, he spoke. 'You know gold is the one precious metal that has an almost mystical attraction. All through the ages the possession of gold has given comfort in times of insecurity. There's an atavistic urge for people to own gold, as if it were a talisman to ward off disaster.

'That's why you always get a run on gold when there's a crisis in the world...'

'...Like what?'

'Well, for instance the price shot up when the Shah of Iran was overthrown...Then there was the seizure of the US embassy in Tehran...The Soviet invasion of Afghanistan...More recently the invasion of Iraq, the 2008 banking crash…that sort of thing. Uncertainly can lead to panic-buying of gold, pushing the price into orbit.'

I said, 'So, if someone knew there was going to be an international crisis they'd buy gold in advance. Then when catastrophe struck, they'd be sitting pretty?'

'Yup. But I can't think of anything looming that might fit the bill.'

I thanked Geoff and asked him the latest on the Pronova deal. He hesitated. 'I knew I should have kept it to myself. JJ's not supposed to be telling the world and his wife. Security for my old age is wrapped up in Pronova.'

I told him I was thinking of having a small flutter myself. I asked casually, 'We're not all going to be done for insider trading are we?' He said huffily, 'My dear girl, I have some integrity left. In 30 years in financial journalism I have never abused my position. But I decided to keep my eye open for a good prospect for an honest punt.

'My Pronova "inside information" is a combination of painstaking research, good fundamental analysis, the odd straw in the wind and a hunch born of long experience. Add all these together and you've got the next best thing to a cert. But I have no actual knowledge of any putative takeover so my tip is just that - a tip. An absolutely legitimate stockmarket practice.'

'So when should I buy the shares?'

'Tomorrow, dear girl. I feel it in my water. Tomorrow's when the balloon's going to go up.'

I thanked him again and asked him to transfer me to JJ. I wanted to see if he'd managed to confirm any connection between the lottery murders and Bixby's presence in the areas.

'Sorry, Emma, no can do. Bugger's not been here all day. Shall I leave him a message.' So much, I thought, for JJ's protestations about not getting his weekends off. 'Yes, tell him I called. He's got my mobile number.'

I ended the call and dialled my sister. I'd forgotten to give her my current number in case she wanted to get in touch. As soon as she heard my voice Wendy burst into tears. In between bouts of sobbing she told me that Oscar and Kate were dead.

'It was last Thursday. I...I...found them on the doorstep. They'd been...they'd been...Oh Emma...' I heard Harry's voice muttering something. Then he must have taken the phone out of Wendy's hand because suddenly he was on the line. His voice was steady, but carried a note of sympathy mixed with outrage. 'It was a terrible shock. Lucky the kids were both at their ballet lessons. Wen just opened the front door and there the cats were stretched out on the step. I'm afraid their throats had been cut...'

For a moment I couldn't take in what he was saying. 'Throats cut? You mean some vicious bastard just killed them for fun?' Harry mumbled something I didn't catch. Then I could feel the blood drain from my face as his words got through to me. He said, 'We told the police and they said it didn't seem like your average sadist out for a thrill. They seemed to think the way their throats were slit...er...I mean the way they were...er...dispatched, indicated some kind of ritual killing.'

I wanted to throw the phone down and collapse on the settee and weep my heart out. But I forced myself to remain calm. 'What do they mean, ritual killing?'

Harry said, 'You know, the sort used in black magic rituals or devil worship, that kind of thing.'

'Do they get a lot of that in Hornsey Rise,' I asked, unable to keep the sarcasm out of my question. His voice took on a defeated note. 'No, not really...The police did have another theory. They said it could have been a kind of warning to us. Someone sending us a message.

'But Wen and I talked about it for hours and couldn't think of anyone we knew who we might have upset. Or anyone nutty enough to kill our pets. So I rang the police and told them it didn't hold water. After that they seem to lose interest.'

'Thanks Harry and I'm so sorry you've both been through such an ordeal on my account...'

'Your account. What do you mean?'

'Well, they're my cats and if I hadn't asked Wen to board them for a few days the madman, whoever he is, wouldn't have done what he did.'

Harry stammered that looking after my cats had always been a pleasure and the kids loved it. I promised to ring again in a day or so when Wendy was less upset. When I put the phone down, I let myself go and for the next half an hour the tears flowed unashamedly for the two companions who'd shared my life for the last two years.

Twenty-eight

By the time Nick arrived at nine o'clock I'd got my emotions back under lock and key and had washed my face and put fresh make-up on. My eyes were still slightly puffy but I didn't think Nick would be observant enough to notice.

I was right. He swept through the door in high good humour bearing a take-away chinese meal. As we ate and shared a bottle of white Bordeaux we brought each other up to date on events. I told Nick I was up to speed on the Pentecost state of mind - thanks to Gideon's briefing.

'So now we've got the elusive motive,' Nick said excitedly. 'The classic one of revenge, pursued by someone who's - how did Gideon put it - morally insane?

'Which presumably means he'll stop at nothing to achieve his ends. Add this to the power he wields and we've got a pretty formidable situation.' I said, 'Changing the subject, What's this WWW you left me a message about on the computer? Something about a seminar to keep up-to-date with the latest?'

He waved his hand deprecatingly. 'Oh, it was a sort of acronym code for a refresher on the latest internet technology. As you know, when the network was just used by the scientists back in the late sixties, they all knew how to access each other and the information they wanted. But after that, as the spiders web grew, millions all over the world came on line and its getting more and more complicated with more and more risks and threats like viruses and phishing scams. So WWW was their quaint way of labelling the seminar – a way of taking us back to the beginning when WWW stood for World Wide Web.

'The trainers moved on to present day and took us into the future.' His face turned serious. 'For once that cliche about something being a miracle of modern science is accurate when it comes to the Internet.'

I shook my head, 'It's impossible to visualise all the uses its being put to these days. '

'I know. We were shown how to download directly onto our screens confidential information from the White House, the CIA and Homeland Security databases, NASA's communications with the International Space Station or, and this is top secret, the minutes of meetings of the Chinese Politburo. It's incredible.

'And, of course, the other side of the coin is hackers could access restricted information on our files, or China's plans to invade Taiwan or Emma Holgate's tax return…I tell you, it's a cyber jungle out there.'

I said, 'It's really quite frightening how much we've come to rely on computers for the smooth-running of our lives. I can't help thinking there's a disaster waiting to happen somewhere.'

Nick poured the last of the wine into both our glasses. 'As the Good Book says "...Sufficient unto the day is the evil thereof..." Let's talk about happier things. Allardyce told me you spent today splicing the mainbrace with Matthew. How did you get on with the captivating cap'n?'

I retorted, 'Judging by your air of quiet elation, as well as you with the simpering Sophie...'

'Ouch!' Nick's expression became serious. 'To tell you the truth Sophie and I just...well...hit it off. On the flight over I felt completely at ease with her. We just talked and talked. And later we spent a very romantic time in a wine bar.' He looked sheepish. 'I'm sorry about the previous subterfuge. But, on Allardyce's orders I had to suss out whether Sophie would be any good as an insider for us in the Pentecost setup.

'Apparently, she's a patriot and feels strongly about her country. This is why we approached her in the first place. But we had to be certain. After talking to her I judged we could trust her so we decided we had to tell her what I really did for a living and what you and I were doing here. I told her of our...um...pretence.' He said pleadingly, 'Emma, I know you've told me to back off. But I still feel guilty that somehow I've betrayed you.' He added suddenly, 'Not that we did anything more than talk and hold hands.'

I said reassuringly, 'As far as I'm concerned there's nothing to feel guilt about. In fact I'm glad you've said what you have because Matthew and I hit it off rather well, too, so that makes us even.' Nick visibly relaxed. 'So we can go on being friends?' I nodded.

'That's just as well because after what Sophie told me, all three of us might be working together...' He held up his hand to forestall a comment from me. 'Seriously, she's worried about developments at Pentecost.'

'What kind of developments?'

Nick explained that Sophie was being excluded from all discussions and decisions on two projects under way. One was being called 'Operation D-Day' and the other 'Operation Wipeout'. Nick said, 'Whenever Sophie mentions D-Day and Wipeout, either Hugo or Bixby changes the subject. She's convinced there's something sinister brewing.

'She's tried to find out more, but all she's managed to come up with so far is that D-Day's to do with a shipment of some kind and Wipeout's connected with computers. I tried checking with the NCA database but there's nothing on the files.'

I said, 'So where do we go from here? '

'Well, Sophie reckons she can hack into Hugo's computer terminal when he's not there. He doesn't know it but she found the indentation on a slip of paper of his current password when she was in his office recently. She thinks the word is "PLAGUE".'

I said thoughtfully, 'Plague? If you play word-associations you might well get "virus". I wonder if there's any significance?'

'Hopefully, we'll soon find out because Sophie's going to log on to Hugo's terminal and try locating D-Day and Wipeout. Whatever she gets she's going to download it onto a memory stick and bring it to us here.'

Twenty-nine

The grief I'd felt over the deaths of Oscar and Kate had turned into a smouldering hatred. It had now become personal. My journalistic detachment had been replaced by an aching desire for revenge on the man whose brutality had invaded my life.

The call I'd been waiting for came the next morning after Nick had gone off to meet Gideon. It was Sir Hugo's secretary asking me to present myself at the Pentecost offices at 3pm. The Chief would be pleased to show me the offshore end of his enterprises and introduce me to Mr Bixby.

I'd just ended the call when it rang again. This time it was JJ. It still hadn't come to me what had nagged at the back of my mind during our last phone conversation. I knew it was an inconsistency of some kind which I wanted to ask him about but I couldn't recall what.

He was in buoyant mood. He said he'd been obliged to take Hugo's London secretary out for lunch 'for old time's sake' and one thing had led to another and he hadn't gone back to the office. In fact he still wasn't there. He was ringing from his mobile on the way to another police media conference at Scotland Yard.

'But I found out what you wanted. And you were right, Emms. As far as I could gather, without making Sandra too suspicious, Bixby was away from the office around the times the murders were committed. Apparently, he'd been secretive about where he'd been going but he always said he'd keep in touch via his mobile. Not a lot to go on I know but, at least the dates coincide.'

A thought occurred to me. 'He wasn't by any chance in London on Thursday?'

'Mmmm, as a matter of fact he was. I know because Sandra said they'd been expecting both Hugo and Bixby to stay in Guernsey until the weekend. Suddenly Bixby turned up apparently to deal with some sort of crisis. He told her the company jet was on standby to whisk him straight back to the Channel Islands the next day. Why do you ask?'

So, I thought, Bixby could have killed Oscar and Kate as a warning of some sort to me. If he could murder innocent human beings without turning a hair, he could butcher a couple of cats easily enough. My stomach turned over at the thought. I told JJ what had happened. I said, 'The circumstantial evidence is getting stronger. Bixby's tied in with the murder scenes and he was in London the night my cats were killed.' I explained what had happened to Oscar and Kate.

With sympathy in his voice JJ said, 'What a ghastly thing for you...and for Wendy for that matter. It's certainly starting to look like our Mr Bixby's a very dangerous character. Whatever you do, Emms, don't take any chances.'

I told JJ that it was increasingly certain Hugo was also implicated but that it was going to be difficult to prove. In the meantime Nick and I had found out Hugo was planning two big operations but we hadn't the faintest idea what they were.

There was silence on the line as JJ thought. Then he said, 'Wow! Sir Hugo the media mogul could actually be Public Enemy Number One - involved in murder, drugs smuggling and money-laundering. This is going to be some exclusive...' I smiled to myself. I'd almost forgotten that JJ and I were set to write all this up as the story of the decade.

JJ said excitedly, 'They might even make a film about us, like they did for Woodward and Bernstein in All The President's Men. They could get John Boyega to play me and Michelle Dockery might make a reasonable stab at portraying a famous female investigatory journalist.'

I said reprovingly, 'Yes, well don't let's get too carried away. First things first. We need to button this whole business up before indulging in flights of fancy, tempting though it might be to some people.'

'You're just no fun any more.'

I felt better after that call. It was good to enjoy a bit of banter with JJ. It restored a sense of normality, somehow. But my mood was shattered when my phone rang again. I recognised the echoey crackling before anyone spoke. I'd been researching on-line about this weird distortion with calls from The Phantom, or Bixby, or whoever it was. I'd learned anyone can buy an app to distort the voice. This would have a double advantage for the caller – the listener wouldn't have a clue who it was and, if a mobile phone recording was passed on to the police, it would foil their voice recognition software.

A dalek in a subterranean cavern deep under the earth said, 'Did you think I'd forgotten you? I left a message with your sister. Have you got it yet? In fact, I left two messages...'

The voice continued in a matter-of-fact monotone, 'If you don't want Wendy to share the fate of dear Oscar and Kate do not press your luck with me any further. One million pounds has been paid into your bank. There will be no more. And I want the other half of the ticket today, delivered by you in person.'

'But I'm in Guernsey,' I said.

A chortle. 'And so am I. Bring your half with you in a plain brown envelope and meet me inside the old German watchtower at Pleinmont Point. Be there at 11.30 this morning. If there is anyone else about, pretend you are a sightseer. Go down the steps and remain inside. I will instruct you what to do next.'

I said angrily, 'If I have your million, and you're not going to pay any more, why should I take the risk of meeting a homicidal maniac?'

'Don't waste my time with insults. The simple fact is: if you don't do as you're told your sister will be the next to die...And then it will be dear little Nicola and Vicky. So, please, no more talk of another million...And don't be tempted to confide in your paramour. Come alone. Your sister's life is in your hands.'

The speaker sounded sinister enough, but it was as if he was playing a part in some low-budget movie. If I didn't know he'd already killed eight people, and was probably a lunatic, it would be faintly comical. But, murderer or not, maniac or not, I wanted to see his face.

I replied, 'I'll be there. But you did say you've paid one million already?'

'Check with your bank. We have fulfilled our part of the bargain. All we ask is that you do the same.' Then the line was dead. My hands were trembling as I stared at my phone. So Oscar's and Kate's killer was The Phantom. And he seemed to know all about Wendy and the children. I dare not risk telling Nick or Matthew. But, why had The Phantom bothered to pay the one million? He could have got me to hand over the ticket just by threatening Wendy. So much didn't make sense.

I dialled the bank's number and asked for Mr Boutillier. Within seconds he was oozing charm down the phone. Yes, the money had been received, transferred from another anonymous numbered account, this one in Belize.

I told him that Senator Le Page would be calling to check that I had the collateral for a business transaction he was undertaking on my behalf. 'No problem Ms Holgate. And do, please, call me Francis.'

Next, I rang Matthew.

'Matthew Le Page.' A ripple of pleasure ran through me as I heard his voice. I hoped he hadn't changed his mind about taking me on as a client. I said as neutrally as I could, 'Hello, Matthew. Thank you for yesterday.'

I felt a surge of relief when his tones lost their brisk efficiency and became warmer and more intimate. 'I enjoyed it too...' And as if he could read my mind he added'...It was the happiest day I've had in years. '

'Me too.' I was content for the present to leave it there, so changed the subject. 'You remember that transaction we discussed yesterday? Well, the collateral's now in my bank. If you'd like to verify that with Le Boutillier and then start buying those shares I mentioned...'

He said he would get onto it straight away and would keep me posted.

Thirty

As I drove out of St Peter Port, climbing up through cobbled streets and past clusters of white shops and cottages, it seemed impossible that I was on my way to meet Britain's most wanted criminal. I must be mad, I thought. But I couldn't see any other way of handling the situation I was in. I was telling myself to keep calm at all costs, but inside I was jelly. I wished Matthew was with me in the passenger seat. But that just wasn't possible. I felt an irritating itch. Mark the scar was definitely disturbed about something.

Steering westwards, past golden-coloured cows and ancient churches, the peace of the countryside bathed in warm summer sun belying the violence with which my life had become involved. As I pushed on through ever-narrowing lanes, I saw a German watchtower looming ahead. I turned a corner to find myself almost on the cliff's edge.

In front of me was the sentinel-like outline of a World-War Two bunker topped by what could be imagined as a huge concrete funnel. Built by the Germans with slave labour, it stood as a permanent reminder of man's inhumanity to man. With its sinister, slitted eyes, it still stared out to sea ready to warn of an invasion that would now never come. I remember someone telling me that the island was riddled with tunnels, bunkers and towers. And there was even suppose to be a labyrinth of passages right under St Peter Port town itself.

I parked the car and walked towards the structure. There was nobody else around. Seagulls wheeled overhead and on the horizon what seemed like a toy launch butted its way past the Hanois Lighthouse. As I nervously descended the steps, the heat of the sun changed to cold as the dank atmosphere seeped from the interior.

I stood in the doorway peering into the gloom. As my eyes adjusted to the shadows I saw beyond the entrance a circular platform from which, 80 years ago, Hitler's gunners had manned part of Fortress Europe. Some steps led to another level - probably a labyrinth of compartments where the troops were housed during their tours of duty. Suddenly, the spooky silence was broken. An amplified whisper which seemed to come from everywhere and no-where filled the air.

The voice had the same familiar, distorted quality of The Phantom's phone calls so at times the speaker could have been a woman, a man, a boy or Bugs Bunny. 'Have you got the envelope?' The question hissed and swirled around the walls. I realised my adversary was using a microphone and speaker of some sort.

'Yes.' I was surprised that my voice was so steady.

'Good. Throw it down the steps ahead of you and then go back to where you are standing now.' I did what I was told. I called defiantly, 'Why don't you show yourself? If you're going to kill me, at least let me see your face.' I heard the envelope being ripped open. A long, amplified sigh drifted through the bunker. Then another distorted whisper. 'I'm not going to kill you, yet. You see I need your services. You will now instruct your bank to repay the million we've loaned you.'

'Loaned me. But I thought that was a payment for the first half of the ticket...'

Echoey whisper. 'You don't really think we'd hand over a million pounds for something that is ours anyway, do you?'

'Then why go through all the charade of transferring money out of Belize, just for the pleasure of putting it back again?'

'We needed a temporary haven. A rather persistent investigator was becoming a nuisance. So where better to hide the money from further scrutiny than a private account in the Channel Islands? And it had the added advantage of gaining your co-operation.'

The whisper took on a harder edge. 'We've played along with your little game but now we require our money back. You'll find the account number for the transfer in an envelope on the shelf below the slit to your left. Take it and go.'

Sizzling syllables. 'If you need an incentive, remember your dear family.' The anger welled up inside me. I said incautiously, 'I know who you are. And if I do, so do others. You think you're one jump ahead of everyone but you're not. The police are closing in on you and the rest of your pathetic gang.'

Derisive clapping echoed through the labyrinth. 'Don't be tiresome, Ms Holgate. The authorities, such as they are, are about to have more momentous concerns. Like The Apocalypse...'

Where the Pentecost City headquarters stood as a symbol of opulence against the London skyline, its Channel Island base was tastefully discreet.

The building itself was in a quiet side road reached via an arch from the High Street. The offices had been built with Guernsey granite a hundred years before by one of the island's shipping families. From the upper floors it would have a picture postcard view of the Victoria and Albert Marinas and the islands of Herm and Sark.

A small brass plate on the wall, by the double glass fronted doors, testified that Pentecost Holdings could be found within. As I waited in reception I tried to shake off the memory of my almost-meeting with The Phantom. Confused thoughts chased around in my head. But there was one thing I was sure of - I was not going to transfer a million pounds anywhere.

I wrenched my thoughts back to the present and remembered to push the 'on' button of my phone's recorder, which was in a discreet pocket in my handbag, turn the phone upside down and back to front to get the mic into optimal position and then put it into flight mode to block any incoming calls. The record function was a useful tool as it could surreptitiously capture up to three hours of material before its memory was full. When this happened I had set it to automatically send the audio file to my computer for me to, if necessary, edit later.

I was all set. Although I still made notes at interviews, using my own brand of shorthand, I'd found over the years that a recording of what was said was a handy way of rebutting any allegations of inaccuracy after publication. I always kept the recording unobtrusive because it tended to have an inhibiting effect on interviewees. But this meant I sometimes lost parts of the conversation through distortion. Well, nothing was perfect in this life.

My musings were interrupted by a severe, middle-aged woman who introduced herself as Mrs Ozanne, Sir Hugo's Channel Island secretary. Unsmilingly, she conducted me into the lift and along a carpeted corridor on the top floor. The entrance to one of the offices was open and as we swept past I saw Sophie poised over a keyboard and staring into her screen. I wondered if she'd managed to access Sir Hugo's computer system yet.

We came to double doors and Mrs Ozanne gave a discreet knock before pushing them open. The room was decorated in pastel shades and full of light from a window that stretched the full length of the wall opposite. The carpet on the floor was thick enough to wade through and the furniture was a contrasting dark walnut. Behind his desk, with his back to the view and looking like a snappily-dressed Buddha, was a smiling Sir Hugo.

He said sonorously, 'Emma, dear lady, delighted to see you again. Forgive me for not entertaining you before now but I've had a few pressing matters to attend to. But, no doubt, you've been spending the time profitably with your young man...And now here we are, no harm done. No harm done at all.'

I took my notebook out of my handbag and for the next hour we played our respective roles - he the benevolent media grandee and me the supplicant scribe. Every time I broached the subject of his father, he switched the conversation to other things. When we'd finished, he had talked a lot but revealed little. I said tentatively, 'You mentioned I might meet your computer genius, Mr Bixby...'

'It so happens,' he replied genially, 'we're lucky on that score. George had to fly out to Zurich and then on to London to deal with some tedious problems. But, he arrived back this morning and...' He consulted his watch '...just about now he will have finished his hook-up with Miami.'

'Miami?'

'Yes, I own a couple of TV stations there and I'm thinking of downsizing the operations. George has been working on the figures for me.'

Miami, I thought. Crossroads of the world's narcotics trade. I wonder..?

Sir Hugo heaved himself to his feet and beckoned me to

follow. We went through a side door, down one flight of stairs and into an office with no windows and only one anglepoise lamp for illumination. The troglodyte's lair.

And there was the cave-dweller himself, his features eerily lit by the glow of his computer screen. I could feel my heart thumping so loudly I thought they both might hear it. Was this The Phantom? Was this the creature who killed human beings without remorse? Was this the animal who'd pitilessly slaughtered my cats? Had I just had a close encounter with him in the bunker? He looked up when we entered.

'George,' Sir Hugo boomed heartily, 'a visitor to see you. This is Emma Holgate, The Globe reporter I've been telling you about.' George Bixby slid off his chair and waddled towards me. He gave a stiff bow and held out his hand. His head came up to my chest so to look at me he had to crane his neck backwards. 'Pleased to meet you,' he said.

His voice surprised me. I suppose I'd expected something squeaky or child-like to go with his diminutive proportions. But instead it was harsh, gruff, something more appropriate to a nightclub bouncer. Could this really be The Phantom? Although he was small, he was muscular with broad shoulders and long arms. His clean-shaven face was curiously cherubic and could have been mistaken for that of a schoolboy. His gibbous eyes under a mop of dark hair gave him a permanently surprised look.

As we stood there, disappointment clutched at me. My certainty that he was The Phantom began to evaporate. Somehow I couldn't equate this Toulouse-Lautrec with a rampaging mass murderer. I said awkwardly, 'I hear you're a genius with computers...' He inclined his head in acknowledgement. The cultivated politeness of his reply was at odds with the gravelly delivery. 'Forgive me if I don't respond with a ritual show of modesty. You're right, I am.'

I stared at him and he lifted his shoulders and dropped them again. 'As you can see, physically nature has not been kind to me. While my contemporaries engaged in conventional human activities like falling in love, getting married, having children...I found refuge in creating my own world – in cyberspace.' He said confidently, 'I understand it and am master of it...' His eyes stared over my head into the middle distance as he said enigmatically, 'In the future, computers will rule the world and I shall rule the computers.'

Sir Hugo coughed. 'I've told Ms Holgate a little about Rainbow. But tell her how you've not only invented a "vaccine" to combat computer viruses but also a way of getting it to thousands of users direct.' I looked at Bixby curiously.

He pointed at the keyboard and monitor on his desk. 'Through that I can access any other computer in the world, as long as it's on-line.' I nodded encouragingly. Getting into his stride he said, 'It's like a spider's web connecting me to millions of people. Up to now cures for viruses have been confined to anti-virus software fitted to individual systems and devices.

'But I have devised a unique way of injecting my cure via the Internet which can combat thousands of infections at the same time.' I said I remembered some of the details from Sir Hugo's dinner party. Bixby shuffled back to his chair, climbed up on his seat and swivelled to face his screen. He said opaquely, 'Rainbow and its method of delivery is my greatest achievement so far - except for one.'

I asked him what that one was but Sir Hugo intervened silkily, 'That, I'm afraid, is not yet for public consumption but when it is, dear Emma, I promise you will be among the first to know.' He turned to Bixby and said, 'I think we'll leave you to your brave new world, George, while Emma and I enjoy a well-earned cup of tea.'

Back in Sir Hugo's office we sat in armchairs and Mrs Ozanne appeared carrying a large, silver tray. She placed it and its plate of biscuits on the table between us before withdrawing. Sir Hugo poured the tea, and for the next few minutes we sipped and nibbled and made polite conversation about George and his cyber-world.

Gradually, I became aware something was wrong. A light-headedness was enveloping me. I wanted to laugh hysterically. A strange idea jumped into my mind. I don't know why I hadn't thought of it before. Its brilliance made me feel quite elated: I should tell Hugo the truth. That he was living on borrowed time and the whole of his criminal empire was about to fall.

He'd be so interested to hear that law enforcement agencies throughout the world were poised to swoop at the NCA's signal. He needed allies and I could be one. When you came to think about it, we were both pawns in the same game. If we joined forces we could let both sides slug it out while we walked off with the loot. What a dazzling plan. We could cash in the winning ticket and invest it all in Pronova. I heard myself giggling with delight.

It was all so simple: we could syphon the Venture cash - as soon as it hit the Pentecost account in the Western Bank - into the secret account I had arranged with Le Boutillier. With the million I'd already got, plus the proceeds from my successful Pronova investment added to the jackpot money, Hugo and I would have nearly twenty million pounds.

We'd split it down the middle and he could arrange for himself a safe passage to South America. But, before he left, he could put on a memory stick all the details of his laundering companies and the Hell's Angels network. And make a statement incriminating Bixby in The Phantom murders. Then he'd use his private jet for his getaway, I'd be rich and the NCA could claim a triumph for law enforcement.

I shook my head to clear it. What had got into me? I peered at Sir Hugo. He was leaning back with a faint smile playing at the edges of his lips. His hands were clasped across his stomach. Had I spoken aloud what I'd been thinking?

Sir Hugo began to speak, but his words appeared to be coming from the same place as The Phantom's phone calls...He leaned forward dropping his avuncular air. 'There's a great deal at stake, young lady, and you're not going to be allowed to jeopardise it. So we're going to get inside that pretty head of yours and find out what's going on...'

He leaned back. 'I know it's a cliche beloved of modern fiction writers but the fact is - it works.' His voice was becoming hypnotic to listen to. 'You're probably feeling a little drowsy by now. That will be the gamma-hydroxybutyrate, otherwise known as GHB... In fact describing what you have just imbibed as GHB is not strictly accurate: it's a genetically-altered derivative, mixed with scopolamine, and is a most efficacious product of modern neuropharmacology, in case you're curious.'

I looked down at my teacup. Pentecost had slipped something in it and I had drunk it to the dregs. I went to say something but nothing would come out. My body had become paralysed. Hugo's voice was insistently intruding into my fading consciousness '...While it is active it depresses the central nervous system. But, a useful side effect, for us, is that its subject is obliged to tell the truth. Perhaps all politicians should be required to take a daily dose, eh? Ha-Ha!

'But fear not, there are no permanent side-effects. You will first slip into unconsciousness. But that will last a mere few minutes. When you awake again your brain will enjoy a heightened perception. And you'll positively desire to answer all our questions.'

His words were being swamped by a rushing sea of blackness at the edge of my mind. 'And, do you know what the beauty of this drug is? When it finally wears off, you won't remember a thing. It will be just as if you've been asleep. You and I can go on as before with no recriminations or inhibitions to sour our relationship...'

I couldn't concentrate any longer on what he was saying. I felt a curtain fold around my mind and I slipped into a velvety darkness.

Thirty-one

When I woke up Pentecost had been joined by three others who'd pulled up chairs and were sitting round me like indians encircling a pioneer's waggon. I saw by the clock on the wall I had been unconscious for 10 minutes. I was still sitting in the same position and Hugo was still beaming at me from the other side of the table.

To my left - a scowling Francesca Botero and George Bixby, whose legs were dangling incongruously. To my right sat Charles Manderson, Western Bank's top man. It didn't surprise me. After all, to accomplish all The Hell's Angels' dubious financial dealings Hugo would have needed a financial insider.

I still could not move. But my mind was pin sharp. It was like waking up to a technicolour world after dreaming in black and white. But my perceptions were distorted. I seemed to see my four interrogators through a fish-eye camera lens. But when Hugo spoke, part of my mind focused obediently on every word, like a dog attending to his master's voice.

'As I was saying earlier, dear Emma, we're rather anxious to know what's going on. We believe we have the true situation up to date thanks to our...ah...contacts. But there are one or two areas about which we need to reassure ourselves...'

I was curiously aware that his voice was having an hypnotic effect on me. I loved the mellifluity of it, the cadences, the olde worlde charm. I could have listened to it all day. All I wanted was to hear him talk and to please that voice.

He began my interrogation by asking me what I knew about 'Wipeout'.

'It's the codename for something Pentecost Enterprises is involved in but I don't know what.'

'What about Operation D-Day?'

'Again, I don't know.'

Manderson said, 'If they don't know about either operation they don't know anything.' He sprang from his chair in jubilation and walked behind me. He slipped both his pudgy hands under the lapels of my jacket and kneeded my breasts.

I was still unable to move. All I could do was swivel my eyeballs upwards but he was behind me and out of sight. He let out an explosive sigh. 'I've been longing to do that since your dinner party Hugo. They're wonderful tits, so firm...' He squeezed my nipples between both index and middle fingers. 'And she likes it too. Her raspberries are begging for more.

Pentecost waved him back to his seat. 'This is neither the time nor the place to give rein to your animal instincts, Manderson. We're not out of the wood yet. She and her policeman boyfriend know enough to seriously endanger our plans. Emma, my dear. I believe you think you know the identity of The Phantom. So, do enlighten us...'

I tried to point across the table but my hand remained stubbornly in my lap. I said, 'It is George Bixby.' There was a moment's silence before the room exploded with laughter. Bixby was looking even more astonished than usual. Eventually he said in his hoarse voice, 'How...why...do you think I'm The Phantom.'

'Because you have been in the vicinity of all the murders when they happened, you were in London the night someone killed my cats and being a midget you could easily gain people's confidence before shooting them.' Bixby looked genuinely perplexed.

Manderson said jocularly, 'You must admit, George, it does seem plausible.' Bixby's face darkened as he turned back to me and said, 'Earlier this afternoon we talked about Rainbow and the Internet, but what do you know about my other invention?'

I wrinkled my brow. 'What other invention?' I asked eventually. Bixby looked at Hugo in triumph. 'There you are, we're watertight. She doesn't know about the virus or Wall Street. Or the armada...'

Manderson blew up. 'Are you mad, Bixby? She doesn't know so don't tell her.'

Pentecost waved his hand placatingly. 'I've told you, she'll remember nothing of this conversation when she wakes up. It'll be expunged from her mind. Even hypnosis won't be able to breach the barrier this drug erects around the memory.'

Slightly mollified Manderson said, 'I suppose you've thought of the possibility that she might have a tape recorder with her?'

Pentecost replied, 'It was the first thing I checked as soon as she went under. In her handbag are the usual female accoutrements. And her mobile phone of course – What would the journalists of today do without their mobiles, Eh? I remember the time when you'd have to find a phone box before dictating your scoop to a copy-taker. Another planet Indeed... another life.'

It was then that Francesca signalled she'd had enough of Hugo's stroll down memory lane. She said, 'What do you know, Emma, about money-laundering and its connection - if any - with Pentecost Enterprises?' I replied ingenuously, 'Sir

Hugo's companies are believed to be involved but there is not yet enough evidence to prove it.'

At this Pentecost sat up erect in his chair. He said casually, 'You say not yet enough evidence. What steps are being taken to acquire this evidence?'

'When you cash in the next lottery ticket, the police will trace all the addresses you send the money to and these companies will be raided. It's expected that those arrested will implicate the Pentecost empire in both money-laundering and drugs smuggling.'

For a second there was absolute silence in the room. Then Manderson gulped, 'My God, they're right on our heels. What're we going to do..?'

Pentecost held up his hand, 'Before you start panicking just remember one thing. That £17 million will bounce straight out of those overseas accounts - half to purchase the last of my gold and the other half to complete the funding of the Armada.

'And as soon as that happens we launch D-Day and Wipeout. At this point the UK police are going to be far too busy containing riots in the streets to worry about us. And by the time they do get round to worrying, it'll be too late. I shall be in command...'

Manderson said anxiously, 'But I thought D-Day and Wipeout were going to take several weeks yet to get in place.'

Pentecost replied, 'Thanks to George's inspiration and not a little perspiration we've managed to bring them forward so now we're only a tad away from the off.'

Francesca ticked the days on her fingers. 'Correct me if I'm wrong, Hugo, but now we've got the lottery ticket, Venture's validation procedures will take two days after which we get our cheque. That takes us to Thursday. With special clearance the

£17 million can be in Manderson's bank and out again the same day to buy the gold and pay off the Cali people. So by Friday we'll be ready.'

Hugo nodded. Turning to Manderson he said, 'So now's the time to keep our nerve. The police have nothing to act on at present and by the time they run a trace on the £17 million it'll be too late. All we have to do is act normally until Friday and stay alert.' He turned to Bixby. 'George, is Rainbow installed in all Pentecost's systems?'

'Yes, nothing will damage our computers...' He smiled in mock sorrow. 'But I can't say the same for the dealing rooms of the world...' Manderson threw a look in my direction and said apprehensively, 'Are you sure she won't remember anything. Wouldn't it be safer to...er...keep her under lock and key?'

'And alert all her friends in the world of law enforcement,' said Pentecost. 'No, this drug's been tried and tested and never failed. It's better all round if Emma returns to her normal routine. We can play them along for a few days more...'

Manderson wrung his hands. 'I wish I could share your certainty about all this. It still sounds to me like something out of science fiction. Surely Wall Street and the City of London and Tokyo and Hong Kong and all the other stock exchanges are tamper proof? They must have hired the best brains in the world to protect their security systems...'

Pentecost said phlegmatically, 'Oh, they did...Well almost the best brains. George relished pitting his skills against theirs. But, frankly, he was disappointed. Is that not so, George? They'd become complacent and negligent in their duties. Not many people realise that some High Street banks have security systems dating back thirty years...Yes, unbelievable I know. And its this kind of sloppiness and complacency that George is about to exploit.'

Bixby said patiently, 'I seem to have explained this with monotonous regularity Charles. But, for your peace of mind, I'll go over it again. Every system, however sophisticated, has its weakness. I have designed my virus to seek these weaknesses out. Then it slips through and into the electronic body and, once that happens, the host is doomed.

'And there's absolutely nothing that's been so far invented that can stop it. That's because I'm the world's foremost expert on both hardware and software. And, for reasons of my own, I have decided that the gamekeeper should turn poacher...'

Manderson was still looking doubtful. Bixby changed tack. 'To use an analogy, I have cultivated the AIDS virus for computers. And I've also developed its antidote - Rainbow. But, so long as I have the original of Rainbow and the only back-up copy's in your bank's vaults, this new AIDS epidemic will infect all the systems I target. And there'll be no cure.

'As soon as I launch it from Nemesis, all the finance centres of the world's banking systems will implode just as dramatically as if a bomb had gone off.'

Her eyes shining Francesca continued the theme. 'Capitalism, which revolves around the Yankee dollar, will collapse and with it will go the so-called democratically-elected governments.' Pentecost chipped in, 'And for my part, in the UK we will give added impetus to this collapse by simultaneously flooding the major cities with free cocaine, heroin and amphetamines...'

'...which are currently hidden offshore and awaiting collection by our fishing fleet,' completed Bixby. 'What a deadly combination we make, Hugo, if I may say so.'

Pentecost acknowledged triumphantly, 'After D for drugs Day, our confederates, the traffickers and dealers, will obligingly add to the havoc with gang wars breaking out all over the land as their prices collapse. And, when the monetary system implodes, my gold will make me the most powerful man in Europe.

'All my media outlets will re-enforce the message that only I, and my army of well-placed friends, can hope to restore order. And George will activate all the contacts he's made already in his cyber-world to co-ordinate a global meeting of minds. The upshot will be: a new world order...' He sighed heavily '...And revenge.'

In the silence that followed Manderson coughed. 'On a more mundane level, Hugo, what will happen to The Phantom, so-called?'

'Don't curl your lip like that, Charles. The Phantom so-called has served us well. My mercenary has carried out my bidding with admirably professional detachment. And now I've practically completed buying my gold, there's just one more task to perform...'

Manderson, Bixby and Francesca all looked at him expectantly.

Pentecost continued sombrely, 'It has just come to my notice that a certain member of my staff has been attempting to gain unauthorised access to both my, and George's, computer files. For what purpose I trust we are about to find out.'

He swivelled towards me. 'Depending on your answer, dear Emma, it will either be thumbs up or thumbs down for my head of public relations. Now, tell me, why has Ms Baxter been interrogating our databases?'

I answered obligingly, 'To find out more about Operations D-Day and Wipeout. She was suspicious of your exclusion of her in discussions and agreed with Nick to discover anything she could.'

Pentecost shook his head mournfully. 'Ah. Such a pity. Loyalty appears to count for so little these days. And any fool knows an unauthorised user can easily be traced. Tut tut she has become a risk we can ill afford at this stage of the game.'

With a note of high anxiety in his voice Manderson said, 'But did she find out enough to damage our plans?'

'Have no fear, Charles. Ms Baxter didn't even get past our security codes.'

Pentecost turned his attention back to me. 'Sadly, Emma, for Ms Baxter your honesty is not going to be the best policy. Now, apart from your theory about poor George, have you or your associates, any other thoughts as to The Phantom's identity?'

A lethargy was sweeping over me again. I tried to blink away the soporific state I was sinking into. Haltingly, I replied, 'George Bixby... my own idea...don't know what other theories... police baffled...' It took all my strength to answer as waves of tiredness engulfed me.

Pentecost said, 'He will be gratified to know that, I'm sure. Just one more job and he can retire a rich man.'

Before my eyes finally closed I saw Pentecost turn his head to consult the clock on the wall. From the end of a long tunnel I heard him say, 'The drug's wearing off. A textbook demonstration of our little helpmate's efficiency.

'When Ms Holgate wakes up she must find this room exactly as it was when we were having tea together so I suggest you all return to your respective tasks...'

Pentecost's tones began to lose their charms and I slept.

Thirty-two

'Emma, my dear. Emma, wake up.' More insistently, 'Emma, stir yourself.' Someone was shaking my shoulder and a voice was calling from the bottom of a lift-shaft somewhere. Then it got nearer and I recognised it but the name of its owner eluded me.

As I opened my eyes a face was peering into mine. 'I must say, dear lady, you appear to have been well and truly burning the candle at both ends. Never before has one of my reporters fallen asleep in the middle of an interview with me.' Slowly the features swam into focus and I remembered where I was. I looked down at the table to see a teapot and two empty cups with a skin already formed on the dregs at the bottom.

'I'm...I'm sorry, Sir Hugo, I've never done that before. I...I...felt rather strange and must have blacked out. How long have I been asleep?' I looked at my watch and then at the office clock to check. It was nearly six o'clock. The last thing I remembered was coming back from seeing Bixby at a quarter past four and sitting down for tea and biscuits with Sir Hugo playing mother. Why had I fallen asleep? And for over an hour?

'As I say, my dear, you've been overdoing it. I left the room to take a phone call and when I returned you'd dropped off.

Frankly, you looked so peaceful that I didn't have the heart to distrurb you. I believe we'd concluded our business so I thought it would do no harm to leave you there. Even the formidable Mrs Ozanne could not conceal a smile. However, the working day is now nearly at an end so I thought I'd better waken Sleeping Beauty.'

'You must think me very unprofessional.'

'Think nothing of it. No harm done. But take a little advice from someone old enough to be your father. Spend the next few days relaxing. Don't think about work. Just concentrate on that young man of yours and enjoy yourselves.'

The first thing I did when I got back to the cottage was ring Wendy. She was still sniffling a bit when I mentioned Oscar and Kate, but otherwise everything seemed normal. I'd given Matthew my landline number, in case my mobile was out of signal range at any time, and he'd left a message on the answerphone to call him back as soon as I got in. I dialled his home number, assuming he would have left work by now.

'Emma. Terrific news. Your Pronova shares have gone into orbit. Do you want me to sell when the markets open tomorrow morning, or do you want to give me a stop loss and hang on in there?'

Just hearing his voice made me feel warm and secure. I said, 'How much have I made today then?'

There was a muttering as he made a few calculations in his head. 'Give or take the odd few hundred I'd say you'd doubled your investment.' Half a million! I remembered a saying of Geoff Travis's: Always leave some profit for the next man. So that's what I'd do. 'Yes, Matthew, sell.'

'Right. And where have you been all day? I've been trying to ring your mobile but you seemed to be out of range. You're a cool one. I expected you to be ringing me every hour on the hour to check on your investment.'

He said good-humourdly, 'But I suppose making half a million in an afternoon is nothing to get excited about for someone accustomed to living the high life with all those metropolitan movers and shakers.' I went to say something but Matthew cut in...'How about coming round to my place tonight. I'll cook us dinner and we can tell each other about our day.' I looked round at the cottage. It was more like an office with all the computer paraphernalia. And Nick was still out.

I said, 'I couldn't think of a nicer idea.'

Thirty-three

When Matthew opened his front door he'd changed from his formal office clothes into black cord trousers and a blue crew-necked sweatshirt. From my limited holiday wardrobe I'd chosen a long and loose-fitting oatmeal cotton dress which I thought struck the right balance between casual-ness and elegance. I still had a faint headache lingering from my session with The Chief.

We smiled at each other and our eyes locked in a moment of remembrance and mutual desire. Matthew's home was a converted Guernsey farmhouse. While the traditional features had been kept, the inside had been tastefully refurbished in a modern style. He took my hand and led me into the sitting room. I perched on the sofa as he poured us both a drink. My nose twitched at a seductive smell coming from the kitchen.

Matthew explained, 'Tagliatelle with sage, pimentos and garlic. I'm not much of a cook but that's one dish I've managed to master. It was one of Laura's favourites so I thought I'd see if I'd still got the knack.' He handed me my gin and tonic and we both toasted each other silently. He said, 'So, where have you been hiding all day?'

'Oh this morning I had an assignation with The Phantom and this afternoon I interviewed his boss and for some inexplicable reason fell asleep for over an hour...' Matthew laughed but his grin died when he saw my expression. 'You are joking...I mean, about The Phantom..?'

I took a long gulp from my glass and began to feel better. I shook my head. 'No, I'm not joking.' I reached out and took his hand. 'Matthew, darling, I haven't been totally honest with you but I can't go on any longer. I need to talk to someone. Will you listen?'

He nodded gravely. So I started with my phone call from Annie last Monday and, apart from one exception, told him everything right up until my session with Sir Hugo this afternoon. Matthew didn't interrupt, apart from occasionally leaping into the kitchen to prevent the tagliatelle from being ruined. When I'd finished he blew out his cheeks in one long expulsion of breath. 'Phew. I need time to think about all that. Let's have dinner while my creation's still edible and you can answer my question between mouthfuls.'

For the next hour we ate and talked and shared nearly two bottles of Pouilly Fume, at the end of which I felt easier in my mind than I had been for a week. And the alcohol was having its usual, predictable effect. Whether deliberately or not Matthew had been attentively re-filling my glass every time I'd taken a sip. Consequently, I was floating on a sea of well-being. Matthew affected not to notice that I was staring at him with lust in my eyes. Over coffee he said thoughtfully, 'One thing puzzles me. You say you behaved completely out of character by falling asleep during your interview with Sir Hugo...But why?'...I mean why did you fall asleep? Did you notice anything strange either before you lost consciousness or when you woke up?'

I dragged my thoughts back to dreary matters. 'While we were drinking our tea I did have this weird feeling, with funny thoughts running round my head. The next thing I knew was Sir Hugo shaking my shoulder to wake me.'

'You say this happened after coming back from seeing Bixby in his den?'

'Yes. Hugo's PA wheeled in the tea trolley, Hugo played mother and we sipped and made polite conversation.'

'Do you think you might have been drugged?'

I stared thoughtfully across the table. It would make sense. 'I suppose if Hugo is a drugs baron I dare say it'd be easy for him to lay his hands on something that would knock me out.' Matthew rubbed his chin reflectively. 'Yes. But why? For what purpose? If something was going to happen that he didn't want you to see he could have called off the appointment. No, he needed you there in his office AND drugged. Are you sure you were asleep the whole time?'

'Are you saying I could have woken up and said or done something and then completely forgotten it?'

'It's been done before. Some drugs are capable of producing amnesia so the person's lost all recollection of where they've been and even who they are.

'I suppose it's not impossible. But what would Hugo want to blank out an hour of my life for? He doesn't strike me as the sort of man who gets his kicks from drugging women and then having his wicked way with them.'

Matthew sighed. 'Ok, let's leave it there for the time being. But I think you must tell Nick and Jack all that you've told me…' He looked at me sternly '…especially about your contact with The Phantom.'

I tried not to slur my words as I said insistently, 'No Matthew, you're the only one I want to know. And I have to trust you on that. Please say nothing to anyone. I can't explain but that's how it's got to be.' He gave me a sideways look and then reluctantly agreed.

After we had stacked the dishwasher and tidied the kitchen, Matthew led me back to the sofa.

'A nightcap?'

'I don't suppose you've got such a thing as a Calvados? I asked.'

Matthew laughed. 'Your wish is my command.' A minute later he handed me a sherry glass filled to the brim with an amber liquid. He said, 'This is a special brand. It's called eau-de-vie and is guaranteed to take your mind off your troubles.'

He poured himself an Irish whiskey and sank down at the other end of the sofa. I raised my eau-de-vie in an exaggerated toast. We clinked glasses and both took a swallow. I nearly coughed a mouthful over Matthew's cream-coloured carpet. The spirit seared its way down my throat and tracked to my stomach.

I put the glass down on the coffee table and turned towards him. Heat was beginning to pool in my groin, reaching out to touch every nerve-end in my body. I heard myself say in a tiny voice, 'Matthew I want you.'

Matthew was looking at me, his expression a mixture of hunger and love. He pulled me to him and kissed my hair. My head swam as the tang of his aftershave mingled with the scent of his male-ness. His left hand slid off my shoulder to cup the fullness of my breast. A deep sigh escaped from his lips. 'It feels so good to hold you,' he said.

Suddenly we were kissing passionately. My nipples had already grown hard and swelled to the size of raspberries as we held each other. Matthew's eyes were closed and the front of his trousers bulged with his desire. I teased my nails across his chest and down over the tensed muscles of his stomach clearly visible through his sweat shirt. He moaned and rolled his head.

His left hand had dropped to the bottom of my dress and was now working its way slowly up the inside of my leg. In a spiralling motion his nails lambently caressed the tender flesh of my inner thigh. Involuntarily, I squirmed and opened my legs a little wider.

He eased the elastic of my briefs outwards and slipped his middle and forefingers beneath the material. Like the legs of a cartoon character they ran frenziedly on the spot. I gasped in delight as pulses of ecstasy radiated through me. Using both hands I impatiently unbuckled his belt and flipped undone the button of his trousers and slid the zip downwards.

I pulled at the top of his underpants and stared in wonderment that something so flaccid in repose should assume such an impressive length and girth when aroused.

As I stared I could feel waves of bliss rippling outwards from my loins. I fluttered my tongue as Matthew's moans grew louder in time with the tide of exquisite pleasure rising in me.

Together we pounded in harmony as our convulsions reached fever pitch. Nerve-ends screamed for release as electric shocks of sensation shot through us both.

Finally, as my body was racked by a cascading orgasm Matthew gave an animal cry and his body jerked with juddering pulses. Later, with a smile of satisfaction, and for the second time that day, I drifted into a blissful sleep.

Thirty-four

I got back to the cottage just before midnight. As I stood on the step and groped in my handbag for my keys I could hear the sound of a man groaning. I opened the door and a sickly smell, like an overflowing cesspit, greeted my nostrils. Nick called out brokenly, 'Don't put on the light...'

I saw through the gloom a scene of devastation. In the front room, furniture had been turned over, books littered the floor and the computer was smashed with our files scattered everywhere.

Lying amidst the mayhem was Sophie. Her eyes were open and staring, unblinking, at a point on the wall over my shoulder. Her beautiful features were twisted into an unnatural gape. It was plain that she was dead but, just the same, I knelt beside her and felt for a pulse. There wasn't one.

Her skirt was pulled up over her waist and she had obviously put up a struggle before she died. The pool of blood spreading out across the carpet, like an ink stain on blotting paper, told its own story. The Phantom had been here, in our temporary home.

Nick was slumped against the overturned settee shaking his head and staring at me in bewilderment. 'I only saw her at lunchtime today. She seemed so...so...alive. I couldn't believe it was her when I walked in tonight. I still can't take it in now...' I put my arms round him and pulled him to me. I don't know how long we stayed like that in the darkness together. Eventually instinct took over. In normal circumstances I should call the police. But, instead, I rang Gideon's number and told him what had happened.

Within what seemed like only a few minutes he was walking through the front door closing it carefully behind him. He took one look around and at Sophie's body and said, 'Dear God!' He poured a heavy slug of brandy from a bottle on the sideboard and handed it to me. He pressed another glass into Nick's fist and gruffly ordered him to drink it.

Gratefully, I swallowed a mouthful and felt the spirit burn its way down my throat. I began to stop shaking. Gideon poured himself a measure and looked at Sophie. 'Wasn't she your insider - Pentecost's publicity girl?'

I said, 'Yes. We met the other night at a private dinner party and, despite being recruited by Nick,' I nodded in Nick's direction '...They did become good friends.' Gideon grunted and knelt down performing the same ritual as me. Then he went upstairs reappearing with a duvet he had pulled off the bed which he draped across Sophie's body.

Nick stared sightlessly into space. 'But why..? Why would The Phantom want to kill her? I mean, they couldn't possibly know what we were planning, could they?' Gideon shrugged. 'Who knows? She was obviously endangering their setup in some way. Can either of you think of anything?' A dreamlike scene in which Hugo knew all about Sophie's involvement with us, jolted through my mind and then it was gone. I tried to recapture the thought but it stayed just outside the limits of my consciousness. I shrugged and told Gideon about Sophie's offer to Nick to dig into what was behind Operations D-Day and Wipeout.

'So, she could have discovered something, come here to tell you, was followed and then killed before she could pass it on.'

I said, 'Nick, how did she get in..?' He sighed heavily, 'I gave her my spare key. She told me she'd tried, but failed, to penetrate the security on Hugo's laptop. But she came up with this brilliant idea to smuggle the whole thing out and bring it here.'

Nick explained, 'The plan was that she'd wait until she thought she could remove it, out of office hours, without anyone noticing it was missing. Pentecost always left it in his safe but Sophie knew the combination – God knows how – so she planned to remove it, bring it straight to me for us to download its contents and squirt them on to the NCA. Our boffins could work on cracking the codes and she would return the laptop with no-one any the wiser.

'I told her that she'd be safer if I gave her a key so she could let herself in if we weren't here. I just didn't think she'd manage it so quickly.'

'So she lets herself in not knowing that she'd been rumbled and The Phantom was only a step behind,' said Gideon.

Suddenly Nick was the professional investigator again. 'But, if The Phantom followed Sophie, and somehow pushed his way in, she wouldn't have had time to hide the laptop. It would have been staring him in the face. So why turn this place over?'

'Just suppose,' suggested Gideon, 'that Sophie suspected she was being followed and as soon as she let herself into the cottage she hid the laptop somewhere. Along comes The Phantom, there was a struggle which caused some of the mess and then his ransacking resulted in the rest.'

I said, 'So the question is, did The Phantom find what he was looking for and, if not, is Pentecost's computer still here somewhere?' Gideon said, 'That would be too much to hope, but I suppose it's worth a quick look in all the likely places - just in case.' He held up both his hands. 'A prosaic thought, I know, but strictly speaking this is a crime scene and we'd be contaminating evidence. However, in the circumstances, I don't think we have any choice. But, if you do find anything that might be useful for the Senior Investigating Officer point it out to me.'

For the next half hour we hunted everywhere but found nothing. Eventually Gideon exploded with frustration. 'Why is nothing ever easy? Now we're still no nearer knowing what D-Day and Wipeout are... You two get some things together. We'll put you up overnight in a hotel while we clear up this mess.'

He reached out and put a hand on my shoulder. 'By the way, Emma, you were right to call me. I'll smooth everything over with the local plod. With luck we can keep the lid on this. If we can somehow find out what those two codenames mean, maybe Sophie won't have died in vain.'

Thirty-five

Nick and I had breakfast back in the familiar surroundings of The Breton. Our conversation was stilted, our thoughts elsewhere. Politely, Nick asked me about my afternoon with Sir Hugo and I told him the curious way in which I'd fallen asleep.

At the mention of this Nick reluctantly dragged his thoughts away from Sophie and asked me to go over in detail what had happened. I told him as much as I had told Matthew yesterday evening. But nothing about Annie, the ticket or The Phantom.

'If you were drugged, do you think it was to interrogate you?'

'Interrogate me? What, while I'm asleep.'

'I'm being serious. There are plenty of drugs around these days that put their subject into a kind of hypnotic trance. Afterwards, you think you've been asleep while all the time you've been under the control of the hypnotist.'

'You mean I could have been made to tell all I know but not be aware of it afterwards?'

'Exactly. You say you were asleep for over an hour and Hugo says he was so captivated by the charming sight of you snoozing in his chair that he couldn't bring himself to wake you. Does that sound like our ruthless media tycoon?'

'Hmmm. When you put it that way, it seems unlikely. But,

how can we know? If I did go into a kind of drug-induced trance couldn't we retrieve the information through hypnosis - like they're suppose to do with people who claim they've been abducted by aliens?'

'Very fanciful. And strictly for sci-fi anoraks.' Nick shook his head. 'Science, I'm afraid, has taken over from witchcraft. With drugs like, for example, GHB the amnesia is always automatic and virtually impenetrable.'

'You mean if I was put into another trance I still wouldn't be able to recall the missing hour?'

'Just so. It was for that purpose the drug was developed. Once it's been administered you tell all but no-one else will ever be able to discover how much you revealed.' I looked at him glumly. 'I don't like the idea of carrying around with me a missing piece of my life in which I did, or said, God knows what...'

Then I remembered. My mobile phone! Of course. I'd set its record function before being collected from reception. If the batteries hadn't given out, it should have surreptitiously recorded the whole of my visit to Sir Hugo's offices on my voice memos App. And as a failsafe it would have automatically bounced the whole file to my computer. Could I have captured the whole afternoon? My heart jolted joyously at the thought. Then, reality quickly asserted itself. Surely this would just be too good to be true

As usual, I had followed habit and, after the interview, had automatically grabbed my bag and put it over my shoulder without a thought. Normally any recording would only be retrieved later as an aide-memoire or if there was some dispute after publication.

I scrabbled in the pocket where I had left it before my Pentecost session and there it was. I looked up, my face

Ticket to a Killing

flushed in triumph. 'I think we're about to solve the mystery. The drug might be designed to wipe a human memory but it's not versatile enough to do the same to a digital recording.'

'You mean you're still using that devious ploy..?'

'Strictly in the pursuit of truth. And aren't you glad I am?'

We went back up to our room, where we'd slept in separate twin beds, and walked out onto the verandah. We hunched over the phone as I pressed playback. Yes! There was my dutiful interview with my proprietor. Fast forward. Bixby's voice claiming the future was already with us and how nerds would one day rule the universe. Forward further. Mrs Ozanne bringing in the tea trolley.

I was exhilarated. Now came the bit I had no recollection of. It was weird hearing myself as if I was someone else. Nick shot me a look of concern at a loud rustling right by the microphone followed by Manderson gloating about wonderful tits.

I shuddered as I realised he'd been pawing me. I felt a wave of gratitude when I heard Hugo order him to curb his animal instincts. The recording moved on. We were now at the point where I talked of my suspicion that Bixby was The Phantom and the gales of mirth that followed.

I felt sick when I heard myself giving away the the NCA plan to track the payout of the £17 million back to all the Hell's Angel outlets. And 'Operation Starburst', the international effort that would follow to close down the drugs network. As we listened and the entire Pentecost Plot unfolded pictures began to form in my mind to go with the words I was hearing. Gradually, despite the GHB, the blanks were being filled in.

Nick reached out and touched pause. He whispered, 'This is dynamite, Emms. Look we'd better get Gideon in. He should hear everything on that phone and now.'

Thirty-six

Half an hour later we were seated in the police conference room at the old, converted St Peter Port hospital which now served as the Headquarters of Guernsey's Law Enforcement and Border Agency. Gideon had been joined by Matthew, who looked across the table and twitched a wink at me. Nick and I sat opposite and we all made ourselves comfortable. I placed my phone mid way between us all and pressed Play.

We heard the whole of the missing hour, including Francesca's calculation that they'd be ready to launch D-Day and Wipeout by Friday, Bixby's boast of having invented the computer world's AIDS virus, the proposed attack on the capitalist system and Hugo's intention to order Sophie's murder.

As the playback lapsed into an empty silence, Gideon spoke. 'Pentecost's totally and utterly insane. He's a megalomaniac. It would be pathetic if he wasn't one of the most powerful media barons in the world. As it is it's bloody frightening'

Matthew said, 'Yes, and with his resources and contacts, he could just pull it off.' Gideon held up his hand. 'First let's analyse what we're up against and then devise some plan of action. I want something I can recommend to the Commander when I speak to him later on the secure satellite link.'

Gideon hunched his shoulders as he concentrated. 'Now, have I got it right: They know all about our plans to trace their network. They also know that, until we can trace their network, they're still in the clear. So they're feeling pretty damned cocksure. They think they're several jumps ahead of us. And by the time we catch up, if we ever do, their conspiracy will have made our petty efforts irrelevant. Agree so far..?'

We all nodded. He continued, 'But...The one advantage we've got is: They know. But they don't know we know they know. Now let's look at what we're faced with under separate headings...

'First, D-Day: That's obviously the armada of drug ships which will sail for the UK shoreline as soon as Pentecost gives the word. It's all meant as a diversionary tactic while he initiates Wipeout. It sound as if he's got the drug shipments already but his last payment to his suppliers will come from the lottery money...'

Nick said, 'So what if we stopped the payout at source somehow. His suppliers would cut up rough and may want their property back. That could cause all sorts of chaos.'

Gideon shook his head. 'Unlikely. They've probably built up a trust of Pentecost over the years and he'll just say there's been a hitch and he'll pay later. In any case, we need that money to go into his account before we can trace it to his outposts and close the lot down.

'No, regrettably, we've got to let him get his hands on that £17 million.'

I said, 'But how are we going to track his spider's web of accounts, and identify the recipients, if the information's sitting on his computer and we haven't got the computer?'

We all looked at each thinking the same thing at the same time – poor Sophie had died in vain. Gideon coughed awkwardly. 'I feel damn bad about it because we've come up with a solution which, if we'd thought of it before, Sophie, poor girl, might still be with us.'

We looked at him expectantly. 'It's really quite simple. We tap direct into his server at the server farm. We've got our IT team there now monitoring all outgoing traffic. As soon as Pentecost orders money transfers, we'll be recording every keystroke and digital code and by the time he's finished we'll have a twin of his master files...'

Nick said, 'I've just thought of something. Why can't our IT geniuses use the same technique to block Bixby's virus? That would give us game, set and match.'

Gideon said, 'Would that it was that easy. Sorry, Nick, but the source of Bixby's virus could be anywhere. For just this kind of eventuality they've probably located his master server cluster somewhere entirely different. It could be anywhere.'

I said, 'Going back to the drugs. Surely we're not going to let them into the country?'

'No, once the £17 million is on its way to his overseas network we can get the Royal Navy and Border Agencies to intercept Pentecost's fleet. That's no problem. It's this Wipeout that poses the greatest threat.

'If Bixby really can inject a destructive virus simultaneously into all the stock exchanges, there's little doubt it would bring capitalism to its knees. Money markets would collapse, cash would be worthless, governments would fall and there'd be riots in the streets.

'In all that chaos ordinary, decent folk would welcome the restoration of law and order - in what ever form it came. Hence Pentecost's delusion that he and his chums could take over with the popular support of the people.'

Nick said, 'Via his media operations Pentecost would

promise to bring to bear the combined weight of his wealth, through his gold acquisitions, and influence, via the Great and the Good he's already tapped up, to re-establish a civilised society. And he'd be able to ram the message home using the same newspapers, broadcasting and on-line outlets.'

Gideon hauled himself to his feet. 'Coffee anyone?'
Refreshed by a shot of caffeine and nourished by a plate of constabulary biscuits we assessed where we'd got to. I said, 'We were grouping what we're up against under various headings. So far, Jack, you seem fairly confident about intercepting the drugs, and the money-laundering will be neutralised by the raids on the Hell's Angel outposts and Pentecost's overseas holdings...'

Gideon nodded. I went on, 'But we still haven't come up with a way of preventing the virus attack and we still don't know who The Phantom is.'

Matthew said, 'Surely, after the drugs and money-laundering networks are closed down, someone will be prepared to shop The Phantom in exchange for a lesser sentence?'

'Possibly,' Gideon replied. 'But, with due respect to his victims, his identity's not crucial at the moment. Our priority has to be to prevent Bixby spreading his virus and attacking the stock markets. For all we know he's injected his virus into the system already. So where the Hell do we go from here..?'

Nick said vehemently, 'Why don't we arrest the lot of them now, today? We've got this recording as evidence. At least that way we'll have some sort of control. If the virus has been programmed to activate on a certain day, we might be able to sweat it out of Bixby. And, if Pentecost knows we've got rock-solid evidence he might be persuaded to co-operate...'

Gideon said bleakly, 'Arresting them would achieve precisely the opposite of what we'd intend. For starters that recording would not be admissible in court. And we haven't got any actual evidence as such. Pentecost's lawyer would know this and have him out of custody in hours. Then we will have shown our hand.

'Sir Hugo and Bixby would be on the alert and our entire operation would collapse. No, somehow we've got to allow them to go ahead with their plans and only swoop when we've got enough to shut down all the syndicates and put Pentecost and Bixby behind bars for a very long time.'

Matthew said, 'It seems to me that we've got no choice. Bixby's the key to stopping the virus. He invented it and if it's already in the system ready to be activated, the only one who can de-activate it is Bixby - ergo we must persuade Bixby to co-operate.'

Nick said, 'Maybe we can't arrest Sir Hugo and get away with it. But what about grabbing Bixby and keeping him incommunicado on any trumped up charge. Without his genius sidekick, Pentecost would be impotent...'

Various other ideas were discussed over the next half hour. We reluctantly decided that, in the absence of a better idea, we'd go ahead with the 'arrest' of Bixby. It would take all day to get the necessary legal formalities in place but he'd be in custody by tonight. In the meantime, I knew what I had to do.

Thirty-seven

When we left the HQ Nick said he'd see me back at the cottage. Meanwhile, I was to be shadowed by two plain clothes policemen from Guernsey CID for my own protection, now that The Phantom had surfaced in the island. I could go where I wanted but they'd always be there. Meanwhile, he was relieved to say, Sophie's murder had not got into the Guernsey media.

Earlier, Matthew had taken me to one side to tell me the good news that I was now £516,436 better off, thanks to my Pronova sale. I still hadn't arranged the transfer of The Phantom's million but since he was now in the Channel Islands he couldn't get at Wendy, so I knew my sister was safe. For the time being, at least.

I said I'd ring Matthew at his office to arrange our next date. Then, I walked down St Peter Port High Street into Marks and Spencers. I threaded through the store and down the stairs emerging onto The Esplanade. After I made sure no-one was following me I went to a phone box and rang Sir Hugo Pentecost's offices.

After a few moments of arguing, I persuaded Mrs Ozanne to fit me in to see Sir Hugo before his first afternoon appointment. I reversed the charges on my other call and talked for fifteen minutes. When I put the phone down I couldn't suppress a smile of satisfaction. If my plan came off, I was going to be a very rich woman.

When I emerged from the yellow call box a pair of hands covered my eyes and a high-pitched, strangled voice said, 'Guess who?' I turned round and standing there with a smug smile on his face was Jeremy Bartholomew Jerome. I threw my arms round his neck and kissed him enthusiastically on the cheek. 'JJ...Am I pleased to see you! But what are you doing here? I can't see Theo funding a sojourn in the sun for both of us.'

'Hah! So you admit your leisure time, not to mention your love life, is being subsidised by the poor old Globe, Eh?' Prodding him in the ribs I said playfully, 'That's not what I meant and you know it. I've not exactly enjoyed a rest cure while I've been here...But, there have been developments in my love life, as you call it…'

'…Do tell me more.'

'It's a long story. I've got a date with our revered boss at two. But, if you're up to buying me a pub lunch I think I've just about enough time to reveal all.' I slipped my arm through his and propelled him in the direction of the Prince of Wales.

JJ said, 'Why were you phoning from a call box - what's happened to your mobile?'

I didn't like being untruthful with JJ but I didn't want to say it had been temporarily confiscated by the police. 'I left it behind at Matthew's last night...'

'Matthew's Eh? And who might Matthew be?'

'Patience, all will be revealed.'

As we walked up Smith Street's steep cobbles JJ explained that he'd flown into the island that morning after persuading Sandra, his old flame and Sir Hugo's London secretary, to allocate him a seat on the company jet which was back in Gatwick on Pentecost business. Theo had reluctantly agreed that both his reporters might find it helpful to compare notes face to face.

Most of the pub's drinkers were standing around in groups on the pavement in the sunshine so JJ and I took our halves of lager and ploughman's specials to a dark corner inside, which we had to ourselves. I then told JJ everything that had happened since we spoke last, leaving out only who else I'd been ringing from the phone box. And I still kept to myself my involvement with Annie and the lottery ticket.

When I'd finished his grin had gone and he whistled softly. 'Jesus, Emms, how can you be so cool after what you've been through? This is heavy-duty stuff. You take a confrontation with a serial killer as casually as if you'd just had a chat with the vicar.

'Then you're drugged and now you intend to go back and confront the very man who's behind it all...If I was a target of The Phantom's, I'd be a jibbering wreck cowering under guard in some cop shop.'

I said, 'Don't think I'm not scared. But, apparently, I'm being shadowed by two undercover cops. As I haven't managed to spot them, they're either very good at their jobs…'

'…Or you've given them the slip already,' JJ laughed.

When we finished lunch, I left him to explore the town while I kept my appointment with Sir Hugo. I noticed Mark the scar was trying to draw my attention to something.

This time Mrs Ozanne showed me into the Pentecost boardroom. Hugo Pentecost sat in a swivel seat at the head of a long, mahogany-topped table. He looked controlled and quizzical as I paced up and down by the window assembling my thoughts.

'I must say, dear Emma, you're looking very serious. I trust there's not been a rift in the lute..?' I swung round and said bitterly, 'You can cut the crap, Sir Hugo. I know exactly what went on when I came here last.'

He furrowed his brow. 'As I recall, we had a fairly innocuous chat and you were discourteous enough to fall asleep.'

'Yes, after you had slipped some sort of drug into my tea...' Hugo sat up straight and blinked. I went on, 'I see I'm getting through to you. You're wondering just how much I know. Well, the answer is: Everything. You see, when you searched me you missed my mobile phone which I always use to record my interviews…'

For a moment Sir Hugo's self-assurance evaporated '...I don't believe you. You're bluffing.'

I took an identical phone out of my pocket that I had borrowed from Nick and slid it down the table in front of him. 'As you can see it's what you might call State of The Art. And, ironically, funded by Hugo Pentecost's Globe.' His face dropped all pretence and became a mask of anger. 'What have you done with the contents of that recording?'

I slid into a chair next to him and looked him in the eye. 'A couple of hours ago it was being analysed by Jack Gideon and Nick Marlowe, of the National Crime Agency and Matthew Le Page, head of the island's government.'

In the quiet that followed I could hear the murmur of traffic streaming continuously along the seafront. Then Hugo's face broke into a smile. 'Do I assume from the fact that no blue-uniformed heavies are swinging sledgehammers against my door, and that you are sitting here conducting a civilised conversation, it means that you have a proposition?'

'As you might say, very perspicacious. I'll come straight to the point. I'm prepared to tell you their plans to combat D-Day and Wipeout in exchange for certain...um...considerations.'

'And they would be?'

I ticked off on my fingers. 'One: I want the entire £16 million of the remaining lottery money transferred into my private account...' His face suffused with blood and he opened his mouth to speak. I held up my hand, palm outwards. 'Two: I want the identity of The Phantom.'

He sneered sarcastically, 'Why don't I also tell you how to stop the virus and where the drug shipments are to be landed?' I leaned back and regarded him coolly, 'There wouldn't be any point, because I'm not interested. I just want the money and I need to know who your hired killer is...I have a score to settle.'

'I don't believe any of this. Your sudden change of character doesn't ring true. I suspect a trap. Perhaps you're carrying another one of your ubiquitous voice recorders?'

'No trap. And I'm not recording anything. It's just that I've been thinking and I've decided I've got to seize the moment.'

'And, if seizing the moment means betraying your friends - even your lover..?' I looked at him hard-eyed. 'Moralising's just wasting time. It's simple. I'm covering my bets. I want to be rich and I intend to come out of this with something, whatever happens. So your £16 million is my insurance.'

I said, 'How's this for a deal? If you agree to pay it, I'll give you back half - £8 million - in exchange for The Phantom's name and you can carry on with your plans. You can either use it to complete payment on your gold, or the drugs.'

'Where does insurance for you come in?'

'As I see it, your mad scheme might just come off. If it does, my nine million might not be worth much if there's a currency collapse. If that happened I'd expect a lucrative role in your new world order, in exchange for my silence.'

'Your silence over what? The law will already have traced

my association with certain...ah...extra-curricular activities. I am prepared for that but they'll be in no position to pursue their case in the chaos. So what else might I have to fear?'

'Your implication in the murder of at least eight people. The Phantom has been working for you and I will know who The Phantom is. The police might find it difficult to assemble a case against you for drug smuggling and money-laundering. But, once they have The Phantom, they'll have you. And even in your new, exalted position, you won't be able to avoid going to jail for a very long time. But, in exchange for your patronage, I'll keep my mouth shut.'

Sir Hugo made a steeple of his fingers and squinted at me through half-closed eyes. 'I see now there's a definite method in your madness. If - and heaven forfend - my master plan fails, you will still have my eight million. Hmmm! A pretty scheme.'

I said, 'Not to forget the one and a half million I already have - the £1 million down payment for the ticket plus proceeds of a rather successful share deal. Nine and a half million should ensure a comfortable future. Plus, of course, I shall have the kudos of having helped bring you to book and, by the time JJ and I have finished serialising it in The Globe, I'll be a household name too.'

Sir Hugo looked at me admiringly. 'My my. You are indeed a worthy adversary young Emma. So, an all or nothing throw of the dice for me, then. But you seem to have overlooked one small possibility...'

'Which is?'

'I could throw you to The Phantom. I happen to know you've made him rather cross.'

'Then you'll put your grandiose dreams in jeopardy because, without me feeding you inside info, I wouldn't put the odds of you succeeding at better than 50-50.' He scratched his jaw and stared out of the window. Then, 'Alright, I agree to your terms. I don't suppose you'll trust me enough to tell me what our friends in law enforcement have in mind?' I smiled faintly. 'Oh dear, Sir H, you really don't expect me to reveal anything before I have the money, do you?'

I slipped a piece of paper with the number of my account at the Royal Bank. 'Forgive me if I don't take your word on trust, Sir Hugo. Perhaps you'd be good enough to seal our bargain by telephoning Mr Manderson now and making the necessary arrangements. Of course I realise you won't actually have the Lottery money in your account before Thursday but I'm sure a man with your financial clout can whistle up the necessary from other sources.'

'Now? But...'

'It'll put my mind at rest and will also make me feel obliged to disclose something on which you need to take action within the next few hours.'

He gazed at me resignedly before reaching for the phone. Judging from Hugo's end of the conversation, Manderson was deeply unhappy with what he was ordered to do. But Hugo said it had now become a vital part of his strategy and that immediate steps should be taken to transfer the sum into my account. He put the receiver down on its rest. 'Satisfied?'

'So far so good. When I'm actually in possession of the cash we can have a meeting and you can tell me the name of The Phantom and I'll tell you what the NCA are up to. Between us we should be able to keep your coup viable.'

'But, what's this I should take action over this afternoon?'

'Ah, yes. I suggest you get your tame genius to disappear rather rapidly. They plan to arrest him by tonight.'

He looked at me in astonishment and then reached for the

intercom buzzer. 'Mrs Ozanne, please ask George to see me immediately.'

Thirty-eight

Tee-shirted holidaymakers drifted in colourful waves down the cobbled High Street as I walked against the tide to the Royal Bank. Within minutes I was sitting in Le Boutillier's office getting the Uriah Heep treatment again.

'I'll come straight to the point Mr Le Bou--er Francis, I'm expecting £16 million to arrive in my account at any time between now and Thursday via the Pentecost account at the Western...' He tried to remain expressionless but couldn't stop his eyebrows from trampolining upwards to meet his hairline '...And shortly after it is, I'll be instructing you to transfer half of it back again.'

Le Boutillier coughed. 'I'll just recap to make sure I've understood you correctly. You'll be receiving £16 million from Pentecost's bank, half of which you will be instructing me to transfer back to the originating account.'

I smiled encouragingly at him. 'Exactly. Any problems?'

'Er, no. It's just that it's irregular, no not irregular, it's an unusual request.'

I promise you, Francis, it may be unusual but the money has an impeccable provenance and if you need reassurance on that point I'd be happy for you to ring Senator Le Page...' Le Boutillier looked uncomfortable. 'That won't be necessary, I assure you.'

'I was going to ask you, Francis, if you would accept Matthew's reassurances on the phone should you have any misgivings in the light of any future...um...eventualities.'

'As I said, Ms Holgate, Senator Le Page has already vouched for your bona fides...However, his word of course would be a 100 per cent guarantee...'

'So, should certain occurrences come to light that might give you cause for concern, personal reassurances from Matthew - even on the telephone - would be sufficient to put your mind at rest?'

For a moment he looked uncertain of himself. Thoughts of trying to explain some massive fraud to his bosses chased through his mind. 'I can't imagine what might fit that category. However, Senator Le Page is the Island's Chancellor of the Exchequer. I'm sure he's not going to turn out to be a Ronnie Biggs...' He gurgled at his own attempt at humour.

'Fine. One other question. Will you accept my authorisation over the telephone for the transfer. Or, for that matter, a countermand, should I change my mind and want something different done with the money?'

'If you sign certain waivers, yes.'

'Good. If you'd care to prepare all the necessary documents, I'll sign them before I leave...'

That done, I took a slip of paper out of my handbag and slid it across his desk. He picked it up suspiciously and his right eyebrow twitched upwards. I said, 'I would like you to carry out those instructions immediately, Francis.'

He said smoothly, 'Well, of course, this particular commodity is a speciality of our branch in Jersey so it'll be no problem at all. I commend your acumen, Ms Holgate. An excellent way to begin diversifying your portfolio, if I may say so.

I regarded him with wide eyes. 'I'm glad you approve, Mr Boutillier. And, not a word...'

'Absolutely, Ms Holgate. And, it's Francis, remember..?'

Thirty-nine

My next stop-off was to the police headquarters in the old hospital building. This time I found Nick and Gideon sitting either side of Jack's grey steel desk comparing bits of paper. Between them was a map of the English and French coasts and their Channel ports. At one end of the desk was a computer terminal which looked somehow out of place in this throwback office, which might have been regarded as modern in the 1970s.

The room was one degree better than dingy, the decor having given up the uneven struggle with time. As I entered they both looked up with preoccupied expressions. Jack grunted and waved me to a seat and Nick gave a tired smile. I looked around. Along one wall was a row of brown filing cabinets on top of which was one dead spider plant trailing forlornly over the side. The window looked out onto another window from the wall opposite.

'How's it going?' I asked.

'We've more or less got an interception plan in place to stop them landing the drugs,' replied Nick. 'We've got a combined Op with the French and British coastguards, police and border agencies and they're already on the lookout for any unusual movements.'

Jack looked up. 'And, so long as Pentecost fires his money off to all his outlets, we'll have a trace on the destinations...But of course he knows that but doesn't particularly care because he thinks we'll be in no position to do anything once the world's monetary system's about to collapse.'

I said, 'So the main thing we've got to do is stop the virus and Pentecost's Doomsday plot will be thwarted. Then all the rest will drop into our laps. Right?'

'More or less. We can stop the drugs, close down the syndicates, arrest Pentecost, uncover the identity of The Phantom and give ourselves a pat on the back for saving the world as we know it...'

Nick added, 'But as you say, Emms, only if we can stop the virus.'

'So, any ideas?' I asked. Jack and Nick looked at each other. 'The answer has been staring us all in the face,' said Jack. 'Bixby's Rainbow vaccine. On your recording, Emma, Pentecost asked if it had been put in place in all his companies. It's obvious Rainbow's the only antidote.

'Someone said there were only two Rainbows in existence - Bixby carried his about with him on a flash memory card and the other was in the Western Bank.'

Nick said, 'If we can get hold of Rainbow, we can squirt it via the Internet to all vulnerable outlets and they can incorporate it into their security systems. That way Bixby's grand scheme will be neutralised - courtesy of Bixby. Then we keep the little man under wraps and out of commission. End of story.'

'Brilliant,' I said. 'But, for the sake of the argument, if Bixby's own version isn't available for whatever reason, how're you going to get the copy out of Manderson's bank vault?'

Jack said, 'A court order. Our people are working on both

that and Bixby's arrest warrant as we speak.' He shot his cuff and looked at his watch. 'We should be ready to carry them out in about an hour.' I kept my face impassive. But I needed urgently to make a phone call. Damn! I'd forgotten the police still had my mobile. But, on the other hand, the one I'd borrowed from Nick for my meeting with Pentecost was still in my handbag.

'I need to...er...powder my nose.' The two men grinned as I excused myself. I walked quickly out of sight round a corner. I keyed in a number. When the receiver was picked up I said, 'You know my voice? '

'Instantly, dear lady, it's so distinctive.'

'Listen and then act fast. Get the Rainbow back-up out of Manderson's bank. It's going to be removed by a court order within the hour. If it is, it's goodbye to Wipeout. Understand?'

The voice was no longer languid. 'It will be done. And, thank you.'

I broke the connection and looked round. A woman police constable had walked past and smiled but otherwise there had been no-one to witness my call. I erased the 'last call dialled' record from the phone's memory and took a few deep breaths and walked calmly back to Jack's office.

Forty

'I just don't understand it. Both gone. It's unbelievable...' Nick was pacing up and down in the cottage - which had been restored to miraculous normality by the NCA's clean-up crew - raving at no-one in particular. He looked at me, sitting on the settee. 'I don't know how you can be so indifferent. It's fucked up the entire operation. Without Bixby in custody and the virus antidote we're stuffed.'

'I'm not indifferent. What did Jack say on the phone?' Nick slumped down beside me and expelled his breath harshly. 'He said when they swooped on Pentecost's offices, Bixby had disappeared. We know for a fact that he hasn't left the island as we've been watching the ports and the Pentecost company jet's still here...Pentecost feined outrage and blustered about police harassment…'

'…What do you mean, feined? I would have thought he'd be apoplectic and ringing the Chief Constable, not to mention the Home Office.'

'Well, that's the curious thing. Gideon said that, underneath his bluster, it almost seemed as if Pentecost had been expecting the police.' He looked thoughtful for a moment and then dismissed the idea with a shrug. 'Anyway, if that wasn't bad enough imagine how we both felt when we presented the court order to Manderson and the cupboard was bare. Apparently, Bixby had been in earlier and signed the Rainbow memory stick out and then disappeared.'

'Maybe he's just taken it home to do some work on it from there.'

Nick shook his head. 'He wasn't there. It looked as though he'd left in a hurry, though.'

I regarded him steadily. 'So what now?'

He said grimly, 'Unless we can find Bixby and both his Rainbows, Pentecost's going to be taking over the world.'

JJ rang later to apologise for not being able to take me out to dinner that evening as we'd arranged. He said he'd been called back to The Globe by Theo who was panicking because the office had been hit by some kind of bug and three reporters were off sick.

Nick went back to police headquarters and I rang Matthew. He persuaded me to go round for the evening and I volunteered to pick up a Chinese takeaway en route.

We'd finished our meal and were sitting together on the settee with an Alfie Boe track playing softly when Matthew said, 'I think I'm in love with you, Emma.'

I twisted to look at him. 'Matthew I...'

'Hush. I don't want you to say anything. I just needed you to know. I've never felt like this about any woman since Laura died...' I put my arms around his neck and we kissed gently. Later, as we lay together in the dark, Matthew began to chortle to himself. 'If they could see me now, my fellow members of the States of Deliberation, behaving like a pubescent schoolboy on the settee...'

I pulled away from him and laughed. I'm sure they'd respect you all the more for being human. We're not doing anything immoral or illegal, after all.' Just then the phone rang. Matthew groaned and hauled himself to his feet, tucking his shirt in as he walked across to pick it up.

'Matthew Le Page...Oh, Hello Jack. What's the latest?' Matthew's jocularity subsided as he listened to Jack's report. Occasionally his eyes darted to me. Then he said, 'No I haven't seen her. But I'll let you know straight away if I do.' He put the phone down, closed the curtains and switched on the table lamp.

I said, 'What was all that about.' Matthew came back and sat next to me and gazed at me with sad eyes. 'They think someone's betrayed them to Pentecost...And...they suspect it might be you. Emma, my darling, what have you done?'

I took a deep breath. 'Matthew, dearest, please listen carefully. First, I heard you say on the phone that you hadn't seen me. But I'm supposed to have two plain clothes men following me everywhere. So Jack knows I'm here. He must have been testing you...'

'...That's not important. I can always say I wanted to talk to you first before turning you in. But, is what they say true?' I reached out and took his hand. 'Matthew. I have reasons for doing what I've done, but I can't explain...You've just told me that you love me. Now I have to put that love to the test...Will you help me? ' Thirty seconds went by as he stared into my face, trying to read what was in my mind. Eventually, his shoulders sagged. 'How can I say I love you if I don't trust you. Yes, I'll help you?'

'Even if it means risking everything?'

He smiled gently, 'What have I got to lose, except my position, my reputation, the respect of my peers. But then at least I'll be married to a millionaire.' I prodded my forefinger into his knee playfully. 'Aren't you rushing your fences a bit, Senator Le Page. Who said anything about marriage?'

'Well, a chap can only hope a lady might be persuaded to show her appreciation...When the time is right, of course.' I said, 'In the meantime a chap might have to go through hell and high water...'

'So, how can I help?'

I told him what I had in mind. When I had finished, Matthew nodded curtly. It would be done. For his part he revealed that Jack's suspicions began when my two shadows reported my visit to the Pentecost offices. Which had happened after I had been party to discussing counter-measures in the police boardroom. That, in itself, wasn't conclusive.

But Gideon's fears had grown after a policewoman had reported seeing me this afternoon, not in the lavatory, but appearing to be making a confidential phone call. And this, again, had been immediately after I'd been told about the plan to impound Rainbow.

When these events had been followed by the abortive attempt at arresting Bixby and seizing his memory sticks, the evidence had begun to drop into place. But, it still wasn't conclusive. So, they were going to interview again the policewoman, who was now off duty, probably in the morning, before coming to any final conclusion.

In the meantime they were working on trumping up something against Bixby's boss that would keep him out of circulation until the crisis was over.

So, I thought, I had 12 hours to retrieve my passport from the bedroom, pack some spare clothes and warn my new business partner.

Forty-one

On the way back to the cottage I stopped in a layby and used Nick's mobile to ring Hugo's private number. A familiar, fruity voice answered. 'Pentecost.'

I said without preamble, 'Since Bixby and Rainbow have gone to ground an extremely pissed off Mr G is working round the clock to get enough on you to make an arrest. I reckon you've got until tomorrow morning at the latest...'

He replied blandly, 'They've got no evidence. They wouldn't dare.'

'You wanted me to tell you what's going on and that's what I'm doing. Ignore it if you like...see you in jail.'

'What do you mean?'

'I mean that G is desperate. He knows he's got nothing to lose. If he can put you under arrest it might just throw a spanner in the works. And the reason I'm telling you this is not completely out of altruism. They suspect me of leaking their plans to you, so we really are partners now...'

I could hear heavy breathing at the other end as Pentecost weighed what I was telling him. He said, 'But that means you are of no further use to me. I think I would prefer to keep my sixteen million and take my chances. Goodbye, dear Emma...'

'If you put the phone down now, Wipeout and D-Day are

dead and your grandiose dream with them.'

'I must say, dear lady, you are a tenacious one. I'll give you thirty seconds to convince me. If you fail, then we both go our separate ways and take our chances. As I see it, George, his virus and Rainbow are my guarantees. He can put our plans into effect without me and the time bomb is already ticking. In just three days...how should I put it..? I shall be lord of all I survey...'

I said, 'But, how do you know that they haven't got Bixby and Rainbow? They may have been suspicious of me from the start and have been feeding me duff gen. Have you heard from George since he left?'

'No, but I wouldn't expect to.'

'So, he could be in custody. And they're closing in on you right now. Tomorrow, you'll be swept into the net, too. As for Venture's seventeen million. Matthew can freeze it as soon as it hits your account by one telephone call.'

'But why should he do that?'

'Because he's in love with me and would do anything I ask...'

I added indifferently, 'So, as I see it, you lose seventeen million, your empire, your impossible dreams and everything else - all because you were too greedy. Or...we can remain partners and I could get you off Guernsey undetected - they've obviously staked out the company jet. This will give you the chance to contact George and we can carry on working together for our mutual benefit.'

There was a brief pause before Pentecost replied, 'I find your analysis most persuasive, dear lady. Partners it is. And, if what you say is true, my normal mode of transport will be out of bounds. So I'm obliged to place myself at the mercy of your ingenuity.'

'Be at your offices at six o'clock tomorrow morning and be

ready to leave the island by boat.' With luck, I thought, we'd be half way to France before Gideon's suspicions were finally confirmed and he takes out a warrant for my arrest.

Forty-two

Nick was doing his best to act normally, but I could tell it was a strain. He knew I was under suspicion. I pretended not to notice. While he was having a shower before bed, I threw some clothes into a holdall and put my passport in my handbag.

Luckily, the cottage had an adjoining garage accessible from the house, so I could put the grip in the car without my minders, if they were still around, seeing. When Nick emerged from the bathroom, I was already sitting up in bed reading.

'Where have you been?' He asked. I looked up casually. 'I went round to see Matthew. Then I decided to drive all round the island, via the coast road. Do you know, it took me less than an hour...'

I prattled on, 'Then I parked in a quiet little place at the Beaucette Marina to think about my day. Did you know you can see the lights of Alderney and France from there? It's quite romantic...'

For a moment I thought Nick was going to confront me with his suspicions but he said stiffly, 'In the light of The Phantom's presence here Gideon thinks it would be better if I don't let you out of my sight from now on. He needs the two who've been shadowing you for other duties, so you're stuck with me I'm afraid...'

I hardly slept at all. I couldn't set the alarm because I didn't want to wake Nick. So I lay there dozing until dawn began to lighten the eastern sky. I slid out of bed and took my clothes into the bathroom to get dressed.

For the sea trip I chose denim trousers and shirt over which, to ward off the chill of the morning, I could wear the Guernsey I'd already packed. When I'd finished, it was 5.30 and Nick was still asleep. I blew him a silent kiss and tip-toed down the stairs and let myself into the garage.

The up-and-over steel door slid quietly open and I prayed the hire car had been regularly serviced and that it would start first time. It did and I backed gingerly down the drive into the street. Keeping the revs of the engine down, I pottered through the narrow streets.

A few lights were on as early risers set about making breakfast. But I shared the roads with only the occasional car, the odd jogger and two milk floats. Just as I was beginning to breath easier, I noticed the sidelights of a car behind me. I could just make out two silhouettes. My minders hadn't been called off yet. So that's why Nick, normally a light sleeper, hadn't stirred as I let myself out of the house. He knew I had nowhere to run.

There was no point in trying to outwit my followers, so I continued sedately down The Grange, past Elizabeth College and parked half-way along St Julian's Avenue. My shadows pulled up 50 metres behind. Casually, I walked across the road and ducked down a maze of side streets which led to the heart of St Peter Port and the Pentecost building.

A spry Sir Hugo, dressed in a voluminous off-white, lightweight suit, opened the front entrance and hauled me inside the unlit reception area quickly before locking it again.

'Apologies for the unceremonial greeting, dear lady, but we are not alone.' He nodded to the street outside. 'I fear we are the focus of unwelcome attention.' I said I knew I'd been followed but I didn't think they would have caught up with me so quickly.

His chins wobbled as he shook his head. 'You misunderstand. I've been watching out of the window. Guernsey's thin blue line is encircling us as I speak. The concerns you expressed so pithily last night were not misplaced. Oh dear, no. The forces of law and order are closing in.'

I tried to look out of the window but Pentecost pulled me further into the shadows. I said, 'I'm sorry, Hugo. It looks as if our partnership's going to be dissolved before it's started. And I had things all so well planned, too. It's so frustrating – we're only a street away from freedom.'

At that moment the gloved hand of authority began thumping at the door and another pressed the bell. A voice called, 'This is the police. Please let us in, Sir Hugo. The building's surrounded. Open up or I regret we'll have to break the door down.'

Ignoring them Pentecost turned to me. 'So tell me, dear lady, how were you intending to whisk us from the clutches of the law?' The banging was becoming more insistent and orders were being shouted.

I said, 'Well, I suppose there's no harm in telling you now. Matthew's standing by with his cruiser ready to take us to France. From there we'd be able to think through our next move but...' I spread out my hands in a gesture of surrender '...we can hardly walk to the harbour, trailed by half the island's police force, and lead them to their own Chancellor at the helm of the getaway boat...'

As a tremendous crash from the front entrance made a vase of flowers on the reception desk jump, Pentecost smiled. 'Courage, sister. All is not lost. No definitely not. Follow me.' He strode purposefully across reception picking up a case as he went. We hurried down a corridor to a locked room at the end. He took out a key and within seconds we were through and it was bolted again behind us. We clattered down a flight of stone steps into the basement.

Hugo pulled aside some old brown filing cabinets to reveal a small opening in the wall. It was just wide enough to allow him to squeeze his bulk through. I handed him his case and followed, pulling the files back in place as best I could. 'Hugo, where exactly are we going?'

'Patience, dear lady, and all will be revealed. But to satisfy your immediate curiosity we are availing ourselves of a most excellent escape route...' I could just hear urgent shouts above us as Gideon's men swarmed through the ground floor offices looking for us.

Sir Hugo tugged me on and we stumbled our way along a sloping, dank burrow. As we continued downwards Sir Hugo explained that the passage linked the Pentecost headquarters with the Victoria Marina travelling under the Esplanade in the process. The tunnel had been constructed with slave labour during the German occupation of the island.

Between puffs of breath he went on, 'When the German occupiers realised they were losing the war, they decided they might need to make a quick getaway. They planned to slip through this bolt-hole, jump in a boat and escape to a neutral country.

'We've merely adapted their idea and ensured that the tunnel was properly maintained.'

I said, 'But surely it can't have been kept secret for nearly 80 years?'

'Indeed not. These days it also acts as a storm drain. But, because it begins in our building St Peter Port's town authorities reckon it's our responsibility to maintain. So we pay the upkeep...' He dug his hand into his right pocket and pulled out a big, brass key '...But we have rights of access. An investment worth its weight in gold, as it turns out. First George and Rainbow and now us...'

He chuckled lugubriously, 'In a very few minutes we'll be sauntering along the promenade like two early birds with nary a care in the world. The mere fact that we're carrying luggage...Well...we've spent a night enjoying the luxury of a hotel room and we're on our way back to our boat.'

As Hugo talked, a pinpoint of light was growing larger. A minute later we were standing in the shadows behind the grill, which was secured by a heavy padlock. We peered in either direction. In the water below just a few boat-owners going about their business. We slipped through the opening and closed it behind us. We walked along a narrow ledge in the harbour wall to a set of steps. Then for 500 metres we ambled casually along The Esplanade until I spotted Number Four pontoon in the Queen Elizabeth Marina at North Beach.

We strode confidently between the yachts moored each side of the walkways until we came to *Multum in Parvo*. As we stepped aboard Matthew, dressed in jeans and a dark blue Guernsey, with his hair squashed beneath a yachtsman's cap, bustled anxiously out of the cabin and took me in his arms.

'Matthew, darling,' I said. 'We must hurry. Jack's breathing down our neck. We only just got away as it is...' We clung together for a moment with Hugo standing by grinning. Then Matthew stood back with a crooked smile on his face. 'In for a penny...'

He bundled us and our cases below and told us to stay out of sight until we'd left local waters.

Forty-three

As we cast off Hugo lounged back and smiled jovially. 'I do wish I'd had the pleasure of seeing their faces when they found the place empty. It'll probably take them hours to work out how we escaped.'

Matthew set a course for St Malo, a walled coastal city in Brittany. An hour and a half later we had passed Jersey and he said it was safe enough for us to join him in the cockpit. I took a deep breath of the ozone-laden breeze. There was only a slight swell and *Multum* was cutting through the waves effortlessly.

Hugo slid his bulk onto the L-shaped seat and sniffed the wind. 'You know, Dr Johnson was right. Being condemned does concentrate the mind wonderfully. The beauty of the sun and the sea is all the more piquant because one might be deprived of it.'

I said, 'I hate to drag your thoughts back to more mundane matters but, since we share the distinction of being fugitives, how about telling me who The Phantom is...'

'Do you know, dear Emma, your tenacity can border on the obsessive. All in good time. Necessity has made strange bedfellows of you and me and we need some space for trust to grow between us. When you've transferred my half-share...all will be revealed. In the meantime, I intend to find George...'

I stared at him searchingly, then shrugged. 'Ok. I've got us off the island as I said I would. Where do we go from here?' Hugo looked sideways at Matthew, placidly steering the boat southwards. 'Inestimable though Matthew's services have been, I assume he'll be returning immediately to Guernsey. Therefore, I'm loath to discuss any plans I might have within the hearing of someone who is...shall we say...not one of us.'

Matthew leaned towards us both, still holding the wheel with one hand. 'Oh but I am one of us, Hugo. I'm coming with you...All the way.'

Startled I said, 'Oh Matthew, I'd love you to, I really would. But it wouldn't make sense. At the moment no-one knows your involvement with us. As far as anyone back in Guernsey's concerned, if you're missed you've just been out for a sail...'

Hugo chimed in, 'She's absolutely right, my dear sir, you'd have nothing to gain and everything to lose by assisting two fugitives. I suggest you drop us at St Malo and return, as swiftly as you can, to your life of mundane respectability.'

Matthew shook his head, 'No deal, sorry. Either I'm coming with you both or I turn this boat round and take you back to face the music. I'd be able to come up with some convincing story. After all, who would you believe: Two escapees or one of the island's most respectable politicians?'

'But, Matthew, darling, you'll lose everything you've ever worked for once it gets out that you helped us.'

'Aren't you forgetting one thing, Emma? I'll lose nothing if Hugo pulls it off. And at this moment I would think the odds are distinctly in his favour. He's been one step ahead of the NCA ever since all this started. And look at the shambles we've just left behind. Pretty pathetic wouldn't you say?'

I stared at him. Hugo exploded into laughter. 'A true

politician, my dear sir, pragmatic to the end. To coin an apposite phrase, welcome aboard.'

About a mile off the French coast Matthew cut the throttles and pressed a button which sent the anchor rattling into the depths. He turned to us both. 'I think it's cards-on-the-table time. Hugo, you're probably thinking that once you're on French soil you have no further use for us. You slip into the crowds, get a taxi to Dinard Airport and you're away. Right?'

Hugo gave a wounded look. 'I cannot deny it crossed my mind.' He looked at me. 'You were bluffing last night when you said the enemy might have George and Rainbow. They haven't have they?'

As I looked at Matthew, he nodded slightly. I said, 'No, as far as I know George and Rainbow are free.' Matthew interjected, 'Which from your point of view Hugo removes the incentive to continue any partnership arrangement with Emma here. After all, what's in it for you to have us both along if George is all set to press the Doomsday button?

'And. your drugs armada's standing by and any discovery by us of the Phantom's identity could implicate you in murder?' Hugo said drily, 'Put like that, dear sir, very little's in it for me.'

'So you'll forgive us if we take certain precautions to make sure our partnership remains intact. Once we land in St Malo you have to believe it's in your best interests to keep us in tow.'

'So, what are you proposing?'

'First of all let me see if I've got something correct. You need at least eight million to pay the balance on the gold you've been buying and/or the drugs..?'

Hugo assented. 'Eight million's the bare minimum.'

Matthew went on, 'But, even more importantly, besides paying your debts, the money ensures the continuing and vital goodwill of your suppliers and those on whom you'll be depending for support if you're to be some sort of Commissar for the UK. Right?' Hugo nodded silently. 'Commissar, Governor, President…The title matters not. But the position does. I shall have control of the levers of power.'

'So, here's the deal. And, unless you agree it I turn round now and go straight back to Guernsey: First, you'll make a call to Manderson via my satellite phone here to check if the lottery money's been paid in yet.' Matthew pointed an accusing finger. 'Emma and I know that you probably reversed your previous instruction to him about transferring money from your account into hers as soon as Emma left your office...'

By the resigned expression on Hugo's face I could see Matthew had hit the target'...So this time you'll wait on the phone until he says the money's there and you'll order him to transfer the entire £17 million into Emma's account. Then Emma will contain her impatience to know the identity of The Phantom.'

Hugo wasn't happy and was shaking his head. Matthew held up his hand. 'But...and this is where your incentive to keep us stuck to you like glue comes in...when we've all arrived at our destination, and we're in the company of George Bixby, Emma will authorise the re-imbursement of your account with all £17 million, not just half of it, so you can carry out your original scheme without impediment.'

Hugo looked suspiciously from one to the other of us. 'Forgive my lack of faith in human nature, my dear sir, but why should I trust you?' I said, 'Because you have no choice and because you've got nothing to lose.'

Hugo expelled his breath in a long, weary sigh. 'I do believe you have me, as they say, over a barrel. Give me the phone...'

'One final thing, Hugo,' said Matthew. 'I'll have the phone on speaker so we'll hear every word of both sides of the conversation.'

Forty-four

An hour later, I checked with Le Boutillier and the money had finally arrived in my private account. Which meant that Venture's validation procedures, and clearance of the cheque, had probably been given a helping hand by Manderson. I told Le Boutillier not, after all, to transfer half the £17 million back to the Pentecost account, but to await my further instructions.

So, by that lunchtime, as we moored in the Breton port, I was a multi-millionaire several times over. I hoped Annie would understand and forgive what I was doing.

The three of us made an odd-looking trio as we walked into St Malo. My denims and Guernsey went well with Matthew's yachting gear. It was Hugo strutting alongside us looking as though he'd walked off the set of Casablanca that drew the eye.

We checked into a hotel outside the walls of the old city. Matthew and I shared one room and Hugo was three doors down, along the corridor. We all arranged to meet later for a meal, at which point Hugo had promised he would tell us our destination.

Matthew and I spent the afternoon as tourists. We walked along the ramparts of the encircling wall and then wandered, hand in hand, around the ancient, narrow streets, looking at the shops. Just two lovers, enjoying the charm of a French, medieval town. Yet, we were fugitives from justice. As we ambled, I found Matthew's closeness was having an alarming effect on my libido. I looked sideways at him wondering if he was feeling the same.

We chose a restaurant and booked a table for the three of us. At eight o' clock that evening, over our plates of Fruits de Mer and two bottles of Chablis, Hugo announced our plan of action for the following day. 'I hope you've all got your tropical kit packed, because we're off to the Caribbean...' Matthew and I stared at him in disbelief. 'The Caribbean?' I said. 'Is that where George is now?'

Hugo beamed at us both. 'Why do you think I was wearing my lightweight suit? Yes, by now George should be ensconced in *The Nemesis* just off Antigua, which is where I planned to join him for the grand launch of Wipeout.' Matthew and I both began to speak at once. 'Calm yourselves children, one at a time if you please.'

I said, 'How...How... did he slip through the net in Guernsey and get all the way to the West Indies? And without the company jet?'

Hugo was enjoying himself as he saw the perplexity written on our faces. 'You saw half our escape route this morning, Emma. Thereafter, George slipped into the launch we've been keeping ready for just such an emergency.

'From there he sailed to this very port where it was child's play to engage the services of one of our regular air taxi companies which had him, and Rainbow, half way across the Atlantic before poor Jack Gideon even realised he'd gone.'

'And we follow suit tomorrow?' Said Matthew.

Hugo inclined his head. 'We are. It's all arranged. We leave first thing in the morning from Dinard.' Something vague stirred in my mind. I'd heard the name of *The Nemesis* somewhere before, but I couldn't quite remember. 'You said he was ensconced in *The Nemesis*. What exactly is that?'

Hugo seemed to relish the words as he replied, 'Nemesis is the Goddess of retribution. The word itself means retributive justice. Which is very fitting. Because our *Nemesis* is 50 million pounds' worth of ocean-going electronics. It's a veritable floating GCHQ'.

He went on, 'And, it's from there that George will launch D-Day and activate the virus, all via a Pentecost satellite transponder which will receive our signal. Once received, it will encode and amplify the instructions and then re-transmit them back to our network of computers linked to every major stock market. The messages they receive will appear to be innocent buy and sell instructions. Hidden in their algorithms, though, will be our AIDS virus.

Hugo's face took on an almost Messianic expression. 'It would seem, dear partners, as if very little can stop us now.'

Back at the hotel Hugo excused himself and went to his room leaving Matthew and I to have a nightcap in the bar. We talked for an hour about how we should handle the next two days. Then Matthew took my hand. 'I don't know about you darling, but my brain can't take in any more. I've been longing all day to hold you close and make love.'

He pulled me to my feet and whispered something in my ear. The words sent a ripple of desire through my body. Minutes later we were standing at the foot of our bed. Matthew filled our glasses with Veuve Clicquot, which had been delivered with Gallic gravity by the concierge, and we toasted our futures.

I felt a surge of elation that we were together and it was all going to be alright. The adrenalin that had been pumping round my veins since early morning seemed to have an enhancing effect on my fantasies. We both became so elated we went on toasting things, like a couple of giggling schoolkids, until the bottle was empty.

Matthew said, 'Darling, you satisfied me so wonderfully last night. Now it's your turn...' As his lips kissed the arch of my neck, and I felt myself trembling with anticipation... Later, gasping like two asthmatics, Matthew and I collapsed together on the bed in a contented heap of arms and legs...

Forty-five

Matthew was languidly running his hand from my breast to my thigh when there was an urgent knocking at the door. It was early the next morning, an unlikely time for room service.

Matthew padded across the carpet and let in a bustling Hugo. 'I bring you disturbing tidings...' He seemed not to notice my nakedness covered by a sheet, which I hastily pulled up to my chin. He looked from Matthew to me and back. 'I've just been listening to the breakfast news on the radio.

'The local station in Guernsey is full of murder and mayhem and Emma and I have the dubious privilege of being prominently featured in their bulletins.'
'What do you mean, murder and mayhem?' I asked, a knot of fear gripped my stomach. Hugo lowered himself into a chair. 'According to Radio Guernsey, police in the Channel Islands and mainland Britain are seeking a man and a woman following the discovery of a woman's body in a holiday cottage.

'The newsreader went on, dear lady, to talk about you, who was said to have lived in the cottage. I myself was described as media tycoon and business associate of Fleet Street journalist, Emma Holgate...'

Matthew asked, 'What about me? Was there any mention of me, or a Guernsey politician?'

'Not that I heard. But our friends in the police are obviously less than pleased that Emma and I eluded them yesterday so they're tying us in with a murder. Very neat. Very neat, indeed. With one Press release they gain maximum publicity by hinting we're fugitive killers, without having to say anything about the real reasons they want us both.'

I looked at my watch. The taxi was due to pick us up in an hour. If the bulletin talked of the Channel Islands and mainland Britain it seemed unlikely anyone yet knew that Matthew's boat was missing or that we might have gone to France in it. With luck we could still make the airport without hindrance.

I said to them both, 'We must act normally. We should go down to breakfast and behave like any other tourists. Then, we pay our bill and leave in our taxi. It's a safe bet that most French people living here don't listen to English radio, so they won't connect us with a UK manhunt.'

Hugo commented admiringly, 'I've said it before and I'll say it again, dear Emma, you have a cool head in a crisis.'

Matthew said, 'And I'll settle the bill with cash – I always keep a spare stash of Euros on board for my regular trips abroad - so they won't be able to trace any credit card transactions to France. Which should give us a bit of extra time.'

Half an hour later we were emerging from the dining room when I heard a voice speaking my name. I turned in the direction of the sound and saw Matthew's face staring at me from a television screen in reception. Probably, I realised, as a service to all its English-speaking residents the hotel kept the set permanently tuned into Jersey TV.

The woman breakfast presenter was talking over pictures of Matthew, Hugo and myself. She was saying '...And police believe Senator Matthew Le Page might have been kidnapped by the wanted man and woman, who were desperate to leave Guernsey without the knowledge of the authorities.

'According to police the two escapees might have forced Senator Le Page, who knows our waters well, to take them to an isolated hiding place before slipping across the Channel, either to mainland Britain or France.

'Helicopters and a spotter plane are searching the area now but so far there's been no sign of Senator Le Page's sail-cruiser, the *Multum in Parvo*...Meanwhile British law enforcement agencies are enlisting the help of their Interpol and Europol colleagues in a widening search...'

I'd heard enough. I looked round to see who else was listening. Amazingly, no-one appeared to be watching the screen but us. The receptionist was dealing with a family checking out. The father appeared to be arguing about the bill...

Matthew recovered quickly from the surprise of seeing himself on the screen. Then he started laughing quietly. 'They think you two have kidnapped me. I'm still the respectable Senator Le Page, not a desperado on the wrong side of the law.

'A week ago my life was a humdrum round of money-markets by day and political work by night. Now, I'm involved with alleged murderers and, what's more, I'm being abducted to a tropical paradise.' He gestured to Hugo. 'Lead on McDuff...'

The taxi driver, a pungent French cigarette dangling from the corner of his mouth, arrived and wordlessly put our cases in the back. My grip-bag now contained a change of clothes and some shaving gear for Matthew, bought from the hotel shop.

Just as we were about to drive off I screamed, 'Oh, my God. I've left my passport in our room. I took it out while I was rummaging in my bag for something...' I leapt out of the taxi and shouted over my shoulder, 'Give me two minutes.'

It was actually three minutes later before we began our journey to Dinard airport, Matthew grinning in a superior way and Hugo frowning. When we were about 50 metres down the road, a column of police cars with blue lights flashing and hooters wailing, careered past in the opposite direction.

All three of us craned our necks as we watched the vehicles skid to a halt, their gendarmerie occupants spilling onto the pavement before bundling through the hotel's front doors. 'My God,' hissed Matthew. 'Someone must have recognised our pictures and reported us.'

Hugo whispered drily, 'What a good job I insisted on special clearance through the airport formalities. With a moiety of luck we may still stay one jump ahead.'

For the rest of the trip the driver, oblivious to our tension, barely spared us a glance. As we drove out of the town he hung on the steering wheel peering at pretty girls walking on their way to work in the town. As we wound through the hedges and fields of the flat countryside he whistled softly along to an American pop song playing on his taxi radio.

I thought that any moment an announcer would break excitedly into the broadcast to warn his audience to be on the lookout for two kidnappers who had abducted a senior Channel Island politician. But the music played on uninterrupted.

At Dinard the eight-seater Bombardier Global 8000 charter plane was already waiting on the runway, the company obviously anxious to keep the patronage of one of Britain's richest men. A police siren was wailing in the distance as the three of us nonchalantly flicked our passports under the nose of a sleepy-looking airport employee.

When he saw it was Sir Hugo himself, he snapped to attention and with exaggerated gestures beckoned us through the gate. We marched briskly across to the aircraft and took our seats. Hugo barked something at the pilot and the plane started to move.

With my heart thumping I looked out of the window as we gathered speed. A line of blue lights, just visible above the hedges, were converging on the terminal building. But...too late. We were airborne and on our way westwards.

Forty-six

Eight and a half hours later, when we emerged through customs in Antigua and stepped from the air-conditioned airport terminal, it was 1.30pm Caribbean time. A gust of hot wind blew an eddy of dust around our feet.

Hugo waved away a red uniformed porter and hailed a taxi. He told the sweating Rasta driver, 'Nelson's Dockyard.' From the airport road we turned south, the battered Renault Espace weaving occasionally to avoid potholes and the smiling children playing cricket with cheerful abandon at intervals along the narrow highway.

Looking back on the flight, it had been sheer luxury. But, at any minute I had expected the plane to turn round and head back to Dinard having been summoned via radio by the forces of law and order. But nothing. Either we were incredibly lucky, and the police hadn't traced our movements. Or had, but the airport staff had covered for us. Or, more likely, the pilot was on Sir Hugo's payroll and was being paid handsomely for his services. I let my thoughts drift back to the present.

Our taxi driver introduced himself as Michael and launched into a well-rehearsed travelogue about the island's historic links with the British Empire. Hugo and I were content to let his words wash over us. But Matthew insisted on keeping up a dialogue of intelligent questions. Forty teeth-rattling minutes later we halted half way up a hill outside a hotel called simply The Inn.

Hugo, his white suit now looking so appropriate for the tropical climate, said, 'My favourite Caribbean watering hole.' He waved his hand at the millions of dollars' worth of yachts lying placidly in the bay below us. 'As you will come to appreciate it offers not only panoramic views across English Harbour but also the privacy of one's own cottage.'

'But I thought we were supposed to be joining you and George on your floating GCHQ,' I said irritably.

Hugo paid off Michael, ostentatiously doubling his fare in return for the history lesson. Then he ushered Matthew and I to the side of the road overlooking the azure waters. 'Patience, dear lady...' He pointed beyond a cluster of expensive craft.

As I followed his gaze I could see, tucked under one arm of the bay, what appeared to me to be a slightly smaller version of Roman Abramovich's super-yacht *Eclipse*, that decadent temple of self-indulgence. Like a Russian spy-ship, Hugo's slight less self-indulgent *Nemesis* bristled with antennae and there were two satellite dishes pointing in opposite directions.

I could just make out a small figure moving casually along the deck. There was something familiar about the walk. Mark the scar had seen it too and was trying to tell me something. I shook my head. I was hot, tired and hungry and in no state to match wits with Hugo.

He said, 'That's *The Nemesis*. George is going to need another 12 hours programming his computers before we'll be finally ready for Wipeout. And, of course, you Emma my dear need time to arrange the transfer of my £17 million.

'But, as the banks in Guernsey will have closed by now, might I suggest we check into our cottages, have a rest, meet for dinner this evening and review our final arrangements. Then, all being well, we'll join George aboard in the morning...And you can both be witness to...' He coughed '...And I don't believe I'm being unduly melodramatic when I say this...A new beginning for civilisation.'

Matthew must have read my mind. 'Hugo, let's keep our feet firmly on the ground for the time being. I agree, there's nothing to be gained by disturbing George now if he's making his final calculations, or whatever...We'll do as you suggest and meet for dinner.'

We were shown to two separate chalets. Hugo chirpily disappeared off to his, looking remarkably fresh considering the transatlantic journey. All I wanted was a shower, a change of clothes and a light lunch - in that order.

By the time I'd finished my fresh lobster salad, followed by melon slices, washed down with two pina coladas, I felt a lot better. As Matthew and I sat on the balcony overlooking the bay, it struck me for the first time what a beautiful place it was. I reached out and squeezed Matthew's hand. 'Any regrets, so far.'

He shook his head but an expression of sadness chased across his face. Then his lips quirked into a smile. 'No regrets. But, I hope you know what you're doing.'

I said cheerfully, 'As someone I know so recently stated: 'In for a penny, in for a pound...' Our eyes locked. I looked all around and said coquettishly, 'It would be an awful pity to waste such a romantic setting.' I pulled him to his feet and led him back into the cottage. I adjusted the blinds so the double bed was thrown into shadow.

As I turned, Matthew took a step towards me and held me at arms length, his hands gripping both of my shoulders. He gazed gravely into my eyes. 'Darling, I do want you. But, quite honestly, I'm not in the mood. I suppose I'm tired after the journey and, well, I'm finding it difficult to come to terms with what you're doing...'

I bent my head to kiss the back of his hand. I said, 'I understand. Your life's been turned upside-down in the past week. It's no wonder your emotions are in a jumble. Let's just lie on the bed and rest together...'

We both undressed and lay back naked, side by side. We held hands as we became wrapped in our own thoughts. Eventually, Matthew broke the silence. 'Emma, I know you said for me to trust you but I can't believe you've turned criminal - even for the promise of millions of pounds.'

I went tense and I felt my face turn to stone. I propped myself up on one elbow and squinted down at Matthew's troubled expression. I said bitterly, 'You've told me that you love me. But, apparently you can't trust me. I didn't ask you to come with us, you insisted - remember? So, either you're in this with me one hundred per cent or you're not with me at all. It's your choice, Matthew...'

Matthew looked stricken. Different loyalties were battling inside him for supremacy. He could see what I was thinking: that it had been so easy in the heat of passion to pledge undying love. It was different, though, when that love called for sacrificing everything you believed in.

In one movement he pulled me down on top of him and clutched me fiercely. 'Oh, my darling, I'm sorry. I'm being unforgivably weak. You're right. I can't hunt with the hounds and run with the hare. I made my decision back there off St Malo and I'm going to stick with it, come what may.'

He said sadly, 'I've let myself down in your eyes. You think I failed you as soon as the going got tough. But, from now on, if you'll let me, I'll be there by your side. No backsliding, I promise...'

I could feel the tears pricking my eyes. Poor Matthew; I was putting him through a special Hell. I kissed him gently on the lips and said, 'I understand how you must be feeling. Don't reproach yourself. We're both going through a testing experience. But, we'll survive as long as we have each other...'

Forty-seven

That evening the three of us ate out on the hotel balcony. Glittering splashes of light reflected in the water from the yachts and the warm breeze smelled of nutmeg.

'I trust you two had a restful afternoon,' Hugo said mischievously, looking at us both in turn. Playing along with his game Matthew and I adopted innocent expressions. I lowered my voice conspiratorially and leaned forward, 'We feel strong enough to take over the world.' Hugo blinked. '*Touche*, dear lady. So let's get down to business...'

He looked about him and kept his voice low. 'As I see it our...er...association is about to come to fruition. Tomorrow morning I will take you on board *The Nemesis* where you will find George all ready to press the button, as it were. That will be my part of the bargain fulfilled. You, Emma my dear, will then use our satellite telephone to ring your bank and authorise the return of £17 million into my account...'

'...At which point,' interrupted Matthew, 'Manderson squirts the money all round the world to your various outposts in final settlement of your gold and...um...other purchases...'

'...Correct. Which will then be a signal for George to activate the Wipeout virus, from which point the world will never be the same again.' He sat back, a look of sublime satisfaction on his features.

I said, 'Sitting here, in these idyllic surroundings, it's hard to believe that such a cataclysmic event's about to happen.'

Hugo leaned forward. 'Look at it this way, my dear. It's a cataclysm that will ultimately benefit mankind. For years we've been losing our way. We need to get back to basics. People require, nay positively yearn for, a firm but fair hand to guide them.' Hugo's expression again began to take on a messianic mien. His eyes glittered like diamonds.

'In these troubled times nations must have strong, purposeful and valiant leadership. The UN and NATO are busted flushes. So-called democracy has run into the ground. We've been taken over by faceless bureaucrats whose lunatic policies are causing untold suffering.'

'What policies?' I asked curiously.

He snorted derisively, 'They're all around us, every day. Look at what happened in Syria. Thousands of innocents caught up in a civil war, begging for help. But, help came there none. Then there was Mr Putin's territorial ambitions in Georgia, the Ukraine, Crimea. NATO blathered but did nothing. Looking back further, exactly the same inaction caused untold suffering in the Balkans when Yugoslavia began to disintegrate. The UN sat on its hands and passed resolutions while the Bosnian Serbs carried out unspeakable atrocities.

'The civilised world could have nipped it in the bud by imposing order through a brief but overwhelming show of force. But what happened? Prevarication, meetings, talk, and fudges. Then the Croats revenged themselves on the Serbs and, again, the innocent suffered. And again there was a plethora of hand-wringing. When action finally came, it was three years too late'.

Hugo was getting into his stride. 'Insanity's sweeping the

earth. How else can you describe the existence of wine lakes and butter mountains and food dumps while half the world is starving? Vested interests have suborned the democratic process and have brought back the law of the jungle...The rich get richer while the poor get poorer.

'Now is the time to restore the balance of human affairs. The world cries out for someone to follow to a new, promised land...'

'...And that someone's you, Hugo?' I prompted.

For a moment Hugo seemed in a trance. With a physical effort he pulled his attention back to the present. 'What's that? Oh yes, me. And a number of like-minded associates. Everything's in place. When the dominoes start to fall, we'll be ready. Ready to sweep away all the mistakes of the last 80 years.'

I said, 'It all sounds very laudable, Hugo. But why couldn't you simply have used the immense power and influence of the Pentecost media empire you've built to work for your new Jerusalem? Why did you become involved with the dregs of the underworld to fight your cause?'

He replied evenly, 'At one time I might have done just that. But those I respected turned out to be duplicitous hypocrites, prepared to throw an innocent man - my father - to the wolves to save their own skins. And that's when I realised they were no better than criminals themselves. In fact in some ways they were worse. They compounded their sin by being weak as well. You ask, dear Emma: Why the underworld - as you so anachronistically put it.

'I'll tell you: that is where the strong abide. The weak shilly-shally about talking of equality, fraternity and justice but that's all they do - talk. The people of action are to be found in organisations like mine, the Russian Mafia, the Japanese

Yakuza, the Italian Camorra, Mexico's Sinaloa, China's Triads...' He jestured about him '...Even in this seeming paradise you have the West Indian Yardies. Add to all this, the occasional Middle-Eastern and African dictatorship. They all have one thing in common - action, not talk. They act first and talk later...'

Matthew said, 'But these are people with no morals. They think nothing of killing, raping, treating their fellow human beings worse than animals. Surely these are not your new Messiahs?'

Hugo said evenly, 'Ask yourself why they are like they are. They have been driven to it. Driven to it by being deprived of their heritage by a succession of weak governments conspiring with other weaklings to keep the spoils for themselves.

'So, now is the time for us to strike a crushing blow and then establish a new world order...'

Abruptly, the maniacal stare was gone from Hugo's eyes and he was all smiles again. 'Let's have a nightcap shall we? And then to bed. We have a busy day tomorrow.'

Forty-eight

Later, in our room, Matthew flung himself into a chair. 'He's certifiably insane you know. Mad as a box of frogs. When he starts talking about establishing a new, world order he reminds me of those old newsreel pictures of Hitler addressing the Reichstag.'

I lowered myself onto Matthew's lap and put my arm round his neck. 'Yes, maybe he is mad. So was Hitler. But look how close he got to global domination. And, if the Fuhrer had the kind of media at his disposal that Hugo has, who knows what he might have managed.'

Matthew stroked my hair and let his fingers trail down my face until he cupped my breast and squeezed gently. 'Am I forgiven for my lapse earlier?'

'Which particular lapse? Your disinclination to make love to me or your doubtings?'

'Both.' He smiled invitingly. 'I told you earlier my doubts are over. Now can I prove my libido's back at full strength, too?'

'Are you sure you've got the energy. It's been a long day, after all.'

'Just try me, young lady...'

Matthew shifted his position so my shoulders were level with his chest. I was wearing a loose-fitting dress whose front buttons Matthew began now slowly to undo. As he shifted slightly, I felt a swelling in his trousers burgeoning against my ribs and an old joke jumped irreverently into my mind.

It was Groucho Marx's invitation to a girl to relax. 'Just sit on my lap and let's see what comes up...' I smiled inwardly and brushed the thought away. Poor Matthew was trying to make amends. He made love wonderfully so who was complaining?

He flicked aside the material and slipped his hand inside the top of my bra. 'Oh, Emma. You're so beautiful...' It was strange. In all our closeness Matthew had not once mentioned my scar. Perhaps it really wasn't very noticeable. As I became conscious of it, it began to redden with excitement.

I leaned up until our lips met and our tongues began to slide together in greeting. Matthew breathed a long sigh through his nostrils. He pulled me closer and levered my breast out of its cup. He slid his left hand over my shoulder and tweaked my hardened nipple between his fingers. A jolt of pleasure shot through me.

His right hand abandoned his left to its own duties as it undulated under bottom of my dress and glided into my briefs. His fingers found it easy to burrow into my inner recesses.

With satisfied little grunts Matthew's fingers flickered in time with pulsing squeezes with his left fingers. A pooling chill of a gathering orgasm centred in my abdomen. I could feel Matthew's hardness, seemingly as big as a cucumber, pushing against my chest. I squirmed, shook myself away and leapt to my feet. Matthew's closed eyes sprang open in confusion. I pulled him to his feet and said, 'What are you trying to do to a girl? Drive her wild with frustration?' I unbuckled his trousers and pulled his shirt over his head until he stood naked, except for a pair of blue boxer shorts.

I said in wonderment, 'What have you got in there, a truncheon?' In a voice trembling with pent-up passion he laughed, 'All the better to beat you with...' I sank in front of him and his face had a dreamy, faraway look. A minute later I got to my feet and led him, like a prize bull, to the dressing table and stood for a moment gazing at our reflection dimly visible in the moonlight shining through the shutters. Matthew looked like some satyr about to ravish a sacrificial virgin.

Matthew seemed hypnotised by the sight. Abruptly, I turned, bent forward and pushed my backside towards him. Matthew grunted and clutched my hips between his hands and pressed forward. I gasped as his massive girth slid home.

'Now...now...my darling,' I begged. Matthew bent his legs and then, as if a starting gun had been fired, he began withdrawing and ramming, withdrawing and ramming. Faster and faster. Jolts of divine electricity radiated throughout my being. I was in heaven and he was my god.

The satyr in the reflection was bringing a taste of paradise to his virgin. Together, our bodies synchronised. We pushed, pummelled, gyrated and pounded until, finally, in a chorus of ecstasy, we howled like animals as a liquid bliss exploded through our bodies and we became one spirit, floating among the stars of infinite space.

Forty-nine

As we puttered towards *The Nemesis* that Friday morning, my stomach was in knots. I hadn't been able to face any breakfast, except a cup of coffee. Today I would know the identity of The Phantom.

I thought back to when Matthew had been in the bathroom, humming happily to himself as he shaved. I still had Nick's phone and I used the privacy to make a hasty call. The person at the other end had seemed baffled at first but had finally agreed to do what I asked.

I glanced at Hugo. Calm as a statue, he was scrunched up at the rear of our RIB like Buddha holding the tiller. Matthew and I had arranged ourselves either side of the boat to balance it. I kept telling myself that after the next few hours my life would never be the same again.

All around, floating palaces and their owners were going through their morning routines, oblivious to my thoughts of destiny. Some were still breakfasting on their sundecks, others already anointing themselves with factor fifteen in preparation for another gruelling day of indolence.

I wondered if they'd be so complacent if they knew capitalism was on the brink of an abyss. The occasional sailboard whizzed past us as their owners took advantage of the offshore breeze. I tried to take my mind off coming events by calculating how many millions of pounds-worth of status symbols were bobbing about here in English Harbour.

Matthew tapped me on the back of my hand. When I looked at him he winked encouragingly. As we got nearer *The Nemesis*, I marvelled at the size of her. Then I marvelled at what could drive a man, who could afford such luxury, to embark on such a lunatic crusade. But that was it of course. Lunacy.

Hugo throttled back and cut the engine, and we glided the last few metres to the ship's stern. I secured our rope next to another inflatable there and the three of us climbed the aluminium steps to the deck.

There was no-one in sight. Except I just caught a glimpse of someone's back as he dodged down a hatchway at the bow. Apart from that the whole boat had an eerie quality to it, as if it was holding its breath waiting for something to happen.

Hugo said, 'In case you're wondering, the crew are all ashore. We thought it best to have the ship to ourselves...I'm sure you agree.' We followed him along the companionway, which had openings leading to cabins to the left and right.

He ignored them all and continued until we reached a pair of double doors at the end. When we'd caught up, he paused for a moment and then gripped the handles before theatrically stepping through. I couldn't stifle an involuntary gasp.

What would normally have been the stateroom was crammed with electronic equipment. Facing us, as we stepped over the threshold, were banks of screens controlled by a series of different keyboards and joysticks.

To either side of the main desk were two smaller panels with more screens. Sitting in a padded, leather chair amidst it all, his legs dangling like a diminutive cathedral organist, was George Bixby. Clasped round his ears was a pair of headphones. I

Ticket to a Killing

don't know what he was listening to because a speaker on one of the panels was hissing with static. Occasionally, the metallic voice of a radio operator somewhere burst unintelligibly through.

He turned slightly as we entered but his only acknowledgment of our presence was a faint smile. Then, once again, his fingers began dancing across several keyboards at once - a virtuoso turning electrical impulses into a language which flashed around the globe in seconds.

'I see George is not quite ready,' Hugo said equably. He consulted a row of clocks on one wall which displayed the times in all the main financial centres of the world. 'It's 2.30pm in Guernsey.' He plucked a phone from one of the desks and proffered it to me. 'So I suggest, dear Emma, you ring your bank now and return my money.'

Matthew looked startled. Hugo's eyes held mine in a steely challenge. Slowly I took the handset from him and punched in the international code followed by Le Boutillier's private number. As I waited to be connected Hugo pressed a switch on the wall and immediately I could hear the dialling tone coming out of one of the speakers. Hugo said silkily, 'I think it might be advisable if we're all privy to both ends of the conversation, don't you agree?'

On the fourth ring Le Boutillier's unctuous voice came on the line, 'Royal Bank, how can I help you?'

'Hello, Francis, it's Emma Holgate.'

Instantly, Le Boutillier's voice became guarded. 'Ms Holgate. I...er...this is...most unexpected.'

I said innocently, 'Unexpected, Francis? I told you I might get in touch.'

'Er...of course...But that was before...I mean...well...this is most awkward.'

'Awkward. Why?'

'In the circumstances it would be...ah...unethical for me to continue this conversation.'

'Francis, what are you talking about?'

His voice gained in confidence. 'I'm afraid I cannot allow this bank to be associated with...er...criminal goings on.'

'I'm sorry, Francis, you've lost me.'

His thin veneer of civility burst under the pressure of his righteous indignation. 'Ms Holgate, you and Pentecost have become headline news here. You're in all the papers, constantly on radio and television. You're being accused of murder and kidnapping and goodness knows what else.

'I feel such a fool trusting you. But as your guarantor was Senator Le Page I felt I had no choice. But I suppose you were blackmailing him in some way. It is all very, very distressing...'

I'd heard enough. 'Now listen Mr Le Boutillier. You don't want to believe everything you read in the papers. Now answer me. Is that £17 million still in my account?'

'It is. but it won't be for long. I shall have to inform the authorities soon. I've been putting it off, hoping that there might be some rational explanation. But you've been missing for two days now and I just can't pretend any longer that what I've been involved in has been all above board.'

I said fiercely, 'Do you remember what I said at our last meeting? I asked if you would act on my instructions if I changed my mind about what I wanted doing with the money. And you agreed. And you said if you had any misgivings, Matthew Le Page's word would allay them?'

'Yes. But you've kidnapped him. How could I believe anything you say now?' I said soothingly. 'No-one's been kidnapped. The media have got the wrong end of the stick...It can happen you know: And I speak with some experience. I'd like you to have a word now with my fiance who, I'm sure, will assuage any doubts...'

'Your fiance? What's he got to do with it?'

I handed the phone to Matthew. He boomed heartily into the mouthpiece, 'Hello, Francis. Matthew Le Page here. Do you recognise my voice? Good. Yes, it's true, Emma and I are engaged and we decided to celebrate with a few days in the Caribbean.

'Whatever's being said back in Guernsey's must be a terrible misunderstanding. Sounds to me like it's good for a few libel suits. Of course I haven't been abducted - unless losing your heart to a beautiful woman can be counted as that...' Matthew turned and winked at me.

Over the speaker came much grovelling and sighs of relief. Matthew continued, 'Now what we want you to do is transfer all £17 million back to the Pentecost account. Manderson's expecting it.

'If you still want an explanation I shall be pleased to give it at length on my return...Oh yes, coming back at the weekend. Yes...So you'll do it..? Excellent. Would you mind authorising it immediately? Most grateful. I'm sure the States of Guernsey will be able to show its appreciation in due course...' Back came Uriah Heep in full spate '...And thank you again Francis...Goodbye.'

Matthew put the phone down and blew out his cheeks. 'Phew! That was touch and go. But you'll have your money in ten minutes, Hugo. Hugo bowed low saying, 'I'm not one given to undue flattery but both your performances were worthy of an Oscar...And may I be the first to offer my salutations...'

I said awkwardly, 'I used a little journalistic licence there, Hugo. Matthew and I are not actually engaged as such. After all we've only known each other just over a week.' Matthew reached out and took my hand. 'I'm sorry darling you've said it in front of witnesses. And to my bank manager, as well. I'm afraid my credibility depends on us going through with it now.'

While we chortled, Hugo dialled his bank. He drummed his fingers impatiently as Manderson checked his computer. While we waited I was aware of bleeps coming from the speaker in front of George. On his screen was a straight line which blipped in time with the bleeps.

Finally a big smile broke across Hugo's face. He said to Manderson, 'You know what to do.' Then he gave the thumbs-up sign to George, who'd been watching impassively. Hugo put the phone down and turned to us. 'The transfer's been made and as I speak the money's winging around the world honouring my debts. My credibility survives, and I hold the biggest personal hoard of gold in the world. Now we can progress to phase two.'

Deftly, he removed his right hand from his pocket. It contained a silver .38 Smith and Wesson pistol which was pointing unwaveringly at Matthew and me. Hugo said smoothly, 'It wounds me deeply to dissolve our partnership so abruptly. But the fact is, dear friends, I am not as gullible as you imagine. I have an instinct for such things and right from the moment you, Emma, began to proffer your services, I knew skulduggery was afoot.

'But I went along with it because I was curious. Why, I wondered, the charade of fleeing Guernsey as a fugitive? And, assuming subterfuge, what was making you so confident that you could thwart plans I've been working on for years..?'

He waved the gun at the bench seat behind a cantilever table in the corner of the cabin. 'Do sit down both of you. But, have a care. The excitement of the moment is making my hand uncharacteristically twitchy. I would hate you to miss my crowning moment, as it were.' A rumble of mirth issued from his throat.

Matthew and I looked at each other and backed towards the seat.

Hugo said, 'So that you may follow the drama as it unfolds, allow me to explain...' He pointed at the speaker in front of George. 'When those pulses you hear finally merge into one, continuous tone the satellite is in its optimum position for our signals. George will then press that black button in front of him and Wipeout will commence.'

For a moment his eyes looked into the middle distance. 'Yes, at 186,000 miles a second an invisible missile will begin its deadly mission.' His attention snapped back to us. 'Does that sound melodramatic? Deadly is the apposite word though, believe me, dear friends. Because its results will be more devastating than if George were launching a nuclear warhead at New York or London...'

I said, 'I won't bother to try to dissuade you from your conclusions about my motives, Hugo. But at least satisfy my curiosity over a few things. For instance, what about Operation D-Day. What's happened to your plan to launch an armada of drug ships at the UK coast?'

He waved his hand airily, 'I set that in motion before I left Guernsey. But the drugs are not important; a mere divertissement to add to the confusion. Wipeout is the key to everything...'

He glanced over his shoulder at the bank of clocks. George was hunched over his controls, his eyes following a blip on his screen, like a heart monitor in a hospital's Intensive Care Unit. The blip was increasing in volume and frequency.

George called over his shoulder to Hugo. 'Thirty seconds.'

The bleeps were becoming frantic, as if produced by some old time morse operator in the final stages of electrocution. Hugo glanced sideways to watch the final few second tick away.

I could feel Matthew tensing his body next to me. I realised too late what he intended to do. Before I could barge him with my shoulder, to throw him off balance, he launched himself across the table. Miraculously he managed to grab Hugo's wrist. But his timing was a fraction too slow. Hugo had seen him coming and swivelled his body to pull Matthew off balance.

For a split second Matthew attempted to twist the gun out of Hugo's hand. As the bleeps became one long wail, Hugo's finger must have been forced against the trigger. A shot rang out and the back of Bixby's head exploded. Blood, bone and brains splattered across the screens and the walls.

Matthew and Hugo froze, staring in horror at the obscenity still sitting upright in its chair. The silence was broken only by the insistent, continuing tone coming from the satellite control panel.

The part of the brain that gave orders to the hands must still have been sending out their electrical impulses. Because George's right palm lifted and hovered. Then it thudded down onto the black button.

As Bixby died the product of his genius took on a life of its own. At the speed of light it shot on its way to wreck the capitalist systems of the world.

Fifty

'Put the gun down very, very slowly Sir Hugo,' A voice ordered from the companionway. A flicker of annoyance passed across Hugo's face and he turned his head towards the door. I called out, 'And about time, too. I was beginning to think you'd gone to the wrong island.'

As Matthew sank back into his seat, Hugo pulled himself up to his full height and smiled benignly. He reached out and dropped his gun on the carpet. 'Do come in gentlemen - I see there are two of you.'

Across the threshold stepped Jim Allardyce closely followed by Nick. Striding across the intervening space, Allardyce waved his gun warningly as he kicked Hugo's silver pistol under Bixby's chair. With a note of genuine compassion in his voice he said to Hugo, 'Sorry about Mr Bixby sir, I know he was a friend and close colleague of yours.'

Hugo shrugged and said colourlessly, 'It was an accident. And if George had to go I'm sure that's the way he would've wanted it. Leaving behind him a world indelibly marked by his genius.'

Allardyce replied cryptically, 'I think he may well be disappointed. By the way, my name's Allardyce and I'm a Commander in the National Crime Agency. You may like to know that we've been scrutinising your activities for some time, Sir Hugo.' Hugo bowed. 'I'm flattered my dear sir. To think that the cream of the intelligence community should show such an interest in a humble Polish *emigre*.'

While these exchanges were going on Matthew was looking from one to the other of us in bafflement. Nick caught the look. He said, 'Perhaps if everyone sits down we can assess where we're at.' Hugo, still beaming benevolently, eased himself round the table and sprawled at one end of the bench seat while Matthew and I continued to occupy the other end.

Allardyce pocketed his gun as he and Nick lowered themselves onto two swivel chairs. Allardyce cleared his throat. 'I ought formally to caution you Sir Hugo, but I'm going to break the rules for the present because there are still some things I need to know...'

Hugo said genially, 'Perhaps as a show of good faith, my dear sir, you might care first to assuage my curiosity over one or two matters.' Allardyce nodded in agreement. Hugo continued, 'Just prior to your arrival on the scene I was accusing dear Emma here of duplicity. I suspected she was not all she seemed. Was I right?'

All eyes turned to me. Allardyce said, 'Your insticts didn't let you down, Sir Hugo. The fact is Emma has been working under my personal direction just after that first day when she came to interview you in Docklands...' Now it was Nick's turn to look surprised. Matthew's face flooded with relief and Hugo half closed his eyes and nodded sagely.

Allardyce went on, 'It all started when I heard Nick had been engaged at one time to Emma Holgate, the distinguished Fleet Street journalist. The same Emma Holgate who wrote a weekly column on lottery winners in The Globe. And, miracle of miracles, the same Globe that happened to be the flagship paper of our prime suspect, you Sir Hugo.'

Allaryce continued, obviously enjoying himself. 'That got me thinking. What we needed was someone on the inside, who could pursue certain investigations without arousing suspicion. Who better than Emma Holgate, the investigative reporter?

'Add to that the convincing cover story of a reconciliation attempt with her former fiance, who happened to be my chief lieutenant, and you have the perfect undercover operative.'

He said apologetically, 'What no-one knew, not even Nick, was that Emma was working as my "double agent" as it were. The day Nick and I recruited her - the same day she came to see you, Sir Hugo - I rang Emma at her flat later that evening and put my plan to her. She was reluctant at first, but I persuaded her it was the only way.'

Nick said stiffly, 'If only I had realised, I might not have made such a fool of myself.' Allardyce said placatingly, 'I'm sorry I had to put both you, and Senator Le Page, through that particular subterfuge, but I dared not widen the circle. I needed Emma to appear to turn money-grubbing traitor and I had to achieve absolute authenticity.'

Indicating Hugo, still reclining phlegmatically, he added defensively, 'And the end has obviously justified the means.'

Nick shook his head in admiration, 'If you don't mind my saying, sir, you're a devious sod. Talk about the right hand not letting the left know.' He turned to me, 'I had to do my share of lying, too, Emms. And I hated it. I know I told you that it was the Commander's idea that I cosy up to Sophie. But on that day we were both going to London I didn't enjoy a cosy *tete a tete* in a wine bar as I pretended to you. I was actually putting her through a crash course at the NCA on how to download material onto our computer system.'

Allardyce cleared his throat and intervened, 'Nick told you

he'd arranged with Sophie to steal details of Operations D-Day and Wipeout. That's true. And Nick was to help her. But, when she couldn't break Sir Hugo's security system, she decided to be clever and steal Sir Hugo's laptop, with its copy of Rainbow, and send the data down the line to our mainframe in London.'

I said, 'So that's actually what she was doing in the cottage when she was murdered?'

Nick replied fiercely, 'What The Phantom didn't realise was that she'd already copied Rainbow to London. When he caught her he must have thought she was about to send it. That's why he killed her and took Rainbow back.'

Allardyce said, 'I didn't tell any of you that we already had Rainbow as I wanted you all to genuinely put the squeeze on Sir Hugo. Happily my stratagem worked.'

Matthew who was looking on in bewilderment spoke at last. 'Just let me get this clear. Emma was working for you, Allardyce, right from the start. But Nick didn't know that. He thought she was taking her instructions from him or Jack?'

Allardyce concurred. Nick added, 'So her apparent traitorous behaviour, when she warned Hugo that Gideon was about to pounce on Bixby and Rainbow, was all part of the act?'

'It was. You see we had to convince Hugo that he could trust Emma. By appearing to betray us she was aligning herself firmly with his camp. We needed Hugo to be lulled into a false sense of security. We'd already planned to mop up his armada - we had all the ships pinpointed and tracked.

'But, we didn't want anything to prevent Hugo from electronically squirting his money to all his outposts so we could trace the addressees, initiate Operation Starburst and raid his traffickers.'

Matthew looked puzzled. 'So, part of Emma's role was to

make sure the transfer of the £17 million happened?'

Allardyce smiled, 'Precisely. That shilly-shallying over £8 million, then £17 million, and the attempt to up the ante from a down payment of a million to two million, was all supposed to add to the authenticity.'

Matthew said, 'But, Bixby's dying act was to press the button to send his virus to stock exchanges world wide. It's gone, by now the virus must be causing havoc.'

Allardyce smiled, ' I'll get to that in a minute.'

Matthew said resignedly, 'It's all so convoluted. So you're operation's been a success?'

'Oh, it's been successful, alright. But more so than you can ever imagine. Because, there was another, important objective.' We all looked on expectantly. He spread his arms wide. 'This. The Pentecost drugs and money-laundering command centre...'

He explained, 'For years he's been giving the authorities the run around. While the world believed his financial headquarters was centred in the Channel Islands, the crooked side was actually run from this boat - the perfect Mission Control.

'Every time we thought we'd tracked it down, it shifted to another tiny anonymous bay, or another atoll somewhere.' He looked at Hugo respectfully. 'He packed it with every electronic gizmo known to man. And in Bixby he had the perfect lieutenant to exploit it to its maximum.

'With all this, and the satellite links, Bixby was able to run the money-laundering and the drugs smuggling like a spider at the centre of a web. Ironically, it was just to amuse himself that he developed his virus, and the Rainbow antidote, as a sideline.'

He looked at Matthew. 'Which brings me back to the virus. Thanks to poor Sophie's sacrifice, we've been able to get it installed in all the world's stock exchange systems ready to repel all boarders - including Bixby's AIDS virus.'

The sound of sardonic clapping came from Hugo's corner of the bench. He wasn't looking as defeated as he should. He said to Allardyce, 'I salute your ingenuity, my dear sir. You were a worthy opponent if I may say so.

'May I presume upon your indulgence just a little longer? Look on it as being magnanimous in victory if you like. Tell me, how did you finally trace us here to *The Nemesis*?'

'We found you here because Emma told us that's where you'd be.'

Once again all eyes turned to me. I said, 'Remember when I jumped out of the taxi in St Malo and ran back to get my passport? I left it behind deliberately so I had the excuse to be alone while I made a phone call. I rang Mr Allardyce's special number and left a message saying where we were going. I must say though I was beginning to wonder if someone had forgotten to listen to the recording.'

Because everyone was concentrating on me, they didn't see what I saw - the shadow of someone lurking in the companionway.

Allardyce sighed with satisfaction. He told Hugo soberly, 'All the play-acting was to achieve four ends. The first was to track down your headquarters, the second was to acquire a list of all your outlets and contacts and the third you forced on us when we discovered your plot to corrupt the financial world's computers.'

'And the fourth?'

'To identify and apprehend The Phantom.'

Allardyce ticked off on his fingers as he talked. One, we've found *The Nemesis*; two, by now an international police operation should be arresting all your associates, Sir Hugo; three, the money markets can sleep easy thank to Rainbow…'

Hugo leaned back, clasped his hands across his belly and

half closed his eyes. He said, 'And the sixty-four thousand dollar question. Who is The Phantom?' Allardyce looked piercingly at Hugo. 'That's what we want you to tell us. Who is he and where can we find him?'

Hugo pursed his lips and shook his head. 'I regret I cannot enlighten you. It would be...ah...betraying a trust...' I said, 'We don't need Sir Hugo, Mr Allardyce. I know who he is and where to find him.' Everyone, including Hugo, looked startled. 'In fact, He's here, right now.' Craning my neck towards the doorway I called out, 'Don't skulk out there, come and join us.'

A fist appeared. It held a nine millimetre handgun, The Phantom's chosen weapon of execution. The arm was followed by the man with whom I would have trusted my life.

Fifty-one

There were gasps of disbelief from around the table. Allardyce went to reach into his pocket and thought better of it when the muzzle of the pistol swung to point steadily at his head. 'Hello, Emms. So you knew all along?' Jeremy Bartholomew Jerome was looking at me with a mixture of admiration and anger.

I shook my head. 'No, it took me quite a while before the penny dropped. It began when you mentioned on the phone about Bixby going to Guernsey. I couldn't work it out at the time but later I realised why it nagged me.

'When I first mentioned his name, you had to rack your brains even to remember who Bixby was. The next second, though, you seemed to know all about his habit of commuting between the Channel Islands and London. You could only have got that knowledge by being closer to Sir Hugo than you admitted.

'Next there was the time I told you about Oscar and Kate, I just had the feeling that you weren't as shocked as you made out.

'Then, I looked at the dates of the murders again. On every occasion you were off duty and out of the office, mostly Sundays. So you could have been at the scene of every crime.

But I became convinced after I thought back to Annie Pearson's murder.

'That day you were supposed to be my leg-man you said you had a dentist's appointment. Do you remember I commented on the fact it seemed to take an awful lot of time for just a filling? Those two hours gave you just enough time to drive out to Annie's Chiswick apartment, kill her and drive back.

'I couldn't understand at first why The Phantom had murdered Annie. She hadn't the ticket in her possession so what was the point? Later, I realised. She'd seen your face and she would tell me you'd called and I'd recognise your description and the game would be up. So you had to kill her.'

I added coldly, 'You must have got a real kick out of all this - working as a reporter on The Phantom story, getting all the police inside information and staying one step ahead, while all the time you were the one they were looking for...'

JJ grinned. 'The best alter ego since Jekyll and Hyde.'

I continued, 'Then there was Sophie's murder. I wondered how The Phantom had managed to avoid his gun being discovered by airport security.

'Then I realised: He wouldn't have needed to pass through security if he was travelling in a private plane. You'd come to Guernsey in the Pentecost company jet. Once you were here, and didn't need the gun any more, you would have disposed of it somewhere.'

JJ was looking at me steadily, a small smile playing about his mouth. The others were transfixed. I pressed on, 'And there was that very clever subterfuge of yours to throw off any suspicions I might have had by ringing me on your mobile phone pretending you were in London.

'But you were actually in Guernsey. That's what you did the morning I rendezvoused with The Phantom at the German bunker. How could it possibly be you, if you were in England?

'Then you said you couldn't meet me for dinner in Guernsey because you'd been called back by Theo. That was a big mistake, JJ. Because I checked with Theo and he knew nothing about a wave of sickness at the office. Now, of course, we know you couldn't make it because you were on your way to the Caribbean with George.'

I looked at him steadily. 'But I have to admit, you did have me fooled for a while about one thing - your voice. I did some research and found you can download Apps that distort sounds. Is this how you disguised your voice on the phone to sound like Bugs Bunny under water?'

He gave a choking laugh. 'You're right, there are plenty of Apps around that do that job. But I wanted something a bit more sophisticated. Anyone can shop down the Tottenham Court Road and buy a gadget that fits on any device and changes the frequency response of all outgoing and incoming messages. You can adjust it so that even your own mother wouldn't recognise you.'

'And you used the same thing on some kind of microphone and speaker in the bunker?'

He nodded. 'Correct.'

As I'd been speaking, Nick was opening and closing his mouth. Addressing JJ eventually he said, 'So you were Pentecost's insider. You were feeding everything you learned from Emma straight back to him.' JJ gave a little bow.

JJ said, 'And, although she didn't know it, that was Emma's best protection. As long as she was a source of useful information she was worth more alive than dead.' I shivered as I realised how near to disaster I'd come.

Allardyce asked JJ, 'Was it you who murdered Magenta?' JJ sneered, 'Hardly, at the time of our dear leader's unfortunate demise I was taking care of Emma in my flat if you recall.'

Nick turned to Hugo. 'I see it all now. Magenta rang you to discuss her scoop and you realised she'd become a threat to your plans so you had her killed.'

Hugo said nothing. Instead he placed both hands on the table and heaved himself to his feet. Involuntarily, Allardyce's hand twitched towards his pocket. But he dropped it to his side as he saw JJ's gun swivel towards him. Hugo held out his hand to the NCA's Commander. 'Very carefully now, dear sir, give me your gun but with the barrel towards your good self if you don't mind.'

Reluctantly Allardyce complied. Hugo clicked off the safety catch and, gripping the pistol firmly, manoeuvred round the table to stand beside JJ.

I said, 'We've answered your questions, Hugo. Could I ask just two more?'

'Do you know, dear lady, I am beginning to get rather bored with this Poirot-esque scene but...' He inclined his head '... since we have shared so much together of late...'

'First, what persuaded Bixby to become gamekeeper-turned-poacher?'

Hugo stole a quick glance at the grotesque form still sitting at the control panel. 'Ah. A story of beauty, the beast and unrequited love. George was utterly and hopelessly in thrall to the pulchritudinous Francesca.

'But like something out of an operatic tragedy, alas, his feelings were not returned. In fact I know dear Francesca was repelled by the very sight of George, the dwarf. But, midget though he was, he was still human, and he deliberately blinded himself to the truth.

'Poor George. He believed power would be the alchemy to sway the heart of his true love. He became a driven man. In his mind my scheme was his key to happiness...' Hugo added lugubriously, '...But, perhaps to die with his dreams intact was kinder than the disillusionment that most surely would have followed.'

I turned to JJ. 'I can hardly bring myself to look at you, I feel so sick. To think that it was you, the person I loved as my friend, and who I thought I knew so well, who killed all those innocent people. And then to be able to behave so normally afterwards...'

He replied flatly, 'It's a natural talent I have. You see there are really two of me. These days they call it Dissociative Identity Disorder – what people in the past called schizophrenia. It allows you one minute to be the sympathetic listener and the next the ruthless assassin.

'People and their puny feelings mean nothing to me. They might as well be trees. If they get in the way, I cut them down.' He looked sideways at his boss. 'It was Hugo who recognised my special ability and we've been a team ever since.'

Hugo cut in, 'Because of Jeremy's...ah...unique bent, he found life on the silver screen preferable to the real thing. On celluloid the highs and lows of the human drama are acted out in all their magnificence. But, alas, the genuine article is but a mere dreary copy. So Jeremy's existence became that of a somnambulist--sleepwalking his way through his days...

'Until I offered him the chance to play that greatest of all roles - God. To have the power of life and death over his subjects. It was then he became truly alive to carry out my bidding as to the manor born.'

JJ jerked his head in a manic nod. 'Those people I killed were just ants...'

Nick said sombrely, 'You're both mad, do you realise that? In different ways, maybe, but at the bottom of it all you're each of you off your heads.'

I shuddered and thought: Hugo had seen through JJ's mask. It took one to know one. I said, 'But why that barbaric way of killing those people?'

JJ examined the muzzle of his gun thoughtfully. 'If Hannibal Lecter can bite his victims to death, I don't see why I shouldn't shoot them.'

'Yes, by why the ritual?'

'I got the idea from The Deer Hunter, you know the film about three friends who go to fight in Vietnam. Well, the uncut version showed how the Viet Cong used to kill their captives by inserting the barrel of a gun into their anuses and pulling the trigger. It was quick and quiet. I adapted the method to the abdomen for more flexibility and simplicity. And it had the added advantage of still being quiet. After I'd done it once, I decided it would make a good trade-mark.'

Allardyce swivelled in his chair. He fixed his gaze on Hugo and JJ. 'You both might as well hand over your weapons. You can't get away.' He pointed laconically at me. 'The resourceful Emma here alerted the Royal Antiguan Police this morning and persuaded them that this boat harboured a highly-dangerous international drugs baron.

'I re-enforced her message later in a brief chat on the phone with the Chief of Police.' He jerked his head at the idyllic scene outside. 'They're probably out there right now.'

Hugo was unmoved. 'That's as may be. But, my dear sir, the game is not over yet. Not over at all.' He turned to JJ. 'Have you done what we agreed?' JJ nodded. Hugo turned back to the four of us and addressed Allardyce.

'I regret I am the bearer of disappointing news. Far from achieving all your objectives, you have failed on all counts.' Allardyce gazed up at him scornfully. Hugo said, 'You're not convinced I see. Then allow me to elucidate:

'One, your international police operation will be still-born, I fear. Because my £17 million went to but one account - a perfectly legitimate bank in Moscow in full payment for a consignment of gold. So, no computer trace on my associates there;

'Two, in...ah...30 minutes exactly *The Nemesis*, my Mission Control as you call it, will cease to exist. I always thought that one day I might need to destroy the evidence, as it were.

'To this end we've been carrying below enough explosives to blow this boat into orbit. All it needed was one primer and one timer, which the redoubtable JJ has already attached and set...

'...And we have ensured our own safe passage out of here by having a small launch available to take us to Guadeloupe and from thence to my new command centre.'

Allardyce said uncertainly, 'You're bluffing.'

'My dear sir, you should know me better by now. I never, never bluff about anything. Three...and this is my *piece de resistance*...Any moment now the world's finance industry will be in chaos; money is about to cease to exist; stock markets will be collapsing like so many houses of cards and with them democratic governments with gratifying rapidity...'

Allardyce and Nick's faces went white. Nick said, 'But that's not possible. We've got Rainbow in place everywhere...'

Hugo shook his head forlornly. 'My dear sir, Rainbow was designed to protect systems at the receiving end of the datastream. But it is powerless if the virus is attacking the *transmission* of the information...'

Matthew said, 'The transmission end? You mean you've spiked thousands of computers, already? I don't understand.'

Hugo pointed at Bixby's slumped form. 'When George pressed that button he launched the virus direct at FINSAT

SIX.' He looked around at our blank faces and sighed. 'FINSAT SIX is the satellite used to transmit all global financial transactions.

'When a bank in the Cayman Islands transfers a million dollars to Credit Suisse in Geneva the data is fired at FINSAT SIX. A computer on board decodes and then encodes the information and onwardly transmits it to the receiving bank. It's all encrypted, of course, and takes a matter of seconds.' Hugo said this technical procedure was known within the finance industry but the knowledge was not widely available.

'Thousands of such procedures are happening every minute. Dear George had his own interactive VSAT transmitter...' He saw our expressions and sighed again. 'For you uninitiated VSAT stands for Very Small Aperture Terminal. With it he beamed his virus to FINSAT SIX and it is now penetrating all encryption codes and wreaking havoc, like a rogue bulldozer in a porcelain factory...'

Allardyce was staring sightlessly at the floor. He looked up wearily. 'So we were pursuing a false premise all the time?'

'Pardon my levity, my dear sir, but you were chasing Rainbows.'

Nick said, 'But what about the recording we had of you and Bixby telling Manderson the virus would be spread through the Internet?' Hugo laughed and then his face became serious again. 'George and I decided we wouldn't trust anyone. Hence the subterfuge. We always intended to strike at the source of the transmissions - the satellite. But that was our little secret.'

He bounced on his toes in excitement. 'We spun the yarn to everyone else that it would be via the Internet. It seemed a plausible scheme.' He beamed all round. 'Moving onto your fourth objective...the identity and apprehension of The Phantom. There you may take some small comfort...'

I said, 'He's your Achilles Heel, Hugo. No matter what your exalted position's likely to be in the new order, your complicity in murder will stalk you just as surely as The Phantom stalked his victims.'

Hugo glanced sideways at JJ who was surveying the scene with amusement. 'As I say, as far as The Phantom is concerned, there you may take some small comfort. As you surmise, he might be an impediment to my future so I cannot allow that to happen.'

Abruptly, before JJ could react, Hugo turned and shot him in the side of the head. A neat hole appeared and a trickle of crimson, mixed with the grey of brain matter, coursed down the side of JJ's face and dripped from his chin onto his shoulder.

JJ's smile was replaced with a look of puzzlement. Then, his eyes glazed over and his body folded into a slumped heap. Residual nerves twitched the gun from his hand.

Matthew, myself, Allardyce and Nick sat stupified, glancing from Hugo to the form on the floor and back again. Hugo straightened his shoulders. 'There, I'm sure that's the best way for all concerned. No expensive trial for the taxpayer to underwrite and no untidy ends for me to concern myself with.'

He glanced at his watch and compared it with the wall of clocks. 'Ten minutes to go...If you'll forgive me, lady and gentlemen, I'll be taking my leave now. I must insist that you remain. As you can see, there's no way out except the doors and they have the stoutest of anti-intruder bars...'

He began backing towards the companionway. Just then I was aware of voices coming from the sea outside. It sounded like orders were being shouted. Still holding the gun, Hugo stepped nimbly over the threshold.

Immediately, there was a dry cough of automatic gunfire and

Hugo reappeared with his back to us. He stood rock still as if in shock at what he'd seen. Then he turned towards us. A look of bewilderment, followed by a rueful sadness, chased across his face. He surveyed us all, ranged in a comic tableau, and attempted a small smile before Allardyce's pistol dropped from his fingers and his 18 stone crashed full length alongside the man he'd just executed.

Fifty-two

'Mah sincere apologies, Mr Allardyce.' The speaker was a short black man who didn't look at all sorry. He was wreathed in smiles and holding a swagger stick. His khaki shirt carried the epaulettes of an officer in the Royal Antiguan Police.

'Ah remember what you say about keeping de low profile but when we heard de shot we pile in. Unfortunately, my men dey're not too experienced in dealing wit' desperadoes and my constable...' he shrugged carelessly '...his finger slip. But, all's well 'dat end's well, Eh?'

Allardyce said agitatedly, 'Not if we don't all get off this boat within five minutes, Inspector. We have reason to believe it's been booby trapped to blow up.'

The wreaths of smiles vanished. It took only a few shouted words of patois for his men to scatter over the sides and into two boats which had been placidly standing by a few metres away.

The four of us ran to the ladder, shinned down it like monkeys, and leapt into the RIB. Within seconds Matthew had the engine started and we were whining at full revs away from *The Nemesis*. The inspector was standing at the prow of his boat, circling and waving sightseers away.

As we approached the jetty Matthew slowed down. He

looked at his watch. 'It should have gone up three minutes ago. I reckon Hugo was bluffing.'

'He told us he never, never bluffed,' said Allardyce. 'And I'm inclined to believe him. He was not the bluffing sort.'

As we bobbed about still watching the scene three hundred yards away I said, 'Mr Allardyce, did you ever find Venture's mole who was leaking all the winners' names to Hugo?'

'We did. It was just one of their telephone handlers who got greedy. She'll be charged with conspiracy.'

'And Manderson?'

'He'll be dealt with by Guernsey's Royal Court. I would guess he'll get several years inside for corruption.'

'What about Francesca?'

'There's no proof against her. And the frustration is: she'll probably pop up within a few months and, with her father, re-activate Hugo's drugs business.

'If Hugo did send the £17 million to one legitimate address, then Operation Starburst would be confined to the small fry. The network'll be ripe for someone with Francesca's inside knowledge to step in and take over.'

As he spoke I was watching *The Nemesis*. Suddenly it seemed to lift itself out of the water, expanding redly as it went. Then a low rumble, like tropical thunder, rolled across the harbour.

As I continued to watch, the boat's outline grew blurred and was lost in a massive plume of water and smoke. When the pall had cleared the superstructure was slipping beneath a sunlit sea, which was glittering restlessly.

I don't know how long the four of us sat and stared. Eventually Matthew looked across at me and said wearily, 'It's hard to believe that the man, and all his dreams, are gone - in one puff of smoke...'

Allardyce dragged his eyes away. 'Speaking for myself, all I can say is: Thank God for it.' He added reflectively, 'But, sadly, Hugo was right. Funny how things go in life. There I was feeling - I have to admit it - a little smug about achieving our objectives. But we've actually failed pretty comprehensively – no Starburst, no command centre, no Phantom to bring to trial and…' He looked back at the spot where *Nemesis* had been…'No business as usual on the world's stock exchanges…'

Addressing me he said, 'And I've an apology to make to you, Emma. When you rang me from the callbox in Guernsey I said Venture had agreed to pay you 10 per cent of whatever you managed to keep back from Hugo. As you gave him the whole lot, and we'll never retrieve it from a Russian bank, I'm afraid you'll get nothing.'

I recalled the million I was paid by The Phantom in the beginning, and the half million I'd made on my stock market flutter. And what I'd done with the proceeds, courtesy of Francis Le Boutillier

I said, 'Oh, I think I'll come out of all this with more than I anticipated.' He saw me look across at Matthew and twitch a wink. Allardyce hurrumphed. 'Yes, I see, of course…you and Matthew…'

Nick said drily, 'It's just as well you weren't expecting any money from this escapade anyway.' We all looked at him.

He explained, 'Well…Bixby's virus could be wreaking havoc as we speak.'

Matthew said, 'In that case well all be back to bartering by this time next week.' In spite of the apocalyptic trend of the conversation, Matthew couldn't conceal the relief he felt over me, which still shone sunnily from his features.

'Not to mention,' chipped in Allardyce despondently, 'riots in the streets and democracy falling about our ears...'

Nick said, 'Let's hope it was all just a desperate bluff by Hugo in a corner?'

Allardyce looked back at the bits of wreckage floating in the bay and shook his head. 'Somehow I don't think so...'

Matthew's wince was replaced by tenderness as he stared across at me. I hoped he couldn't read my mind because lovers shouldn't have secrets. But there was something he didn't know. Whichever way things went we would be alright.

The scar on my cheek began to flush a vivid purple, like an accusing exclamation mark. Amazingly, he didn't seem to notice.

I would choose my moment. Then I'd tell him. The virus could do its worst. But, we had each other...And the £250,000-worth of Krugerrands I'd bought with my Pronova profits, and which were now lodged in my name in a Jersey bank.

Lovingly, I returned my fiance's gaze and pursed my lips in a silent kiss.

One last thing...

If you have enjoyed this book, please would you take a few seconds to let your friends know about it? If it turns out they really enjoy it too they'll be grateful to you, as will I. And if you go the extra mile and take the time to write a review on Amazon, you may encourage an even wider readership to enjoy it too.

And look out for my next novel 'The Kirov Conspiracy' set in an offshore international finance centre. Its theme, the Russian takeover of the European narcotics trade, is all too possible. In fact, it may be happening right now.

Printed in Great Britain
by Amazon